THE UMPIRE

A Novel

WILLIAM FRANCIS

My novel is dedicated to all athletic officials. They perform a thankless job, take the abuse and yet uphold the ethics and integrity of their respective sports.

I also wish to thank Terry and Diane Kestner of Cedar Falls, Iowa for granting permission to use their photograph for my book cover.

Another thank you to Major League Umpire Hunter Wendelstedt for providing the blurb on the back cover.

As always, to Michele.

PART 1

THE SCOURGE OF BASEBALL

CHAPTER 1

I stood outside the boys' locker room at Glasgow High School wearing my Philadelphia Phillies sweatshirt and cap, gray sweat pants, white socks, dirty sneakers and baseball glove. Our varsity and junior varsity players warmed up on brown outfield grass, along with boys like me who hoped to make this year's roster. Most wore red sweats, some gray. Many did calisthenics, such as jumping jacks and push ups. A few ran sprints. Others had paired off to have a catch. The pop, pop, pop of baseballs striking cowhide reverberated in the chilly air.

Oh, crap. Why was *he* coming this way?

"What the…" Joe Forrester said. He stopped and stared for a moment, and then shook his head in disbelief. "Oh, dude, not again. What is wrong with you?"

"The doctors don't know."

"What?"

Musclehead, my secret name for him, never did have a sense of humor. We had met in ninth grade biology, where he proclaimed, "Dissecting frogs is *sooo* cool."

As a sophomore, Joe had been on the verge of removal from the football team because of poor grades. Since I was the "smartest person he knew" he decided to use me to help him cheat on a Social Studies exam. I said no. He then threatened to beat me up and spread a rumor about me and John Higgins locked in a lovers' embrace in the auditorium. Knowing Joe's reputation, and John's, I gave in. The test had been multiple choice. Discreetly, I raised one finger against my thigh if the answer to a question was A, two fingers for B, three fingers for C and four fingers for D. Joe wisely answered a few questions incorrectly, but he still received the best score of his life. Nevertheless, and even though he had promised it was a one-time deal, he continued to threaten me if I didn't help him in the future. So on the next exam, I supplied the wrong answers.

Joe would've dissected me had Miss Grayson, our Social Studies teacher, not intervened. She was no fool. She investigated the wild swing in Joe's grades and eventually had Joe and I testify before the principal. I was pardoned. Joe was removed from the football team and hasn't been back since. He was also banned from the baseball team that year, reinstated only after improving his grades and doing community service.

"I told you I'd be trying out," I said, my knees shaking. "And I mean what I say."

"Yes, but you *suck!*"

I had heard such remarks, and worse, from jocks since elementary school. Despite my best efforts, I hadn't the upper body strength to climb rope or do chin ups. I hadn't the muscle to play football or the coordination for basketball. I had been an easy pin in wrestling. Yet I had been blessed, or some might say cursed, with a passion for baseball. I loved to play or watch the game, to hear the crack of the bat as it made contact with a pitched ball, to hear the crowd cheer when something good happened for their team or hear them moan when something went awry. I loved the intricacies of the sport, the strategy between opposing managers and the one on one battle between pitcher and hitter. The game tested character because more often than not the batter failed in his objective. It was how the batter responded to disappointment that made him worth cheering for or not.

I punched a fist into the palm of my glove and tried not to get emotional in front of this Neanderthal. "What can I say, Joe, I'm a glutton for punishment."

Joe's head tilted like a puppy dog confused by human speech.

I chuckled.

"What're you laughing at?" Joe said. He poked me in the breastbone with a stiff middle finger. It stunned me more than expected and the pain lingered. "You better hope Coach doesn't put me on the mound. I'll drill one through those satellite dishes."

I learned early in life that Nature had a cruel sense of humor. I had already been denied an athlete's body. Why had it been necessary to include large ears, unruly black hair, a couple crooked lower teeth, and a pepperoni pizza face?

"I'm not laughing," I said.

"Damn straight," Joe said. He put a hand on my shoulder. Back in elementary school kids had called me Beanpole and I answered such dumb questions as, "How's the weather up there?" But Joe had to look down a few inches to talk to me eye to eye, and for once his weren't bloodshot. "Do you enjoy making an ass out of yourself?"

I tried to act tough, but I shivered. "Don't you have a dream, Joe?"

"Yeah," he laughed, "Kristen Richardson."

"Oh, man, she is hot."

"Right," he sneered, "like you'd know what to do."

"Well, it's always been my dream to play baseball."

Joe tapped his fist against my forehead a few times.

"Hello, anybody home? How many times do you have to get cut before it sinks into that nerdy brain of yours that it's never going to happen? Tell me, have you ever made a team in your life?"

When I wasn't fantasizing about Kelsey Delgado, I created fictional heroics where I made a greater catch than Willie Mays' over the shoulder grab in the 1954 World Series. I slammed more meaningful home runs than Bobby Thomson's pennant-winning blast in '51. I had thousands of adoring fans. I had money and women. My image appeared on Wheaties cereal boxes and I did television commercials. I gave interviews to sports reporters. I was *spec-tac-u-lar*.

"No, Joe," I said, humble. "I've never made a team."

Joe scratched his dimpled chin. "Doesn't that tell you something? I mean, I'm not the brightest bulb, but at least I know my limitations."

"I've gotten better. I've been practicing."

"All the practice in the world ain't going to help you. Face it, wimp," again with the stiff middle finger to my breastbone, "you're wasting your time." Joe pointed at himself. "You're wasting *my* time." He pointed toward the baseball field. "And you're wasting the coaches' time."

"I have to try."

"Do I have to knock some sense into you?" he said with a fist in view.

I had heard that teenagers felt indestructible. Not me. I was well aware of my mortality because Joe threatened to kill me on a daily basis. His other victims told me that the key to survival was silence. Keep eyes to the floor and never speak. I couldn't do that. Joe might scare me, but I couldn't shrink into nothing. "No, Joe. You don't have to knock some sense into me."

"All right, then. I need to use the bathroom. When I

come back out, you had better be on your way home."

The locker room door slammed behind him.

"You're not the boss of me," I said to the door, my eyes watering. I blamed it on the cold March wind. "I can tryout if I want to."

After all, I was good enough to be on the field with those guys. Plus, I'd look pretty cool in the school uniform. Red and gold, with a dragon emblem sewed onto the sleeves. Wearing that uniform, boys would definitely treat me better and Kelsey Delgado might notice me.

Austin Jenkins, my best friend since middle school, exited the building. He was all bundled up and carrying his book bag.

"Good luck," he said, adjusting his glasses.

"Thank you. I know this'll be the year."

Austin stopped and grinned. He gave me the type of response only a friend would give, laced with sarcasm. "Really, Mike? You're *really* going to make it this year?"

"Hey," I said, "it's something to do."

"You're a strange bird," Austin said, shaking his head.

"A cuckoo?"

"You got it. See you Monday."

"Yeah, see ya."

The locker room door opened and slammed shut. I flinched.

"You still here?" Joe said, shoving me in the back. "Still thinking about it? Then you obviously have doubts. Let me settle it for you. There's no shame in leaving. I mean, better now than after you totally embarrass yourself--*again*."

"It's my choice, Joe."

"Hey, I'm just trying to be your buddy and warn you against doing something so incredibly stupid. You know it's stupid. Right?"

8

Joe was such a poser. I hated when he pretended to be my friend. "No. It's not stupid."

"Damn it," he said, tired of playing. He ripped the glove off my hand and slapped it against my chest, where I held it. "Go home, *loser*."

Joe walked across an asphalt drive that separated the two-story Newark, Delaware school from the parking lot and baseball field. His rubber cleats clicked against the road surface and sounded like a tap dancer.

"I'm not a loser."

Why should I care what Musclehead, the coaches, or anybody else thought about me trying out. I owed them nothing. Baseball meant a lot to me. It was my destiny to play. After all, my initials were MLB for Michael Lawrence Briggs, which matched Major League Base-ball. That had to be more than coincidence.

"And I'm going to prove it."

CHAPTER 2

My heart never pounded as hard or beat as fast as it did when I walked through a gap in the fence by first base and joined my future teammates. Chubby Coach Myers, in his red windbreaker, walked on the dirt portion of the infield and set the bases. I snuck behind him and grabbed a baseball from an open canvas bag left on the pitcher's mound. I looked around for someone to warm up with and approached a short freckled dude who sucked air from having just completed some jumping jacks.

"Want to have a catch?" I said.

"Sure."

I introduced myself and we shook hands.

"Rob Kyle," he said.

"You a Freshman?"

"Yeah."

"Me, too."

What? Why did I lie?

Rob scooped his glove off the ground and onto his left hand. We then separated about fifteen yards along the first base line.

I started with a light toss. Rob caught the ball in his glove, retrieved it in a casual manner, and when he went to throw, his body motion was almost lazy. Yet the baseball came upon me like a speeding missile and I barely got my glove up in front of my face. The leather popped. Pain shot through my hand and up my arm and I did my best to hide any reaction.

"What're you," I said, "a pitcher?"

"No," he said with a grin, "second base."

Liar! The infielder with the shortest throw to first didn't need a cannon for an arm.

I started a return throw, but Coach Myers hollered, "Form three groups by the backstop, last year's varsity, junior varsity, and this year's wannabes."

All of us quickly obeyed.

Coach Myers looked us over. During the week, he was the boy's gym teacher. He claimed to have been quite an athlete in his "younger days," but with his stomach sticking out, little hair on his head and thick glasses low on his nose, I couldn't imagine it. He loved to tell the story about his one and only play in the National Football League. He had signed a rookie contract as a placekicker for the Kansas City Chiefs. On the opening kickoff of the first pre-season game, a night contest against the New York Jets, Coach Myers approached the teed-up football and booted it high into the well-lit atmosphere. The ball spun head over heels and was certain to reach the end zone. It was such a gorgeous kick he stopped to watch it. Just as the flight of the ball reached its apex, the lights went out. Not the stadium lights, Coach Myers' lights. Someone on the Jets had forearmed him under his chin. He woke in the locker room convinced that he should complete his teaching certification.

Mister Bennett, an English teacher, arrived carrying

a clipboard. He had to be the dullest teacher in the whole school, reading poetry to us in a low moan that was enough to put me to sleep. Girls liked him because of all that romantic stuff, and he was single and *cute*. "All right, for you newbies who don't know, I'm the J.V. coach. We have a few open positions this year, so best of luck today. Sound off when I call your name."

He read off a couple names, then mine. When I said, "here," Coach Myers shook his head in disbelief.

"Mister Briggs," he said in a voice that made me cringe. He waved for me to join him by first base. He whispered. "What're you doing here, son? I thought I asked you not to try out."

"I can't help it, Coach. I want to play."

"I can appreciate that, but you don't have what it takes."

"Please, sir, I've been practicing. Let me try. I don't want to be a total loser."

"Michael," he said, almost laughing, "you excel in math and science. You will *not* be a loser. You're just meant to do something else with your life."

"Do you have any idea how much this means to me?"

"I do. I've watched you bust your butt, but effort and desire won't make up for what you lack physically."

"Please," I said, begging.

"You know, Michael, I wish I had a whole team of players with your heart. I'd win states every year. But heart isn't enough. Please leave. Don't make me have to cut you—again."

"Sorry, Coach. I have to do this."

"All right," he said with a shrug. "Don't say I didn't warn you."

The wannabes had been sent into the field.

"Nobody's in right," Mister Bennett said with a bat

12

in his hand.

Little Jimmy Duggan, a friend in middle school until he moved away, said right field was where coaches put the worst player. I didn't care. Having the whole position to myself meant I'd get plenty of chances to prove myself.

Wow, I was a long way from home plate. And with this cold breeze, a fly ball might move all over the place. I hope the coaches realize that just in case I don't catch the ball.

I put the glove to my face and inhaled the sweet smell of leather. It was an intoxicating scent, greater than any perfume.

I jumped up and down to keep warm and to release some nervous energy. "All right, let's go!"

My enthusiasm was met with some snickering, but I didn't care.

"All right," Mister Bennett said at home plate, "around the horn."

He tossed a baseball a few feet into the air and then hit it on its way down, knocking a fast grounder to one of three boys who played third base. The boy fielded the ball nicely, threw a missile to second, where it popped loudly into another boy's mitt. The guy at second then whipped a throw to first, and that boy got the ball and threw a bullet to a standing catcher. The entire process took two seconds.

"All right," I said, punching a fist into my glove, "way to go. That was nice."

After Mister Bennett hit a grounder to each infielder, he hit a fly ball to both boys playing left and center field. They caught the ball easily.

My turn!

Mister Bennett hit the ball, more of a line drive than a fly ball. It started toward right-center. I stepped in that direction. Then before I knew it, the ball made a wicked curve back at me.

Crap!

I flung my left arm out in a pitiful effort to snare the ball, but it shot past the edge of my glove's webbing and landed about ten yards behind me. I turned and gave chase. The ball rolled away as if to mock me. I could actually hear it laughing. Or was that sound coming from the other boys?

I finally reached the baseball when it stopped. I picked it up. The damp grass had put a layer of moisture on the ball. I turned and threw. The ball slipped from my grip and didn't even reach the guy who stood in short right field.

I huffed and puffed, and hit myself in the head. "Stupid, stupid, stupid."

My first chance to prove myself and I totally blew it. Then again, it wasn't all *my* fault. Why had Mister Bennett hit a line drive at me, a curving liner at that? It wasn't fair. He hit a routine fly ball to the other outfielders. Hit me another one. I'd show him.

Mister Bennett did. No curving line drive this time. It was a high floating, as they say, can of corn. I caught it with no problem and immediately resented Mister Bennett. He had taken it easy on me. It was insulting.

The J.V. team was ordered to grab a bat and prepare to hit against Mister Bennett. I stood shivering while the first two hitters popped out to shortstop. The third hitter lined out to Rob Kyle at second base.

I yawned.

A blonde girl wearing a winter coat and ear muffs arrived and leaned against the fence by first base. I wondered what lucky boy she had come to watch. I wished it were me. I'd be a good boyfriend. I'd treat her right. But I was an outsider to relationships. I saw couples holding hands as they walked school grounds or in the halls. I noticed girls who wore their boyfriends' letter jackets.

What?

Everybody was screaming.

A centerfielder ran toward me. "Look out!"

I ducked and covered my head. A baseball landed just inches in front of me. I picked it up, but my fingers were so cold I had no feeling and lost my grip. I picked up the ball again. Then all in a panic, I hurried a throw to no one in particular. The ball landed behind second base and another boy ran after it.

Damn it!

I did suck, big time. I'd certainly hear about it in school. What was wrong with me?

After a couple more batters, Coach Myers and Mister Bennett had the J.V. team replace the wannabes in the field. I jogged in, doing my best to avoid eye contact and suppressing a rising tide of emotion.

"Mister Briggs," Coach Myers said. I cringed, and prepared to be dismissed. "Grab a bat."

Wow, he was letting me stay. Time to show some hitting skills, maybe I could earn a spot as a pinch-hitter.

I hurried to the line of aluminum bats that stood handle-side up against the backstop. "Man, that's heavy," I said of the first bat. I tried another one. It was heavier.

"Let's go, son," Coach Myers said from near the pitcher's mound. "We haven't got all day."

I grabbed the next bat. It felt heavy too, but I didn't want to get yelled at again. I ran to the plate and stood as a right-handed hitter. I held the bat straight up over my shoulders, bent my knees, and stared at a smiling Joe Forrester on the mound.

What?

Why was he pitching? Just to show me up, to put one through my satellite-dishes? And boy, up on the hill he looked ten feet tall, and seemed only a few feet away. Why was everyone laughing?

"Aren't you forgetting something, son?" Coach Myers said.

"What do you mean?"

"A helmet."

"Oh," I said, patting my head and feeling the cloth of my Phillies cap. How could I forget a helmet? They were right there next to the bats.

"Moron," I overheard.

The first helmet covered my eyes. The second one pinched my ears. I worried Coach Myers might yell at me again if I took too long, so I suffered with pinched ears and jogged back to the plate.

"Okay," Joe Forrester said, holding up the baseball for me to see, "here it comes."

Just watch the ball and hit it, like I did at Vinnie's Batting Cages. I had put enough dollars into his pitching machines that Vinnie could retire early.

Joe pitched from the stretch. Before I could even react, the ball whistled right past me about belt high and over the plate. I swung way late. The weight of the bat spun me around and I fell on my butt. Everybody laughed.

I got up, dusted myself off, and stood at the plate. "Remember," I whispered, "you can do this. You've been practicing and practicing."

Joe pitched the ball. I swung and missed to more laughter.

"Perhaps the bat's too heavy," Coach Myers said.

"Yeah," I said, "it's gotta be the bat."

The boys found that hilarious.

I found a lighter bat and returned to the plate. "You

16

can do this."

Joe pitched a mean dirty trick. I was all geared up for his fastball, but he threw a slow, blooper pitch and I swung *before* the ball even reached the plate. A few of the guys grabbed their sides from laughing so hard.

"Terence Shaw," Mister Bennett said, reading from his clipboard. "You're next."

I dragged the bat to the backstop, my head down, eyes to the ground like a sad puppy dog. What had happened? I had worked so hard for so long. When I wasn't cramming for a test, I practiced. Yet I had lost focus and performed worse than ever.

Coach Myers pulled me aside. "You're cut."

I could only nod and head for the parking lot.

"Hey, Michael," Joe said.

Don't look, don't look.

I did.

Joe grinned and held up a fist. "You rock!"

More laughter erupted.

"He tried out as a senior," someone said. "Who does that?"

"He told me he was a freshman."

Ouch. My lie had come back to haunt me.

I could still try out for the baseball team at the University of Delaware, the next school on my academic ladder. Its campus was within walking distance of my house. However, I had promised Mom and Dad that this would be the last sports-related rejection I'd suffer. As Dad had said, "It was time to put aside foolish dreams and concentrate on something practical." He was right. Joe Forrester was right. Coach Myers was right. But letting go of a life-long dream wasn't easy.

I reached my old Ford Taurus and practically crawled into the driver's seat. I grabbed the steering wheel and stared ahead for the longest time, not really seeing anything. My chest swelled. I got a big lump in my throat. I knew it was only a matter of time before the dam busted. So I stopped resisting and opened the floodgates. I let out all my bitter disappointments, not just over failing at baseball, but being so weird and different that boys teased me and girls got sick at the sight of me.

It just wasn't fair. Why I had been born with a passion I couldn't satisfy? Would my life be one of constant frustration?

CHAPTER 3

The next morning, Saturday, I stayed in bed with the comforter pulled completely over me like they did to dead people. How could I ever show my face? I had humiliated myself—again. How could I go to school on Monday? I could already hear the hysterical laughter and name-calling.

Face it, when it came to baseball, I'd only be a spectator. I'd be one of the millions of fans who'd purchase game tickets or watch the sport on television, the internet or listen to a game on radio. Only in my imagination could I put myself in the players' shoes.

Yet as a spectator, I lived in a prime location. Northern Delaware received Philadelphia's media. Between an over-the-airways television station and a regional sports cable channel, all Phillies games were viewable. I generally made it to five games in person. I also had the Baltimore Orioles within an hour's drive and could view their games on another sports cable channel.

There was a gentle knock on my bedroom door that had to be Mom. I poked my head out. "Come in."

19

Mom did. I had her curly black hair, but resembled Dad. She wore glasses and claimed to have three children, me, Dad and the dentist she assisted during the week. "I hope you're not spending this beautiful day in your room."

"It's a trick," I said.

"What's a trick?"

"The weather. It's a tease. One day freezing, one day warm. It'll be cold again tomorrow. It can't make up its stupid mind."

"Well, tease or not, you're not spending all day in your room feeling sorry for yourself. We've all had disappointments. Go out, have fun."

"I'll think about it."

"No think, *do*."

"But Mom."

"I don't want to hear it," she said, waving an index finger like a magic wand. "Get outside. Get some sun on that skin. I swear you look like you're ill."

"Geez, Mom, it's bad enough I get picked on in school. Do I have to get it here too?" That was cruel of me, playing the guilt game. "I'll get up in a minute."

"All right," she said in a softer tone. "I just don't want you in here all day. What's Austin doing?"

"He's away this weekend, remember?"

"Oh, right, visiting his grandparents."

"Right."

Mom nodded and left.

I threw back the comforter, which contained the logos of each major league baseball team, and sat in my briefs on the edge of the bed. My room, this place I've called home since I was five, reminded me of my failure. The ceiling had been painted to resemble a baseball field. The carpet was fake grass. I had shelves stuffed with books about baseball's history, its old ballparks, its famous players and managers. Shoes boxes were stuffed with baseball cards and stacked on my dresser next to a couple dozen player bobble-heads. A Phillies pennant hung on the wall above my desk and computer.

Dad had worried I was too old for such décor and too obsessed with the game until he saw the *Sports Illustrated* swimsuit calendar hung behind my door.

I should put this stuff in the closet. Then re-do my room to fit a soon-to-be college student. Maybe cover the walls with posters of hot women in bikinis. Dad should be okay with it. Mom might object. Yet it would show them I had outgrown, "this baseball nonsense," as Dad liked to call it, and that I was ready to grow up.

***

I put on a clean Phillies tee-shirt and blue jeans, and then pulled my bicycle out from its winter storage in our garage and dusted off the seat.

The garage door had been raised. My bony dad stood in the driveway hosing down his red Mustang convertible, or as he called it, his escape from the world of debits and credits and monthly reports. He could spend all day under its hood or making it shine. My old Taurus rested by the street curb. I never washed or waxed it because the dirt kept it from falling apart, and I wouldn't know the dip stick from the driveshaft.

"Care to go for a ride with your mom and me later?" Dad said.

Spend the day with my parents? Was he kidding? "No, thanks."

"Do you have your phone and house key?"

"Yes."

"Well, be careful."

I got on my bike and peddled in front of split level houses and single story ranches that Dad said had been built just after World War II. They weren't fancy rich houses or run down poor houses, just somewhere in between. I waved at neighbors I hardly knew and hadn't seen outside since last fall. Other cars got washed and waxed. People prepared gardens. Dogs got walked.

I rode behind McVey Elementary, the first school I ever attended and where I once screamed, "I hate school!" I received good grades, which oddly enough caused the other boys and girls to dislike me. It was even worse in gym class. Boys laughed at me. I got picked last for teams. On a cold February day in fifth grade, a couple guys ambushed me on my way from the shower, ripped the towel from around my waist and shoved me outside. I banged and banged on the door and almost froze to death in my birthday suit before Andy Fleming let me in.

McVey had a grass field next to its playground. Some boys, about ten to twelve years old, were playing a pick up baseball game. Small and square pieces of wood had been placed on the ground to represent each base and it appeared they had been set apart at the Little League distance of sixty feet. They had set their diamond so that the batter hit away from the school and toward the corner of South College Avenue and Old Chestnut Hill Road. Both avenues were a safe distance away and shielded by a row of mature trees.

"Are you ready yet," the pitcher said, slamming a baseball into his glove.

"I've been ready," the right-handed hitter said, holding a bat almost as long as he was tall.

The pitcher served up a nice, gentle toss. The ball crossed the plate at the batter's hips and the catcher, who didn't wear protective equipment, stood back apiece and fielded the ball on the bounce.

"What's wrong with that?" the pitcher said, stomping his foot.

"It's outside," the batter said.

"It was not!"

"It was right down the middle, you little dweeb," the shortstop said. "You were struck out five pitches ago."

The pitcher received the ball from the catcher and slammed it into his glove a couple more times. He took a deep breath and served up another soft one. The baseball passed the batter thigh high and bounced to the catcher.

The pitcher threw his hands up so hard his glove flew into the air and crashed behind him. He held up a fist with a thumb sticking up. "You're out!"

"It was inside," the batter said.

"Martin," the third baseman said, "swing the bat or I'll smash your head with it."

I laughed.

"Hey, you," the pitcher said, picking up his glove and looking in my direction, "wanna ump?"

"What?"

"We need an umpire."

"Me? You got to be kidding."

Umpires were the scourge of baseball. They were fat and overpaid figureheads who got cussed at by players, coaches, managers, fans and *me*. They got dirt kicked on their shoes. Their vision and I.Q. were questioned. They were the enemy to anyone who loved the sport. I hated them.

"No, really," the pitcher said. "You know the rules, don't you?"

"Do *I* know the rules?" I said with a chuckle. I had memorized *The Major League Baseball Rule Book* backwards and forwards and owned several worn-out copies. I've watched enough games to be aware of every possible situation. But umpire? Me? I got picked on enough in school. "I don't think so, guys."

"Come on," the pitcher said. "We worked all week to set this game up, but we ain't never going to see which team's better. We promise not to argue."

"Please," came from some infielders and outfielders. Even a few of the batter's teammates begged.

Wow, so this was how it felt to be wanted. It sucked that I couldn't experience this appreciation among my own age group. These boys weren't judging me, calling me nerd, string-bean, beanpole, stickman, or any other name other than my own. They saw me as someone who liked baseball and could help them. I had to reward that.

"All right," I said. I left my bike next to some other two-wheelers and shook hands with the pitcher. "Michael."

"Stephen. We're from Robscott and they're Brookside." Then he shouted to all, "Michael's the umpire."

"We don't need no umpire," the batter said, pouting.

"Do you live in Robscott or Brookside?" a teammate of the batter asked.

"Robscott," I replied.

"He can't ump," a Brooksider said. "He might favor you guys."

"You'll be fair," Stephen said, "won't you?"

"Hey, I don't care who wins."

"Okay," Stephen said. "You're our umpire."

The Brookside team moaned about the decision, but conceded.

"What's the score and inning?" I asked.

"He's the first hitter," Stephen said, rolling his eyes, "and he's been up there forever. We're playing six innings." Then he turned to all, "We're starting over."

I stood off to Stephen's left side and focused on the area above home plate and relevant to the batter's chest and top of his knees.

Stephen's first pitch had more muscle behind it and the ball crossed home plate hip high on the batter and the catcher fielded it on one bounce.

"Strike one," I said, imitating umpires I had seen on television by raising my right arm.

Robscott cheered.

The batter frowned.

I laughed.

Stephen threw the next pitch over home plate knee high on the batter.

"Strike two," I yelled.

The fielders cheered again. I laughed again. What was so funny?

"That was low," the hitter said.

I ignored him. The next pitch bounced in front of home plate.

"Ball one."

"Looked good to me," the left fielder said.

The batter swung and missed the next pitch.

"One out!"

Robscott cheered. I watched them get ready for the next batter with more bounce in their step and more energy in their voices. The Brookside team rooted for their next hitter. The entire mood of the game had become more fun and it had been my inclusion that caused it.

"Wow," I said.

The next batter worked a two ball and one strike count before he hit a fly ball caught by the centerfielder.

"Two outs," I said, and the Robscott players repeated it.

Brookside's next batter hit the first pitch hard on the ground to shortstop. The all grass infield slowed the baseball, but the fielder scooped it up quick with his glove, retrieved the ball with his bare hand and threw hard to first. The Little League distance of sixty feet between the bases made for a small infield. To avoid being hit by the ball, I dropped to one knee and looked at first base as the ball flew by me.

Holy crap! Now what?

How did I best watch the quick action at first base to determine if the hitter was safe or out? Did I look at the entire scene, my eyes taking a snapshot when the ball arrived in the first baseman's mitt? Did I focus on the baseball's arrival into the first baseman's mitt and then look down for the runner's foot on the base? Did I watch the base for the runner's foot and then look up for the baseball in the glove? What was I supposed to do?

At the last split-second, and by pure accident, I had been focused on the piece of wood that represented first base and *heard* the baseball smack into the fielder's mitt before the hitter's foot touched the base. "You're out!"

The Robscott nine celebrated and left the field.

I released a gigantic sigh of relief. "I guess there's more to this job than I thought."

***

Bottom of the fifth inning, Stephen came to bat with two outs and runners on first and second. His team trailed 6-5. He fouled off the first two pitches. Next pitch, the baseball crossed over the plate level to Stephen's breastbone. He didn't swing.

"Ball," I said.

"What?" Brookside's pitcher screamed. "That was right there."

"It was high."

"It was not!"

"Let it go, Clark," the second baseman said.

The pitch might've been close to the top of the strike zone, but I gave Stephen the benefit of the doubt. Then on the next pitch, he smacked the ball deep into the gap between the left and centerfielders and drove in both runs. Stephen reached third by the time the ball was returned to the infield.

"The inning should be over," Brookside's pitcher said with a look of disgust.

Could I eject a kid from a pick-up game?

Robscott scored a couple more runs and went on to win 9-6. The boys collected the bases, their gloves, bats and baseballs. With the exception of Brookside's pitcher, they thanked me over and over for helping them out.

"We never would've gotten out of the first inning if you hadn't come along," Stephen said.

"You made it feel like a *real* game," another boy said. "Our Little League could use you."

"Really?" I said. "Thanks, guys."

The boys left on foot or on bikes. I wandered the grass, felt the sun on my face and savored a feeling I hadn't experienced—respect. I hadn't been teased because of my looks or grades or lack of athletic prowess. I had been accepted, looked up to and admired.

Oh, wow!

I suddenly had an incredible idea. Mom and Dad had been pestering me about a career choice. I was about to graduate high school and had no idea what I was going to do with my life. Dad wanted engineer or chemist. Mom said something medical. But I had to decide for myself and make my own path. And just like that my future became crystal clear.

Why hadn't I thought of it before?

I could be an umpire!

And someday be in the major leagues!

Why not? I knew the rules. I understood the sport. I

27

was used to people calling me names.

From listening to baseball commentators, I knew major league umpire was a full-time career. They made good money too. Along with salary, they received traveling expenses and a meal allowance. They also had a much longer career than a player. I could be in the major leagues for thirty years! Some umpires have been enshrined into the Baseball Hall of Fame.

However, that was at the top level. Such a career required a start in the minor leagues, where salary and other benefits were significantly less. Minor league regular seasons also ended at the beginning of September instead of October. I might need a job in the off-season. There were winter leagues in Latin America, but I didn't speak Spanish.

I had some research to do. I hopped on my bike and pumped my fist. "Yeeha!"

CHAPTER 4

I sped home. Dad's car was gone and the garage door shut. I rode around back, dropped my bike in the yard and used my key to open a sliding glass door that led into the kitchen. I grabbed a bottled sports drink from the refrigerator and hurried upstairs to my computer. I drank, and did an internet search on "professional baseball umpire." The top result was the website for Major League Baseball and the page, "How to Become an Umpire." Step One: I had to graduate from one of only two sanctioned training programs, both in Florida.

After researching the schools online, I liked the Matt Fogel Umpire School in Daytona Beach. Its website displayed a number of endorsements and awards the school had received over the years, along with photographs of its facility and staff of instructors, all professional umpires in either the minor or major leagues and a couple retired. I recognized some of the names. The five week course started the day after New Year's. Tuition of $3000 covered classroom instruction, field work and living at a hotel, meal plan extra.

"Wow," I said, sighing, "that's a lot of money."

Mom and Dad would never pay for it, and definitely not support my decision to attend. They wanted me in college, no argument.

I read: *While knowing the rules of the game is vital, each student has to master the mechanics, such as positioning for each situation, proper signaling and voice control. Each student has to demonstrate a high degree of stamina for the physical and mental demands. He must be confident, hustle, and have the ability to remain calm and handle any situation.*

There are only 68 umpires in the major leagues and 225 in the minors. With the low rate of turnover at the major league level, it's a long shot for an umpire to reach the top. An umpire has to expect to spend a minimum of two seasons at the Short A Rookie Leagues, a couple years at Class A ball and Double-A, and any number of seasons at Triple-A before that call to the majors.

I slumped in my chair. Maybe it wasn't such a good idea. I might be a crabby old man by the time I got called to the majors, if ever.

I almost left the website when I noticed the following: *For anyone serious about starting a career, umpire as many games as possible in and around your community. There are regional umpire associations that handle all levels of amateur ball, from little league to high school and college games, as well as summer leagues.*

What had that boy said? "Our little league could use you." And since when did I let incredible odds stop me? I had to find out if I liked umpiring by doing it.

I searched the internet for Delaware Umpire Groups. A number of organizations popped up, with addresses in various towns across the state. After I read their information, I wasn't sure which one would be a good fit for me. Plus, I didn't want to umpire all over Delaware, just locally in New Castle County. Who umpired around here? I could ask Coach Myers. I made a mental note to see him first thing Monday.

***

There were three televisions in my house, one in the living room, one in my parents' bedroom and one in the basement. When it came to watching baseball, I had viewing privileges in the cellar, which suited me fine. It was a finished basement, complete with a sofa, love seat, coffee and end tables, lamps, two recliners and a rarely used pool table.

I turned on the television to a Phillies spring training game and got comfortable on the sofa. During a record-ed version of the national anthem, I heard footsteps up-stairs. Mom and Dad shouted down that they were home. A few minutes later, Dad came down with a bowl of potato chips and two canned sodas.

"Mind if I join you?" he asked.

I slid over.

Dad handed me a cola and put the bowl of chips be-tween us. "This is just a spring training game, right?"

"Yes."

"Who are they playing and where?"

"Detroit at Clearwater," I replied. "So it's a home game."

"And even though it's only a practice game, you can still watch with interest?"

"Yes. It lets me see what they have this year, and who might play for them in the future."

Dad nodded. He was no dummy when it came to sports, but he preferred golf. He had taken me to a driv-ing range and instructed me on how to hit the ball off a tee. I liked that aspect of the game. It reminded me of batting a baseball, but I kept gripping the club wrong. "No, no, no," he had said. "Don't hold it like a bat."

When I held the club correctly and hit the ball well,

31

he took me to the Newark Country Club for an instructional round. I loved smacking the ball off the tee and seeing how far it traveled. After that, learning how to control my swing in order to hit the ball shorter distances, knowing what club to use, how best to reach the green and putt the ball into the hole, drove me nuts. I had no patience for the subtleties of the sport. So Dad abandoned all hope of me joining him on the links and played only with his golfing buddies. They vacationed every autumn at "golf heavens," such as Myrtle Beach, South Carolina. He has stated on more than one occasion that when he retired he wanted to relocate to that town.

"We missed you on our drive."

"Where'd you go?"

"Amish country," Dad said. "We stopped at a couple farmer's markets, had lunch at the Smorgasbord. What did you end up doing?"

The timing wasn't right to tell him about my decision to try umpiring. "Oh, I just rode around."

"Any news on the scholarships?"

"No."

"Well, I wouldn't worry about it. You'll hear something soon. You're very lucky. "

Oh, boy. This wasn't going to be easy.

CHAPTER 5

Monday before school began, I entered the boy's locker room. It was quiet, only half the overhead lights were on, and although the space had been cleaned, the room still smelled of sweaty gym socks.

It felt odd walking through here at a normal pace. I usually dressed and undressed as fast as possible, darting in and out of the shower, careful not to peek at my naked classmates while ignoring their taunts about my body. I also had to be weary of pranks, such as a towel slapped against my bare butt, or returning to my locker to discover my clothes had been hidden.

The door to Coach Myers' office was open and a light was on. I smelled cigar before I saw it burning in an ashtray on his desk, next to a steaming cup of coffee and three glazed doughnuts. Coach stared at his computer screen.

I tapped on the door.

He flinched. "Christ, Michael, what're you doing here so early?"

"Coach, there's no smoking in the building. Buy my lunch until I graduate or I'll report you to the principal."

"Blackmail me and I'll get Joe to kill you."

"Oh, he'll gladly do it for no reason."

"Care for a doughnut?" Coach said, leaning back in his chair. His tiny office had a red and gold Glasgow High pennant on the wall, a bookcase of sports training manuals, biographies of famous athletes, and a small glass case that contained a couple baseball trophies.

"No, thanks."

"This isn't about you playing baseball, is it? I thought we settled that."

"No, Coach. I was wondering who umpires school ball?"

"A bunch of blind bastards. Why?"

"I want to try umpiring. See if I like it. Maybe turn pro."

"Michael, Michael, Michael," Coach said, shaking his head. "Why do you insist on torturing yourself? Get your degree and go work for DuPont."

"You sound like my dad."

"Well, you should listen to him. We're just trying to look out for you. Kids your age think you know it all, but you don't. Trust me. Trust your dad. You have a gift, but it's not in sports."

"Well, maybe I have to find out the hard way."

"The problem with that is by the time you learn your lesson, life has passed you by."

"I can't help it, Coach. I have to be part of baseball. I can't play it, maybe I can ump it."

"Michael, do you have any idea how enormous the odds are of making a career out of umpiring? It's right near impossible."

"I know, Coach. I've researched it. But before I make up my mind, I want to see if I like it, if I can handle it. So if there's an organization around here that does school ball or Little League,　I'd like to start there and see what happens."

Coach paused for a moment, probably debating if he should help me or not. Then he opened a desk drawer and handed me a business card for the New Castle County Umpire Association, President Randal Spencer. "They ump all the school ball in the county, and most of the summer leagues."

I stared at the card. "Do you know if they're looking for people?"

"I'm sure they are. It's not a popular job."

"Do they pay?"

"Yes."

"Really?" I said, seeing dollar signs. "How much?"

"I don't know, but I hear it's good money for part time."

I looked at Coach. "Thanks. Thanks a lot."

"Michael, don't expect too much. Most of those guys are good and they take the job seriously. But for some it's just an extra buck. They haven't picked up a rule book in years."

"Oh, it'll be great, Coach. I'm sure of it. Bye."

I hurried from his office, clutching the business card as if it were gold. I wanted to telephone Mister Spencer right now, but it was definitely too early. Plus, I'd want privacy. I took a deep breath and decided to wait until I got home.

***

"Hey, Don Quixote," Austin said, arriving at our lunch table with tray in hand. While most students came to school dressed as casually as possible, Austin wore a collared shirt, creased pants and a tie. He took abuse because of his fastidious style, but it was all part of Austin's desire to stand out in the crowd. "Still tilting at windmills?"

"What's wrong with tilting at windmills?"

"It's crazy," he said, sitting across from me.

"Well," I said, "this time it was even worse."

The ends of Austin's lips curled up. He wanted to laugh, but quickly sipped a spoonful of tomato soup. He and I had bought the school lunch, a grilled cheese sandwich, bowl of tomato soup and a glass of chocolate milk. During my entire life in the public school system, whenever the menu had grilled cheese sandwiches, it was accompanied by a bowl of tomato soup.   Just once I'd like to see something different. Why not grilled cheese sandwich and beef barley soup? How about no soup?

"Go ahead and laugh if you want to," I said, debating whether or not to tell him about my interest in becoming an umpire.

"Well," Austin said, "at least you tried. You can hold onto that."

"You don't understand. You love to write and you can do it and have already published a couple short stories. I love baseball and I *can't* do it."

Austin sipped more soup. "Focus on chemistry. It'll make your parents happy."

"I know. I like chemistry, but I don't know if I want to be stuck in a lab all day."

"Yeah, but with the DuPont Corporation right here, you should be able to find work right away and nearby, no problem."

"Yes," I was sarcastic. "Dad reminds me of that fact almost daily."

I ate, and kept a weary eye on my noisy surroundings. Glasgow's cafeteria had round, square and rectangular tables occupied by pimply-faced teenagers who ate their lunches, conversed with a neighbor, texted or chatted on their cell phones.

I located Joe Forrester in his usual seat at the jock section, which incorporated several tables. The bulky wrestlers hung out together, next to the football players. The soccer team had grouped themselves, so had the track and field and cross country, as well as the baseball players.

Joe and I made eye contact. He sneered at me and flashed his middle finger.

The loudest section of the cafeteria belonged to the giggling and screeching popular girls. They were the females every boy wanted to see naked, and some had. They prided themselves on their appearance and wouldn't be caught dead without make up or wearing the latest fashion. Kelsey Delgado sat among them. She claimed to be a quarter Cherokee and I believed her. She had high cheek bones and the cutest dimples when she smiled. Her straight ebony hair fell to the small of her back. I wanted to run my fingers through those beautiful strands. I yearned to have my first kiss with her.

Austin spooned the last drop of tomato soup. "Michael, have you considered being a sports commentator? You're well spoken, well read. You could work for ESPN, or the Baseball Network."

The thought of pursuing a career in television had occurred to me many times. I'd travel the country. I'd show off my expertise. I'd become familiar with players, managers, scouts and office executives. I might even become famous. Some broadcasters were household names and had been enshrined in The Baseball Hall of Fame.

"I thought about it, but I don't think they'd want this face in *front* of the camera."

"Oh, Michael, you're too hard on yourself."

"Just repeating what I've been told."

"Well, stop it. What is it about baseball that intrigues you so much? I think it's so boring."

"Oh, there's something mathematical and cerebral about it. Did you know it's the only team sport where the defense controls the ball? There's no time clock. A team can continue to bat until that third out. There's tension and uncertainty between every pitch."

"And you don't get that tension with chemistry?"

"No. If I mix a certain compound with another one, I know what to expect."

Austin looked away and sighed, "Damn."

Although I had a crush on Kelsey Delgado, every male at Glasgow High fantasized about Kristen Richardson. The blonde strutted into the cafeteria. She displayed her curves in a tight peach-colored sweater and blue jeans.

"Look at her," Austin said, "she knows she's hot."

"Of course she does."

Kristen sat next to the football team's quarterback, Keith Lockhart. The muscular kid squirmed in his seat and appeared uncomfortable with the crowd's attention. Odd reaction, I thought, considering he was the school's sports hero and had the hottest girl.

Joe Forrester appeared disgusted. Or was it envy?

"I hear they're breaking up," Austin said.

"How do you know?" I said.

"Just an impression."

"Why do girls like that always go for the brutes? It's not fair."

"No, it's not fair," Austin said, "but what're you going to do about it?"

"She could do so much better."

"As in yourself?"

"Why not?"

"That'll never happen," Austin said. "And if by some

miracle it did, it would only give Joe more reason to hate you. Face it, she's as unobtainable as your baseball aspirations."

"Oh," I said with a laugh, "now that hurt." I tried to joke. "I might not be much to look at, but I have inner beauty. That's what my mom tells me."

"Mothers have to say that."

I had been so distracted by Kristen and my conversation with Austin that I failed to monitor my surroundings. Joe Forrester snuck up behind me. He slammed a fist against the tabletop. It sounded like a gunshot. My half-empty glass of chocolate milk bounced and almost fell over. Worse, I flinched so badly I fell out of my chair and every student saw it. Their laughter was unbearable. I stared at the floor as I retook my seat.

Joe stood behind me. He squeezed my shoulder and whispered in my ear, "Dumb ass."

Joe raised his arms in victory until the laughter subsided. Then he left with a couple buddies.

"Don't worry about it," Austin said, sympathetic. "You'll graduate soon and never see these fools again."

I had experienced humiliation and embarrassment so often I should be immune. Yet the emotional pangs were as bad as they had been the first time, when Sam Crestfield had pushed me into the mud in first grade. What had I done to deserve this? It wasn't my fault Kristen preferred the quarterback. It wasn't my fault I got excellent grades and Joe was an average student, and cheater at that.

It wasn't my fault!

"Thanks, Austin. But it doesn't help."

CHAPTER 6

That evening, and in the privacy of my room, I tele-phoned Randal Spencer. My heart pounded almost as fast as it did at try-outs. After all, this could be the start of something really, really big.

"Good timing," Randal said after I introduced my-self and stated my reason for calling. "There's a meeting Wednesday night at seven at Trinity Church on Faulk Road in Wilmington. You can sign up and take the writ-ten test."

"I'm only eighteen. Is that a problem?"

"No, that's our minimum."

"I have to buy equipment, don't I? Can I get it at any sporting goods store?"

"Slow down. Love the enthusiasm, but this isn't your ordinary part time job. It's expensive to start. Wait to see if you want to do it. Come to the meeting. Take the test. We then schedule training at William Penn High School. After that, if you still want to do it, I can sell you some used equipment that's in good shape. Don't worry, you'll earn the money back."

"How much can I make?"

"Well, varsity high school is seventy dollars a game."

Wow! Four-ninety a week! I could afford umpire school in no time. And buy a new car.

"But it's rare that we let rookie umpires work that level," Randal said. "You'll do J.V., and middle school, which is fifty."

Three-fifty a week! I'd earn more money umpiring in two to three hours than most teens did in eight hours of fast food or retail.

"Summer leagues range from thirty-five to seventy, depending on the level, which are Babe Ruth for thirteen to fifteen year olds, American Legion and Semi-Pro."

"Little League?"

"No, they use volunteers."

"Do I work every day?"

"No, you'll average about three games a week. Maybe more if we get a lot of rains outs to make up."

"Do I have to pay taxes?"

"No, it's chump change."

"School ball starts their games right after school, and the season ends by Memorial Day, right? And summer leagues start their weekday games at six?"

"Correct."

"See you Wednesday," I said and hung up.

I had asked Randal to confirm the start time and length of the school season because I had a full-time summer job at Lums Pond State Park that started Memorial Day Weekend. Between working school ball and summer league games, as well as my full-time job, I should be able to save enough money to pay for umpire school all on my own.

However, I shouldn't count my money before I earned it. I had the enthusiasm and motivation. Yet my emotions might cloud my common sense. After all, I had already discovered in the pick-up game that there was more to the job than what met the eye. What other discoveries lay ahead? Plus, the amateur level could be a whole different ballgame—no pun intended. I'd confront players who were bigger than me. I'd face coaches and managers as old as my dad. Would I be intimidated and subconsciously have it influence my calls? There might not be security. How would I handle an unruly situation? There'd be nothing to prevent players, coaches, managers, parents, family and friends from rushing the field.

The job seemed better suited for firemen, policemen or ex-military. Jocks hesitated to argue a call if the umpire stood six-foot-six and all muscle. My bony ass would get laughed at.

Of course, there was Mom and Dad. They'd probably commit me to the state crazy house for wanting to umpire baseball. However, I'd be earning money. That would make Dad happy. Besides, if I didn't like it or couldn't handle it, I could always walk away. No harm done. No regrets. But what if I loved it? What if I earned enough money to pay for umpire school? How could I not attend next January? How could I convince my parents to let me postpone college?

Wait. Weren't most colleges on winter break in January? How long was that?

I plopped in front of my computer and checked the academic calendar for the next school year at the University of Delaware. The fall semester started the Wednesday before Labor Day. It ended a week before Christmas. Spring semester didn't start until the second week of February--a seven week break!

"Yeeha!" I said, leaping out of my chair.

CHAPTER 7

After school on Tuesdays, I tutored students who wanted to improve their math scores. The one hour sessions were held in Mister Tressel's classroom. I liked Mister Tressel, although he probably taught Algebra and Calculus to the dinosaurs, and had big bulging eyes that made him appear ghoulish. "Bug eyes" was a popular nickname among the students. He currently hovered around a couple freshmen, Todd Mendenhall and Terence Kramer, who hadn't yet mastered addition and subtraction.

I had Victor Sanchez, a sophomore who whined about quadratic formulas. "Why do I have to know this? When am I ever going to use this stuff? Isn't there an easier way? This doesn't make any sense."

I daydreamed. I couldn't help it. I had something much more exciting to look forward to than listening to Victor complain. In my mind, I stood behind a stooped catcher calling balls and strikes against a high school batter. These fantasies progressed to where I imagined myself in the majors, in front of thousands of spectators, umpiring regular season games, playoffs, the World Series!

The classroom door opened.

Holy crap!

My fantasy ended and another one started because Kelsey Delgado, all five-foot ten of her long-legged figure, entered the room wearing blue jeans and a red sweater. She carried her *Basic Algebra* textbook.

Wow! She needed help with math! My help! Why else would she be here? This was my golden opportunity to prove to Kelsey that I existed. Until now, all I did was fantasize about us as lovers or imagine ways to meet her. I planned stupid situations like bumping into her by "accident," or find some excuse to stand by her locker. Then of course, I'd wimp out.

Kelsey approached Mister Tressel. He already had two students, so he pointed at me. Her black eyes looked in my direction. She frowned. My heart crashed into a mountain, but I swallowed my pain and tried to salvage the situation.

"Hi, hello, Kelsey."

"I flunked my Algebra test," she said in a whisper. "Ugh. I hate this. I understand my other classes, but math makes me feel so stupid. It's useless, you know. When am I ever going to need this stuff?"

"That's what I said," Victor added.

Oh, wow, she talked to me. I should kiss her. Right now, in front of everybody, just grab her and get it over with. She'd probably have me arrested. Who cares? It would be worth it. But all I did was give a lame answer. "You'll need it for college."

"I know," she said with a frustrated sigh. "I mean, my brain gets tired. You know? Why don't they use numbers in these stupid formulas instead of letters? Then maybe I'd understand it."

I glanced at Kelsey's sweater and how it bulged with her shapely chest and imagined what lay underneath.   I couldn't help it. Some have accused her of stuffing her bra, but no way.

"Take a seat," I said, salivating.

My heart pounded. I thought it might burst through my chest. How gross would that be?

As Kelsey sat, she whipped her head about so that her long hair fell behind her, but to me, it all happened in slow-motion, each strand of hair separated and then came together in a great flowing blackness. I almost fainted, and wondered why she couldn't like me. Didn't she know I'd be the best boyfriend ever? And I didn't care about her height. Other boys refused to ask her out because of it. I mean, how stupid was that?

"Can we go over the Quadratic Formula," she said as she opened her textbook.

"Are you and Victor in the same class? That's why he's here."

"No," Kelsey said, looking at Victor and appearing ready to vomit. "It just doesn't make any sense. It's so complicated, but I'm sure it's easy for you."

I smiled, and wondered if it were possible to get high off Kelsey's perfume. I had to find out what she wore so I could buy it as a gift. Then I'd have to find a private moment to give it to her, which would be impossible. We didn't travel in the same social circle and I'd wimp out anyway. So never mind.

"It'll make sense," I said, "once we break it down to its different components: integers, coefficients, polynomials, discriminants and conjugates—are parts of the quadratic formula."

It took twenty minutes of simplifying several equations for the light bulb to go on in Kelsey's brain. Not so for Victor. He scratched his head and repeated, "I don't get it. I don't get it."

I wanted to strangle him.   I wished he'd leave so I'd

be alone with Kelsey. But instead, Kelsey got up. She collected her book and thanked me. She flashed her brilliant smile. Her perfect teeth appeared much brighter set against her dark skin.

I imagined asking her for a date, but chickened out. Why was I so weird? I had the guts to try umpiring and yet couldn't take a risk with the girl of my dreams.

Kelsey thanked me again and left. The room seemed empty. But my crush had spoken to me. I had helped her. Maybe now she saw me as a friend.

I heard a sarcastic cough. "Yes, Victor."

"I know I'm not as cute as she is, but I'm still sitting here."

"Sorry, Victor," I said, my face probably red.

After the session, I stepped into a vacant hallway. Weird, how fast all the drama and noise ended right after final period. Nobody ever wanted to hang out at school, which was fine with me.

I opened my locker. Most classmates decorated the inside of their locker with pictures of famous celebrities, personal art work, or a photograph of a girlfriend or boyfriend. I displayed nothing. I graduate in June. I didn't want anything like ripping down pictures to slow my exit from the building.

I grabbed my backpack, put on a light jacket and exited the school by the locker room. I shivered, and saw my breath. As I had told Mom, the warm weekend had been a trick. It was still technically winter, and I had failed to heed my own warning and left my coat at home.

"Well, looky here."

Joe Forrester, wearing his baseball warm ups, had come around the corner of the building and blocked my way. I hadn't seen him all day and assumed he had skipped school. I wished he had. He didn't appear too steady on his feet.

"Come to try out again?" Joe laughed.

"No, Joe. I tutor."

"Oh, right, I forgot you're a suck up."

"Well, see ya later, Joe."

"Hey," he said, grabbing my shoulder with a heavy hand. "Let me ask you something. You're a dorky guy with a sense of right and wrong, right? Don't you find it strange that a real hottie like Kristen goes out with that dumb ass quarterback? I mean, what a stupid slut. Why does she like him? He don't like her. I don't think he even likes girls."

"You're too good for her, Joe. She doesn't deserve you."

"What would you know," he said, poking me in the breastbone. "Don't talk about her like that."

"I have to get home."

"Home to your dorky mom and dorky dad," he said laughing. He ripped the backpack from my hand. "Whoa, dude. This is heavy. What have you got in here, a body?"

"Just books."

"Just books," he repeated with canines showing. That meant trouble. "You'd think that lugging this around would help you develop some muscles. But you're just a skinny ass toothpick *loser*."

"Please, Joe," I said, knowing I had to be extra nice, "may I have my books. I need to get home."

Joe swung the backpack at my head. I got an arm up to block the strike, but the force of the blow knocked me off balance. I stumbled, and then belly-flopped onto the asphalt. Eight rubber cleats punched hard on my lower back and I yelped like an injured puppy.

CHAPTER 8

Wilmington wasn't a big city, not like Philadelphia, but for a kid from the suburbs, it was gigantic and scary. I drove with a tight grip on the steering wheel, keeping a nervous eye on all the cars, buses and stupid people that liked to step out into the street without looking. I got confused by all the one-way streets and felt like a mouse caught in an urban maze.

I almost pulled over to call Mister Spencer to tell him I'd be late when there it was, Trinity Church. I had somehow ended up at my destination. I parked in back among other cars, collected a notepad and pen and hurried through a double-door that slammed shut behind me. I flinched as the *bang* echoed.

The New Castle County Umpire Association met in the basement. There must've been about fifty metal chairs occupied by all sorts of older men. They looked at me as if I were an alien from another planet that had invaded their private club.

"I need to see Mister Spencer," I said to a couple guys.

They pointed at a slender, balding man in a gray sweater who had a great tan for March. He stood by a lectern on a low stage, sorting papers in an open brief-case.

"Hi, I'm Michael Briggs."

"Oh, great," he said, and we shook hands. "Call me Randy."

He handed me a blank membership form, a set of bylaws, the latest newsletter and a roster sheet that contained everyone's name, home and email address, and phone number.

"Fill out the membership form," Randy said, "and hand it in after the meeting. You'll take the written test at that time. It's ten questions and a couple scenarios that'll test your knowledge of the rules. If you do well and decide to stick around, there's dues of seventy-five dollars, but we'll deduct that from your pay after the first month."

"Wow, I haven't umpired a single game and already owe a lot of money."

"You'll earn it back."

"Is the used equipment here?"

"No, it's at my house. We'll negotiate a price after the training session, if you decide to stay."

"Okay, okay. Are you trying to talk me out of it?"

"No. Thank you for coming. Go ahead and take a seat in the front row. I'll introduce you to everybody."

"Am I the only newbie?"

"This week. We had five last week. Three have already quit."

"That doesn't sound good."

"It's par for the course. Not everybody has the temperament for this. Some think it's easier than it is."

I sat, feeling back pain from where Musclehead had put his cleats. As usual, I told no one. I'd rather suffer than admit I had been beaten up, or be a tattle-tale. Mom would call that stupid macho thinking. Of course, she was right.

"Everyone," Randy said from the lectern, "let's get started. And please turn off your damn cell phones, or whatever cockamamie device you have. I hate them things going off when I'm talking."

"Oh, come on, Randy," a man two rows behind me complained, "what if one of my girl friends needs to reach me?"

"I don't want to hear about your girl friends. It upsets us married guys."

The men laughed.

"Before I get to the business at hand," Randy said, "I'd like to introduce a new lamb to the slaughter, Michael Briggs."

I stood, turned and gave a simple wave. The men applauded with little enthusiasm.

"Hey, Randy," someone in the back row said, "are we so desperate for umpires that we're recruiting babies now?"

Everyone laughed.

"Hey," I said, going along with the joke, "I'm potty trained."

The men were amused.

"Come on, guys," Randy said, "don't chase him away before he has a chance to quit."

More laughter.

Crap. I had hoped to join a group of men who shared a love of baseball. Instead, I found comedians who didn't seem all that serious about the job, and they certainly didn't expect much from me.

***

I arrived home a couple hours later. Mom and Dad were seated on the living room sofa watching television.

They glared at me.

Oh, no. What had I done? I searched my memory banks, but came up blank.

"So," Dad said, using the remote to lower the t.v.'s volume, "how was the library?"

"Okay," I replied, suspicious.

"Michael," Dad said, "if you're going to lie to us, make it a plausible lie."

"What do you mean?"

"The library closes at five on Wednesday. So where were you?"

Good grades had bought me freedom at home. Usually, I came and went as I pleased, rarely questioned, but they had caught me in a lie. Had I blown my trust with them?

"Is your phone broken?" Mom said. "We tried to reach you?"

As Randy had requested, I turned my phone off prior to the meeting, but forgot to turn it on afterwards. Truthfully, I hadn't forgotten. I had hoped to attend the meeting and get home to bed without my parents noticing, a dumb idea.

"Since you didn't answer your phone," Dad said, "we called the library and got the recorded message about the hours. So where were you?"

"What did you call me about?" I asked.

"Never mind that now," Dad said. "Where were you?"

I sighed. "I went to a meeting of the New Castle County Umpire Association."

"The what?" Dad said.

"I umpired a game for these kids the other day and really liked it. So I signed up with this group that umpires school ball and summer leagues."

For what seemed like a minute, my parents stared

at me with a blank look on their faces. I truly worried they might stroke out.

"You can't be serious," Dad finally said with a nervous laugh. "I thought we decided no more baseball."

"No more *playing* baseball."

"How can you even *think* to do that?" Mom said, her mouth hanging open.

"Why didn't you mention this before," Dad said, "instead of lying to us? Were you hoping to hide it from us?"

"No. I was going to talk to you about it after the training session Saturday. I'm not on the payroll yet."

"Payroll?" Dad said, alert. "So you get paid?"

"Fifty dollars a game for J.V. and middle school."

"Really?" Mom said, looking impressed.

"And you'll save the money for college?" Dad said.

"Of course," I replied, not wanting to reveal umpire school just yet. Why would I?

"Michael," Mom said, "you'll have coaches, players and people in the bleachers cussing at you. Somebody might get carried away and start a fight. We read all the time about kids and adults getting out of control at these games."

"I'll be fine."

"You don't know that," Dad said.

"If I can't handle it, I'll quit."

"What about your school work?" Dad said. "Will you be home in time for dinner?"

My parents ran the house on a schedule, even on weekends, probably because Mom dealt with scheduled appointments at her job and Dad's accounting mentality had to apply to everything. Umpiring after school would mean dinner might have to be pushed back a half hour to 6:30. Wow, civilization might come to an end.

"I don't do homework until after dinner," I said. "So

nothing will change. The games are played right after school and over by 5:30."

"What about your summer job?" Mom said.

"I can do both. Summer games start at 6. So it's Lums Pond from 8 to 5, then umpire afterwards."

"I don't know," Mom said, "sounds exhausting. You won't have any time to enjoy your summer."

"I'll be fine."

"But something bad can happen," Mom said.

"Something bad can happen flipping burgers," I said. "Just think of it as a part-time job, which it is. And I might have fun."

Mom and Dad stared at each other. They said nothing, but still communicated in a way I couldn't understand without being married twenty years.

"Earning extra money for college is a good thing," Dad said. "But I don't want you coasting to graduation. If your grades slip, or you can't handle the job, you'll give it up. Right?"

"Right," I said with a grin, "and thank you."

CHAPTER 9

Saturday, I parked behind William Penn High School on Basin Road in New Castle. Four coaches in red windbreakers held infield and outfield practice on a frozen field with twenty-five boys, some in red and black uniforms and some in all black uniforms.

Randy pulled up in a black Chevy Explorer. "Damn, it's cold," he said as he stepped from his vehicle. "I'm glad you made it."

"Yeah, haven't quit yet."

Randy chuckled. He opened the rear hatch of his vehicle. Four cardboard boxes were stuffed with baseball and umpire equipment. From a briefcase, he handed me a piece of paper. "You got a perfect score on the rules test."

"That was the easiest exam I ever took."

"You'd be surprised how bad some guys do. They know the basic rules, but second-guess themselves on the tricky stuff and get confused. You ready?"

"Bring it on."

"I see you took my advice and wore loose clothing," Randy said. "Are you wearing a cup?"

"I am."

"Good. Your training session will be an inter-squad game, the varsity against the J.V. They'll be a lot of breaks in the action because the coaches will want to give instructions to their players when certain situations come up. I'll do the same for you."

Randy dug around in the boxes and found a rolled-up chest protector, two shin guards, a brush, mask, a pair of black steel-toed shoes size 11 and a navy-blue cap that had a shorter brim than the typical baseball cap.

"Put the cap on," Randy said.

I did, and fit it snug to my head.

"Believe it or not," he said, "one of the hardest things a new umpire has to master is removing the mask without the cap coming off his head. If the cap comes off, it might fall in front of your eyes and block your vision. It can also look pretty funny. An umpire never wants to be laughed at."

Randy handed me the mask. It was similar to a catcher's mask, a black metal cage that protected the face and wide enough to shield the ears, backed by black padding and held onto the head by adjustable, elastic straps.

"Girls have told me I should wear a mask," I said. "I guess they were right."

I put the mask on and Randy helped adjust the straps to the size of my skull. The padding pressed against my forehead, chin, cheek and jaw bones. My vision centered between crossbars that were level with my eyebrows and the bridge of my nose.

"This is *so* cool," I said, seeing the world from between the bars.

"Move your head up and down and side to side."

I did, and the mask stayed snug on my face.

"When you're not behind the plate," Randy went on,

"remove the mask. *Never* make a safe or out call with it still on. And the best way to remove it is to grab the front with your left hand. Never your right hand because your right is used for hand signals. Pull the mask out away from your face, then lift up. That'll clear the brim of the cap. Try it."

I grabbed the front of the cage, pulled the mask away from my face, felt the elastic straps expand by my ears and atop my head, and then lifted upwards. My cap stayed on.

"Good," Randy said. "Do it again, this time faster."

I practiced about ten times. My cap stayed on.

"Very good," Randy said. He looked at my sweat clothes. "I should've told you to wear something with a belt."

Randy retrieved a ball bag from one of the boxes. It was a pouch made of blue cloth with three loops to thread a belt. It could hold up to four baseballs. "You'll be lucky if you get three balls to use for an entire game. The home team's responsible for providing them."

He handed me the brush. It had black bristles and a wooden handle, and the entire object fit in a back pocket. "When you brush off home plate, it's customary to stick your butt at the pitcher. And if he's been especially hard on you..."

"Let out a giant fart."

"No," Randy said, laughing. "Although it's not a bad idea."

"Okay, just brush off the plate, nothing more."

Randy gestured at the shoes, shin guards and chest protector. "It's easier to put this stuff on from the bottom up."

I removed my sneakers and used the bumper of Randy's Explorer as a foot stool to slip my feet into the black steel-toed shoes. Once tied, I tapped a finger on the hard front of the footwear. "My toes are nice and cozy."

"I assume your parents have you on their health insurance."

"They do. Why?"

"In case you need the emergency room."

"Wow. I hadn't thought of that." Yet why else would I put on padding and wear a mask? Umpires were hurt every year. What made me think I'd be immune? "How bad could it be?"

"We've had a couple concussions, a broken wrist, an ankle and an arm, and one gentleman who suffered a heart attack and died."

"Seriously?" I said, nervous.

"Seriously."

"Oh," I acted macho, "I'll be fine."

I lifted my pant legs and strapped on the shin guards. They resembled what catchers wore to protect the front of their legs from ankle to knee, a hard molded plastic backed by padding and held in place by adjustable elastic straps. Once they were in place, I pulled my pant legs over them.

"You sure you haven't done this before?" Randy said.

"I haven't, but it's pretty simple to figure out."

"You'd be surprised how many first timers don't."

Before slipping on the chest protector, I removed my sweatshirt and shivered in my undershirt.

"Doesn't your mother feed you?" Randy said, squeezing my bicep.

"She feeds me plenty. I just don't gain weight. I've been skinny my whole life."

"I wish I had that problem," he said, patting his gut.

The black chest protector was a couple inches thick hard padding with horizontal grooves and a pair of plastic shoulder caps. There were straps bound to the back of the chest protector on both sides of an indentation for the neck that connected to a center strap that paralleled the spine, forming a Y-shape.

I held the chest protector above me and slipped my head through the V portion, and put each arm through an elastic ring that backed the shoulder caps. At the bottom of the spine strap were left and right side adjustable belts with a metal clasp. I pulled the straps around my left and right side and hooked them to a metal ring on each lower side of the chest protector. Randy helped adjust the spine strap and side belts until the armor fit snug.

"Cool," I said, "it looks like I'm wearing a bullet proof vest."

"We have a few cops in the organization. They said the same thing. It won't stop no bullet, just lessen the blow of the baseball."

"But it leaves the arms exposed."

"Yeah, that big seat cushion they used back in the old days fell out of favor, even though it protected the body a whole lot better than this does."

I put my sweatshirt on and felt confined. The top of the chest protector rubbed against my Adam's apple.

"You'll get used to that," Randy said.

Then he rummaged through a box and found a yellow plastic object shaped like a kidney that fit in the palm of my hand. It had three windows with a corresponding wheel, the word STRIKE printed above one window, BALL above another and OUT above the third.

"That's the indicator," Randy said, "to keep track of the count. Just turn the appropriate wheel with a finger or thumb until the number you need clicks into the right window. Have this with you even when you umpire the bases."

I turned the wheels, hearing them click, click, click into place. Ball one, ball two, ball three, strike one, strike two, one out, two outs. "*So* cool."

"Ready?"

My stomach made a noise.

"Nervous?"

"A little."

"It's okay to have stage fright," Randy said. "When you think about it, you're part of a show. And you'll be in the spotlight after every pitch the batter doesn't swing at, or after a play at the bases. Just remember you're part of the supporting cast, not the main attraction."

His words did little to calm my stomach. I felt seconds away from puking, and thought about how embarrassing it would be to lose it in front of these strangers who had gathered to help *me* train. "I'm fine."

"A word of advice. You may use it or not, but it worked for me. You're going to meet coaches and players, school officials, parents and even local politicians. You'll see them more than once during the season, in summer leagues too. Be cordial, but do *not* become their friend. As soon as they introduce themselves, forget their name. From now on, you know the players only by their number or their position on the field and call them by their number or position. Call the coaches, coach. I'm not saying you will, but learning their names and having personal conversations could subconsciously influence a close call."

I remembered the pick-up game and the pitcher for Robscott. I had learned Stephen's name. I had talked to him. I then gave him the benefit of the doubt on a close pitch and it led to controversy. "Got it."

"I had a guy who became drinking buddies with the coach at Mount Pleasant," Randy continued. "I got a lot of complaints about how Mount Pleasant seemed to have a favorable strike zone whenever this guy umpired. This may be just school ball, but it's very important to those who play it. I know I joke a lot about new umpires quitting, but this is serious business. Be professional in your behavior. No favoritism. Accept no gifts. Don't do anything that might be construed as suspicious or inappropriate."

"Got it."

We walked to the baseball diamond and a whole lot of strange things started to happen to my psyche. The grass and dirt infield seemed so much larger than the normal ninety-feet between the bases. The scope of the outfield to the home run fence appeared as large as the Grand Canyon. The players looked taller and broader than normal teenagers, and I pictured the coaches in military uniforms.

"Take a deep breath," Randy said, and I did.

Seriously, it wouldn't be the end of the world if I failed today. That didn't bother me as much as the thought of embarrassing myself in front of these strangers. What might they think? What would they tell their friends? Why did I care?

"Is it helping?" Randy asked.

"A little."

We arrived outside the third base dugout.

"He's ready," Randy said to a coach at home plate.

"All right," the coach said to his players in the field, "last one, guys."

The coach underhanded a baseball a couple feet into the air, and then batted the ball on its way down, hitting a grounder to the third baseman. The fielder scooped up the ball with his glove and threw a missile to second. The second baseman caught it, spun toward first and threw a dart to the first baseman.　That boy then rifled the ball to an unmasked and standing catcher by home plate. The entire sequence happened in the blink of an eye.

Wow. Who was I kidding? I had no business being on the same field with these boys. They were athletes. I sucked at sports. Nobody would blame me if I quit. Hell, Randy expected it.

"It's just practice," Randy said, "and everybody knows it's your first time. Just do your best. You'll either love it or quit."

"Quit?" I said, faking a confident voice, "I might faint, but I'm not quitting."

"Excellent," Randy said with a pat on my back. "Good luck."

CHAPTER 10

William Penn's varsity and J.V. coaches joined Randy and me at home plate. My heart pounded and my body shook, and not from the cold. My emotions could best be described as excited fear. I wanted to try this, but it was oh so scary at the same time.

A coach handed me three clean baseballs. Because I didn't wear the ball bag, Randy kept two. I rolled the third to the pitcher's mound. Introductions were made and hands shook. I forgot the coaches' names. They, however, knew Randy and were happy to see him.

"Another season, eh, Randy," one coach said. "You got any good prospects?"

"There's one standing right here," he said.

I smiled, and doubted the coaches believed him because they looked down their noses at me. I could literally *feel* their doubt and apprehension.

"How old are you, son?" one asked.

"Eighteen."

"Doesn't anybody older want to work for you?"

"Age doesn't make a quality umpire," Randy said.

I liked the response, but wondered if I'd be battling this attitude from coaches all season? I wasn't a child. Didn't they see that?

We went over the ground rules. These were special conditions related to the playing field.

"Everything inside the fences is in play," the head varsity coach said. "A fair ball that bounces over the fence is a ground rule double. We also have a gap in the fence in left center caused by some kids that hasn't been fixed yet. If the ball goes through there, it's two bases. Any questions?"

"No," I said.

The meeting ended. The coaches returned to their respective dugouts and gave a pep talk to their players.

"What are the dimensions of home plate?" Randy asked.

"Home plate is an irregular pentagon of white rubber. It has a width of 17 inches that face the pitcher, two parallel sides 8.5 inches long, and 12 inch long lines that meet at an apex, forming an upside down triangle on home plate's lower portion. These 12 inch sides represent the first and third base line, which means home plate is in fair territory. Another inch of black rubber covers the plate's perimeter."

"Ah, yeah," Randy said with a smile. "A simple eighteen inches wide would've sufficed."

"Oh, sorry. Why did you ask?"

"I thought it might help you relax. You know the rules. Draw confidence from that. The rest can only come with experience."

"Okay," I said, my stomach still rumbling.

"Now I'm sure you've seen on television," Randy said, taking me by the arm and placing me behind an imaginary catcher, "where the plate umpire positions himself for each pitch. For a right-handed batter, crouch over the catcher's left shoulder, the right shoulder for a left-handed batter. Stay upright until the pitcher delivers. Once he starts his motion, crouch down level to the batter's chest and *see* the strike zone--which is?"

I started to provide a wordy, rule book explanation, and then remembered to keep it simple. "Top of the batter's knees to the middle of his chest."

"And above the plate."

"Well, of course."

"Create an imaginary rectangle, like the graphic they sometimes show on television, and do *not* move once you're in position. Let your eyes follow the pitch, not your body. If the ball penetrates anywhere in that imaginary rectangle, it's a strike. Belt out a firm strike call and raise your right hand. Just say ball if the pitch is outside the strike zone. And don't forget to set your indicator after each pitch so you don't lose track of the count. Is it a fair ball if the player is in fair territory, reaches into foul territory and touches the ball?"

"Fair or foul is determined by the position of the ball, not the player."

"Good. When the ball's foul raise both hands and yell foul. Say *nothing* if it's hit fair. The players are trained to continue playing unless they hear something. Fair and foul sound too much alike, so *never* yell fair. Somebody might think you said foul and stop."

"Got it."

"School ball uses two umpires," Randy said. "Or we try to use two. Sometimes I can only schedule one, which can happen at the middle school level. My scheduling priorities are varsity first, J.V. second, and then middle school. It's not ideal, but I do the best I can with the numbers I have. Also, they'll be times when I schedule two umpires, but one doesn't make it. Either he's ill, or had to work late, or just didn't feel like showing up. It's a good rule of thumb to always have your equipment with you. Just because you're scheduled to do the bases, doesn't mean you will."

"Does a single umpire get paid more?"

"Yes. Your rate plus half."

"Great. Maybe I should ask to be scheduled alone all the time."

"No, working a game alone is hard. A steal at second base will give you the most trouble because it's so far away from the plate and you only have a split second to get out from behind the catcher. *Never* call a play at the bases from behind the catcher. That's pure laziness, and it doesn't look good."

"And we gotta look good."

"Yes, we do. Image is a big part of it. You have to project a commanding figure."

"So it would help if I were a big dude?"

"It helps, but it's not mandatory. The most important thing is confidence."

"Got it," I said, sticking my chest out.

"In the two umpire system, the home plate umpire is sometimes responsible for third. If there's a runner on first and the batter gets a base hit, and the runner from first heads for third, it's the home plate umpires job to cover third. The base umpire stays with the batter."

"Understood."

"And you're responsible for tag ups at third as well."

"Okay."

"Make sure runners touch the bases. That seems to be the hardest thing for new umpires to remember. We take it for granted that the player will touch each base, but they don't always. So save yourself a lot of grief by making sure each base runner does what he's supposed to."

"Got it."

65

"They're just playing six innings. A normal high school game is seven. You'll call the plate for the first three. The coaches will police the bases. After three innings, you'll do the bases and they'll handle balls and strikes from behind the pitcher. Okay?"

"Sounds like a plan."

The varsity nine took the field.

"Stand in foul territory along the third base line while the pitcher warms up," Randy said, again taking me by the arm. "They get eight practice throws. After the seventh one, tell them last one or coming down."

"Why do they say coming down?"

"I haven't a clue."

I wondered if anyone did. Baseball had some oddities that didn't make sense, or weren't consistent. Like a pitcher's statistics. An official inning meant both teams had batted, yet a pitcher got credited with an inning pitched after he achieved three outs against his opponent, only a half inning. Nit-picky, I know.

The varsity pitcher blew into his right hand to keep it warm and then stepped onto the pitching rubber. He put his glove up to his eyes, wrapped his bare fingers around the baseball that rested inside his glove, and then pitched from the wind-up. Hands together, he swung his arms above and behind his head, his body twisted toward third base, his left leg bent at the knee and lifted high off the mound, and then with a big thrust from his right foot, he pushed off the pitching rubber. His body sprung forward and his right arm whipped about three-quarters sidearm. The ball shot threw the cold air and popped in the catcher's mitt.

"Wow, that was fast."

"Yeah," Randy said, "these kids throw hard."

I counted seven warm up tosses and then chose the jock expression of, "Coming down." The varsity players yelled the same to each other. Baseballs that had been used by the outfielders and infielders for warm up were tossed to the varsity dugout and collected.

The eighth practice pitch was thrown. The baseball smacked into the catcher's mitt. The catcher stood and threw the ball to second. The player who straddled second caught the ball and applied a tag to an imaginary sliding base runner. The ball was then thrown among the infielders before being returned to the pitcher.

"Good luck," Randy said.

He then stood behind the backstop, near a couple of bundled-up and shivering girls who sat on a small set of bleachers. I moved behind the catcher and put my mask on.

"Never look down when you put your mask on," Randy said. "Always head up and watching the ball. From first pitch to last, always watching the ball."

"Got it," I said, taking another deep breath. My left hand shook as I checked the indicator to make certain I had set it to all zeros.

"Remember to stay upright until the pitcher starts his delivery," Randy said again.

The junior varsity's leadoff hitter approached. I had heard umpires start a game with, "Batter up" or "Play ball." The rule book stated a game began with the word *play*. I stuck to the rule book and said with confidence. "Play!"

"Hey, batter, batter," came from some of the fielders and the varsity dug out. "No hitter, no hitter."

"No pitch, Ryan, you got this," came from the batter's teammates.

Wow. My stage fright suddenly disappeared, replaced by a sudden urge to burst out laughing, similar to what happened during the pick-up game. I mean, seriously, the very thought of me in charge of anything was hilarious. Other people, older people, were the boss. I did what Mom and Dad told me. I did what teachers told me. Nobody saw me as an authority figure, including myself. I should quit now before I totally embarrass myself. I didn't belong with jocks. Hadn't I learned that lesson many times?

Stop doubting!

The hitter stepped into the left-handed batter's box. He was a short and scrappy-looking dude and I assumed he was a speedster and a good bunter. The varsity should bring their first and third basemen in closer. Then again, I shouldn't care about defensive strategy. I shouldn't care about the batter's motivation either. I wasn't a fan anymore. I was a neutral judge.

The pitcher nodded to his catcher, and then went into his windup. I crouched over the catcher's right shoulder, resting my forearms on my thighs, and created my imaginary rectangle above the plate and relevant to the batter's stance. The pitcher released the baseball. It spun at me, its red laces a blur. The hitter stuck his bat over the plate as if to bunt, but pulled it back. The ball whistled past him shoulder high. The catcher's mitt flashed in front of my face. The baseball smacked into leather.

"Ball," I said, standing. I looked at my indicator and made certain I spun the correct wheel to show ball one.

"A little louder," Randy said. "And don't flinch. Your body moved. Don't blink either. I know it's not easy, but keep those eyes open."

"Okay."

The next pitch was "down Broadway."

"Steee…rike!" I said, pointing toward first base and marking my indicator.

"Good stance," Randy said. "Good voice, too."

I smiled.

The next pitch appeared to be another missile through the heart of the strike zone, but at the last split second the ball sailed outside. The batter started his swing and stopped.

"Ball."

"Hey, ump," the varsity coach said from the first base dugout. "He swung at it."

My first controversy, how should I respond? I ignored him, and put up two fingers on my left hand and one on my right and raised them above my head. "The count's two and one. Two, one."

"Aren't you going to ask for help?" the coach said.

"I'm the only ump here, Coach, so no."

The coach laughed. "Right. Old habit."

"Very good," Randy said.

The hitter swung at the next pitch and I heard that distinctive *ting* from the aluminum bat as it made contact with the ball. The baseball shot past my right ear and struck the backstop.

"Foul ball!" I said, holding up both arms. "Two and two."

Next pitch, the batter executed a drag bunt that rolled up the dirt strip between home and third base. I pulled my mask off. The cap stayed on. I trailed the baseball and wondered how I'd determine fair or foul without the white line that would normally be in place for a real game.

The third baseman charged in and picked up the baseball with his bare hand. I judged the play to be fair, pointed toward the infield and said nothing. The third baseman threw to first. I focused on the bag. I heard the impact of the ball into leather just prior to the runner's foot striking the base.

"Out!"

"You're out!" someone hollered.

I then remembered the coach who stood behind the pitcher had been put there to umpire the bases. The players and coaches laughed. I hoped my face hadn't turned too red.

"Good thing you both had the same call," Randy said.

CHAPTER 11

After the third inning, William Penn's varsity led the game 6-5. Both teams took a break inside their respective dugouts.

Randy and I went to his vehicle. He opened the rear hatch and handed me a bottle of water.

"Thank you," I said. "I'm surprised it's not frozen."

"You handled yourself pretty good. A little nervous to start, but you got the hang of it. Do you like it?"

"I *love* it," I said after a sip of water. "It's such an awesome feeling, watching that baseball come at me, the batter swinging. And the power I have. I'm not just watching the game, I'm in *charge* of it."

"Yes, but it's power *with* responsibility. Abuse that power and you won't be here long."

"Understood," I said, removing the equipment.

"Leave your cap on," Randy said. "And bring the indicator."

We returned to the field. He led me to first base.

"With no runners on," Randy continued. "Straddle the foul line behind the base." He walked me onto the

71

infield dirt. "When you have a play at first, move to the infield, always keeping your eyes on the ball. Set yourself at a ninety-degree angle to the incoming throw and the base. When the throw gets close to the base, shift your eyes to the bag and *listen* for the ball to strike the glove while you watch the runner's foot land on the base. Don't be in a hurry to make the call. Take a second. Decipher what you saw and heard. Make certain the fielder held onto the ball. Then make the call. Relax. Have fun. And remember," he smiled, "when in doubt, call them out."

"What?"

"It's a joke."

"Oh, and good poetry."

"With a runner on first," Randy said, moving me toward the pitcher's mound, "stand behind the pitcher to the first base side. Stand to the third base side with a runner on second or third or bases loaded. The same ninety-degree angle applies when you have a play. Always do your best to be in the proper position. If they think you made a bad call, but you're in the right place, you won't get as much grief as you'll get if you're out of position. And let them complain as long as it's about the call. If they get personal, like *you* stinking umpire, *you* got no brains, *you* have no business being an umpire, then eject them and report it to the school's athletic director."

"Do I have any protection if a player or coach gets physical?"

"Yeah," he said with a grin, "call 911."

"That's it? Has it happened?"

"A couple times," Randy said. "One was a player, one was a coach. The player got expelled, the coach fired. So the penalties are severe."

"How bad were the umpires hurt?"

"Bruises, black eyes."

"Well, let's hope it never comes to that."

"Absolutely. Oh, I forgot to mention the infield fly rule signal. As you know, infield fly is in effect with runners on first and second or bases loaded with less than two out. When that's the case, and before the pitcher delivers the ball to the batter, each umpire should signal each other with a thumbs up against the chest." Randy demonstrated. "Keep signaling your partner until he replies so you're both aware of the situation."

"Got it."

"Ready?"

"Bring it on," I said.

I took my position behind first base. Randy stood by the dugout. The first batter for the J.V. team was a skinny and awkward-looking boy. He wore glasses. He shivered as he stepped into the right-handed batter's box, probably more from nerves than the cold. I understood this poor kid because I had been in his shoes. The coach let him have one at bat, and in that one at bat he had to prove himself a superstar in order to stay on the team. A boy who looked like an athlete was given multiple chances to shine.

The varsity pitcher threw from the wind up. As expected, the batter swung late and missed on three straight pitches. He dragged his bat to the dugout.

Another righty hit a ground ball left of the pitcher and toward the second baseman. I moved into the infield while the ball was scooped up and established my ninety-degree angle from first base and the expected course of the throw. I watched the ball until the fielder released it, then focused on the base and heard it smack into leather before the batter's foot touched the base.

"Out!" I said with a raised fist.

"Good positioning," Randy said. "Good, firm voice."

I smiled, and wanted more. There was no way I'd hate this job. It fit me like a glove--no pun intended. I had found my destiny.

***

Bottom of the sixth, the varsity, much to their embarrassment, trailed the junior varsity 8-7. One out, they had a runner on first. I stood behind and left of the pitcher, and near William Penn's varsity coach who was calling balls and strikes.

The varsity batter worked the count to two balls and two strikes. Next pitch, the runner on first took off. The batter swung and missed, one out. The catcher stood and made a strong throw to second. I turned as the baseball shot over my right shoulder. The shortstop caught the ball and applied a sweep tag as the runner slid feet first. The glove hit the runner's lower leg.

"Out!"

"What?" seemed to come from every corner of the field.

"I'm out?" the runner said, looking up at me.

"Are you nuts?" the varsity coach said in my face. "What the hell are you looking at? I've never seen such a blown call in my life! He was under the tag by a mile!"

Wow, Coach, get a breath mint. I had the call right. "The glove touched the runner's leg before his foot contacted the base. He's out. No question."

"Are you kidding me?"

"Simmer down, coach," Randy said, arriving. "It's just practice."

"I don't give a shit! That's ridiculous. With umpiring like that, we might as well quit the season right now!"

Was he serious? It had been the right call, no doubt in my mind.

"Unbelievable," the coach said, swinging his arms in

frustration. He gave me a cold stare that could best be described as the evil eye. "Son of a bitch!"

"Coach," Randy said, "that's enough. Let's get on with the game."

"Worst call I've ever seen," the coach said. "I'm warning you now, Randy, you better not schedule him to umpire any of our games."

Ouch. That was a bit extreme. But I didn't get it wrong. I was closer to it than he was. He must've had a bad angle.

"You can open your eyes now," someone yelled from the varsity dugout.

"Let it go," Randy said to the coach.

Randy and I returned to my place behind first base. His odd facial expression made me wonder if I had really blown the call.

"Did I get it wrong?" I said in a whisper.

"We'll talk later."

"That doesn't sound good."

The next batter, on a two-two count, hit a fly ball to left field that was caught to end the game. The J.V. squad jumped up and down and congratulated each other as they left the field.

Randy and I passed the first base dugout. The varsity players and coaches glared at me as if I had murdered one of their teammates.

"Did you flip a coin on that call?" someone said. "Don't donate your eyes to science. They don't want them."

"Just get him out of here," the varsity coach said.

Holy crap. Was all that really necessary? Even if I got the call wrong, which I didn't, how could somebody be so hateful over *one* play? Then again, I hadn't been so nice when I yelled at umpires. None of them heard me because I bought cheap seats in the nosebleed territory, or I watched the game on television and yelled at the screen.

"So," Randy said with apprehension in his voice, "did you like it?"

"I did until that call at second base."

"Oh, don't let it bother you. Those things happen."

"So I got it wrong?"

"From my angle, it looked as if the tag was applied to the runner's *bent* leg. His lead foot was already on the base."

"Seriously? I screwed up?"

"My guess," he said, patting my shoulder, "is you watched the ball into the glove and then stayed on the glove as the tag was applied. Remember to change your focus to the bag *before* the glove comes down."

I replayed the moment in my mind. The catcher threw. I watched the baseball as it sped by. The short-stop caught the ball chest high. He slammed his glove to the ground. It hit the runner's leg. He was out.

"Wait. Now that I think about it, the tagged leg had been bent at the knee." Usually, when a runner slid feet first, one leg was extended while the other was bent and tucked underneath the body. The tag had been applied to the bent leg. The runner's other foot must've been on the base. "You're right. I watched the glove instead of focusing on the base. No wonder the coach screamed at me. Good thing they don't have instant replay. How could I ever face them again?"

"Just learn from it, and don't let it eat you up. You did very well today."

"I guess the job's not as easy as I thought. How can I be perfect when perfection isn't possible?"

"You can't. You do your best. It's moments like this that will either make or break you. So, should I put you on the schedule?"

"You mean I made it, even after that horrible call?"

"Absolutely."

"Wow," I said, clapping my hands. "When do I start?"

"Most schools start their season later this week. Because you're a rookie, I can't give you varsity, but that may change depending on need and how well you do. I won't schedule you against Glasgow for obvious reasons. Are there any days of the week you're not available?"

"Tuesday. I tutor."

Randy opened his car's hatch and retrieved a notebook and pen from one of his boxes and made a notation. "I'll email your schedule either tonight or tomorrow. If you're happy with the equipment you wore today, I'll sell it to you for a hundred."

"I already owe seventy-five for dues."

"I don't need the money now. I'll deduct it from your pay. And get yourself some navy blue pants with wide bottoms, blue pullover shirts that fit and a few that are a size too big, and more caps. We also sell jackets with our logo on the chest." Randy went to his passenger seat and returned with an arm full of navy-blue windbreakers. "Try a couple on." The jackets snapped closed and had a baseball insignia over the left breast that had the initials NCCUA between the red laces. "Wear it while the weather is still cool. They look good and it's good advertisement for our organization."

"I'll take this one, and the equipment. I guess I can't quit until I at least pay you back."

"You won't quit."

"You got that right."

CHAPTER 12

Sunday morning, Randy had emailed my umpiring schedule for the next month. My debut would be this upcoming Wednesday behind the plate for a junior varsity contest at Christiana High School, my parents' alma-mater. How ironic was that? When I told them over breakfast, they acted disinterested and informed me they couldn't attend the game because of their work schedules. No big deal, I had expected that.

However, the anticipation of my first game drove me nuts. I couldn't sit still, or concentrate on anything. I had to do something to calm my excitement. So I drove to the school on Salem Church Road and parked in its vacant lot. The baseball diamond was behind the two-story building. It had a grass and dirt infield, with two opposing, above ground dugouts made of cinder block and painted blue. A four-foot high chain link fence surrounded the field, except behind home plate, where a high backstop dominated and protected a small set of bleachers.

I walked the infield and savored the sheer joy of knowing that soon the grass and dirt would be occupied by baseball players--*and me*. I'd be responsible for the start of the game and its progression to the final out. The eyes of every player, coach and spectator would be upon me. I felt the weight of responsibility, yet refused to be intimidated. My destiny started here. And when I retired from Major League Baseball and received induction into its Hall of Fame, Christiana High School would be noted as the place where I had started my illustrious career. Maybe they'd hang a plaque in my honor somewhere in the building.

***

Monday morning, I parked behind Glasgow High and met up with Austin outside the school. I finally told him about signing up with the umpire association, my training session, the blown call at second base and my debut match up.

Austin's mouth hung open, but he took it in stride. "Incredible, Michael. Do you enjoy getting yelled at?"

"No."

"You must. And you must love chasing impossible dreams."

"It's not impossible. I have a better chance at this than playing."

"Really? There's more players than umpires. I'd figure the odds were worse."

"Well," I said, conceding the point, "I'm going to try. Come on out and see me in action.

"I'll think about it."

"That means no."

"Not necessarily."

"Yes it does."

"Michael, I don't know anything about baseball. I'd probably cheer at the wrong time."

"Nobody cheers for the umpires. Just come out and see me. I've attended your poetry readings."

"That's it, make me feel guilty."

"Well, I shouldn't have to make you feel guilty."

"All right, Michael. Maybe I can watch the first quarter."

"Inning."

"Whatever."

Throughout Monday and Tuesday, my body attended each class, but my mind was on the field at Christiana. I imagined myself behind the plate calling balls and strikes, out or safe. Coaches, players and fans praised me. Then at the end of the season, the NCCUA held a banquet in my honor and presented me with their "Best Umpire of the Year" award—if they had such a thing. I even created a super hero persona. I stood on the diamond in full uniform, hands on hips, and a cape fluttered in the wind behind me as I looked majestically to the sky.

I entered Mister Tressel's room and told him about my part-time job. "But don't worry, I'm still going to tutor."

"That takes guts," he said from behind his desk. "What do your parents think?"

"They think I'm crazy, but they like the money."

There were only two students present. Mister Tressel had Amber Hill, a cute junior who needed help with calculus. I got a chubby freshman I had had before and hoped never to have again, Kellen Pike. I stood over him as he opened his *Basic Algebra* textbook and wished I had a plug for my nose. His thick black hair appeared matted to his scalp.

"Which equation has x=2, y=3 as the solution?" he asked.

I looked at the simple problem and couldn't believe

his dilemma. The book showed the possible answers as (a) 8x-y=12 or (b)2x+3y=10.

"I'm not going to tell you," I said. "Look at the equations and substitute the letters with a number. Write it out if you have to."

I backed off while his mental wheels spun—or I should say stalled.

The classroom door opened. Kelsey Delgado entered carrying her *Basic Algebra* textbook and spiral notebook. Our eyes met. She smiled!

"Can I help you, Kelsey?" Mister Tressel said.

"I need to see Michael."

She asked for me!

"Oh," Mister Tressel said with a grin. "Michael, batter up."

"Oh, good one, Mister Tressel."

"I'll take Kellen off your hands."

"Oh, thank you. Take a seat, Kelsey."

"Can you help me with factoring polynomials?" she said, sitting.

"Hey," I said, and rushed to the desk next to her. I inhaled her intoxicating perfume. I stared at the curvature of her neck like a blood-hungry vampire. "That's what I'm here for."

"You're the best, Michael."

A compliment! My heart pounded. I struggled to breathe.

"Michael, you all right?"

Calm down! Calm down!

"Yeah," I said, with a wave. "I'm fine. Now, factoring polynomials is simple once you find the, GCF, or greatest common factor. In other words, the GCF is the largest number that will divide evenly into that number. For example, the GCF for 24 is 12."

I then had the greatest time. Kelsey looked me in the

eye when she asked questions. I saw my reflection in her pupils. We smiled a lot. We put a finger on the same problem in her textbook and bumped hands. Her touch went through me like electricity, and there was a definite spark.

Wow!

"Is this right?" she asked after completing a problem. "Are you sure I got this?"

"It's right. You know this stuff, Kelsey. I think your problem is that you second-guess yourself too much."

"Well, how do I stop that?"

"Stop doubting yourself. Go with your first thought."

"Easy for you to say. You must study all the time. I can't do that." She whispered. "I have to have *some* fun."

"I have fun."

"You do? You seem so, um,…boring."

Ouch.

"I'm sorry. I didn't mean that."

She meant it, but I let it slide. "I have fun umpiring baseball."

"What?" she said, her eyes wide. "An umpire? You're one of those guys that gets yelled at? Really? That's so cool. But how can you do that?"

"Because I love it," I said, even though I hadn't umpired an official game yet. I stuck my chest out. "I'm a member of the New Castle County Umpire Association and I have the plate for the Christiana J.V. game tomorrow. Someday, I hope to be in the big leagues, umpiring the Phillies, Orioles, Pirates, Yankees, Red Sox…."

"Really?" she said, sitting back and staring at me. "I didn't know that about you. I don't think anybody knows that. Why don't you tell people? I'm sure it'll make you more popular."

Ouch again.

"What time's the game?"

"3:45."

"You know," she said with a grin, "I might be able to make it. No promises, though."

That was practically a date!

"You know," she said smiling, "you really are a nice guy."

"Oh, that's the kiss of death."

"What do you mean?"

"To be called a nice guy. Girls don't like nice guys, right?"

"That's not true. I know plenty of nice guys."

Now, tell her you have the biggest crush on her. Tell her. Confess your feelings. Ignore the others in the room. Step up. Ask her out. Do it!

"Well," Kelsey said, collecting her books. "Thanks again for your help."

Coward! I walked her to the door. I was so tempted to put an arm around her waist, but of course, I wimped out.

"Goodnight, Michael."

"Goodnight," I said, hating my personality. Why did I act the way I did? Why couldn't I speak to her like other boys talked to girls? Was I that afraid of rejection? Why did I assume I'd be rejected? However, if Kelsey showed up at Christiana, it would mean she liked me. Why else would she spend the time to come watch?

I made a vow. If Kelsey showed up at Christiana, I'd ask her out. It would be the greatest doubleheader of all time. My first game as an umpire and my first date!

CHAPTER 13

The calendar stated first day of spring, but it should be sued for false advertising. My inaugural game would be played under cloudy skies and fifty-five degrees, hardly baseball weather.

I opened my car's trunk and started putting on the protective gear. My hands shook so bad that I initially missed hooking the clasps on my shin guards and chest protector. I must've paused a hundred times to take a deep breath and tell myself to calm down. None of these players, coaches, parents or students cared that I was nervous, or that this was my first game, and I certainly couldn't let it show. They might take advantage. I had to walk onto the field as if I had done so a million times.

I wondered if I was more nervous about umpiring or asking Kelsey out--if she showed up. So far, there were some bundled-up spectators on the bleachers. Young blondes and brunettes who must be player girlfriends and a few older adults who had to be parents come to watch their son. But it *was* early. Hopefully, she'd show

84

up by game time. It was also cold. I shouldn't be too disappointed if Kelsey didn't show. In fact, I wouldn't blame her for not coming. Maybe she'd wait until the weather improved. I could tell her my future schedule.

My partner, Jack Parsons, arrived in a white Chevy Cruz. He was a gray haired, beer-bellied individual who shook my hand and asked the obvious, "So, this is your first game?"

"It is."

"I remember my first game," Jack said. He put his hands in the pockets of his NCCUA jacket. "Years ago, it was, at old P.S. DuPont. I threw out their coach in the first inning. He called me a fat slob. I've always had a belly, but I wasn't taking that off nobody. Too bad it's so damn cold. I can't believe they're playing. Can I give you some advice?"

I wanted to say no. "All right."

"Don't act too high and mighty. You have to be tough, but don't be phony. Relax. Don't be intimidated. Be firm. Be direct."

"Got it," I said.

"Ready?"

"Bring it on."

I carried my mask and strutted to the field like a prized peacock. I soaked in the atmosphere of teenage boys gathered to play baseball, with spectators seated on the bleachers or in folding chairs placed around the field. No Kelsey. No Austin.

Christiana's nine wore red, white and blue uniforms and were taking infield practice with their head coach. Their opponent, Delcastle High, had players dressed in navy blue and white uniforms. They loitered around the third base dugout, anxious to get underway.

As for the field, the grass had some brown spots. The dirt of the infield needed a good raking. The white, two-inch wide foul lines must've been put down by a drunk, and the batters' boxes looked crooked, but so what. I was here, and it was about to happen.

"If your smile gets any bigger," Jack said, "they'll mistake you for the Cheshire cat."

"I can't help it. This is *soooo* cool."

Jack spoke to the head coach. "Let's wrap it up, Charlie."

"Okay," the head coach said. "Bring it in, boys."

"You know him?" I asked.

"Of course," Jack said. "After twenty years, I know most of them."

"Doesn't that interfere with your ability to be impartial?"

"Not at all," he said. "There's a time to be friendly. There's a time to be tough. I know the difference. More importantly," he pointed at the coaches, "*they* know the difference."

I doubted him, but I had to do what worked best for me.

Jack and I met the opposing coaches at home plate. Christiana's head man handed me three clean baseballs. Unlike pro ball, I did not receive a line up card from each team. An official scorebook was kept by each team's assistant coach or student manager.

"Damn it's cold," Delcastle's head coach said. "What happened to spring, Jack? I'm sorry, what was your name?"

I repeated it, and although I equaled the two coaches in height, I again had that feeling of being looked down upon. They certainly looked beyond me to Jack. I had to take charge of the situation. After all, I was the home plate umpire. It was *my* game.

I addressed Christiana's head man. "Ground rules, coach."

"Sure," he said, giving me a funny look. "Everything within the fence is in play. If a thrown ball goes in the dugout, it's an extra base for the runners. Any fair ball that bounces over the fence is a double."

After the meeting, I stood along the third base line. Christiana's starting nine took their positions. I removed a baseball from my ball bag, which hung from my belt on my right side, and tossed the ball to Christiana's pitcher. The kid threw right handed, almost side-armed, and appeared to be all arms and legs.

I reminded myself again to stay calm, act dignified, even though my insides churned at a hundred miles an hour. I couldn't let my emotions get the best of me, or let the excitement of competition suck me in.

"Coming down," I said to Christiana's catcher after the seventh warm up pitch.

"Coming down," he hollered to his teammates.

The eighth pitch was thrown. The catcher received it, stood and threw the ball to second. The shortstop caught it over the bag and then the ball was tossed among the infielders before being returned to the pitcher.

This was it. Mask on. I stood behind Christiana's stooped catcher.

"Let's have a good one," he said, "right, ump?"

"You betcha," I replied, looking down at the back of his helmeted and masked head. Then at Delcastle's dugout. "Let's have a batter."

Members of both teams erupted with enthusiastic chatter in support of their teammates. Delcastle's hitter stepped into the left-handed batter's box and got into his stance. My nerves had settled, but I still had enough energy surging through my body to electrify a major city.

Here we go! I signaled to the pitcher. "Play!"

Christiana's pitcher got his sign from the catcher and went into his wind up. I crouched over the catcher's right shoulder and created my imaginary rectangle above home plate. Since the pitcher threw side-armed, the baseball appeared to come from third base. It spun at me at great speed and whistled high and wide on the batter, the catcher had to jump up to grab it. Had there been a right handed hitter, he'd have been drilled in the head.

"Ball," I said, making my first official call, an obvious one, and recorded it on my indicator.

Christiana's coaches, team and fans yelled, "Relax, Ken. You can do it."

I wished that had been true. The boy was wild. He walked the first two batters without throwing a strike. Delcastle's third hitter, a righty, took one close to the zone.

"Ball."

"What's wrong with that one, ump?" Christiana's head coach begged from the first base dugout. "Come on."

"Take the blinders off," a man yelled from the bleachers.

"Get your head out of your ass," another said.

I smiled behind my mask and realized that with the fans right behind me, and how few of them there were, I'd hear everything they said.

"Help the kid out," someone said.

Help him how? Widen the strike zone?

Delcastle's batter had no intention of swinging until Christiana's pitcher threw a strike. He did so on the next pitch. A mock cheer came from the spectators. I wasn't sure if the sarcasm was directed at me for calling a strike or at the pitcher for throwing one.

With a three ball, one strike count, Delcastle's batter

swung at the next pitch. *Ting.* I immediately felt a shooting pain erupt from my left bicep, just above the elbow. My eyes watered as my arm hung limp and numb. A couple spectators cheered.

"You all right, ump?" Christiana's head coach asked.

"Yeah," I lied, grimacing and shaking my arm to get feeling back. "Just give me a minute."

How ironic. I got injured in the first inning of my first game. The Baseball Gods must be laughing. And yes, I believed in the Baseball Gods. All serious fans of the game did, and for obvious reasons. We were superstitious.

"That'll leave a mark," the catcher said. "Right, ump?"

"Right," I said, sarcastic.

After a couple minutes, I got feeling back in my arm. I made a fist, relaxed my hand, and made another fist with little pain. I flexed my arm and had full movement.

"All right," I said, "let's go."

Next pitch, I crouched behind the catcher and placed both arms behind my back. Delcastle's batter hit a sharp ground ball that Christiana's shortstop scooped up near second base. He stepped on the bag and then threw to first for an easy double play.

Christiana's players, coaches and fans were elated. However, Delcastle had a runner on third with two outs.

Next batter, on a two ball one strike count, hit a fly ball to centerfield that was caught. Christiana's players ran from the field and congratulated each other.

Mask off, I stood along the third base line while Delcastle's pitcher warmed up. I refused to rub my injured muscle, just like a ballplayer refused to rub the spot where he'd been hit by a pitch. Yeah, stupid macho stuff, but just another aspect of the game.

More importantly, I had survived my first half inning. I received some criticism, but overall I felt I had done very well and couldn't wait for more.

I scanned the bleachers, and then sighed disappointed. No Kelsey. Oh, yeah, no Austin either.

CHAPTER 14

Top of the fifth inning, Delcastle's lead off batter hit a slow ground ball toward third. Christiana's third baseman jumped on it and made a great throw to first to beat the runner.

"Yeah!" Christiana's players and fans shouted. They quickly changed it to, "No!"

Jack Parson ruled the batter safe. I couldn't believe it, but hid my reaction.

"What?" Christiana's head coach said. "What game are you watching, ump? Everybody else had him out."

"It was close," Jack said. "But he's safe."

"Close?" the coach said. "Like L.A. and New York are close. Are you kidding?"

I had my own issue in the bottom of the seventh. Christiana trailed by a run, 10-9. Their lead off hitter bunted. The baseball only rolled a couple feet in front of home plate. Delcastle's catcher pounced on it like a cat, but hesitated on his throw to first because the batter ran on the infield side of the base line, obscuring the catcher's view of first. When he did throw, the ball sailed down the right field line. The batter reached second base before the right fielder retrieved the ball and returned it to the infield.

Christiana's players, coaches and fans were excited, but this time, I spoiled the party. I stepped to the infield and pointed at the runner on second. "Batter's out for interference!"

"What?" echoed around me.

"Batter interference," I said to Christiana's dugout. "He ran inside the foul line."

The first base line included a three-foot wide running lane that started half way between home and first and in foul territory. When a batter ran to first, he was obligated by rule to run in this lane so that the catcher had a clear view of the base.

"Good call, ump," Delcastle's coach said, clapping. "Way to be on top of that."

"What're you calling?" Christiana's coach said, stomping his feet on approach.

"Interference by the batter."

"What the hell kinda call is that? You gotta be kidding me?"

"The batter has to run on the foul side of the line," I said, showing him the batter's cleat marks in the dirt around home and then onto the infield grass.

"You're going to make that call *now*? At this stage of the game?"

"I'll make that call first inning or last inning."

"Oh, come on! How can you do that? Let the kids play."

"Give it up, Charlie," Delcastle's coach said. "The kid got it right. Your boy was way inside."

I cringed at being called kid.

"Stay out of this," Christiana's coach said. He looked at me, huffing and puffing, and I expected more arguing, but soon the anger disappeared from his face. He lowered his voice. "If you tell anyone I said this, I'll deny it. You're right. It's my fault. I forgot to teach them the rule."

Holy crap! An indescribable sensation came over me. I had calmly explained the rule and my reason for enforcing it and the coach had shown respect and good sportsmanship. Around Joe Forrester, it never mattered if I was right. In his opinion, might made right.

Christiana's head coach returned to his dugout. I put my mask on and smiled. It couldn't get any better than this.

"We have one out," I said. "One out."

Christiana's next two hitters got on base from singles. Then with a two ball, two strike count on the hitter, the runners took off when Delcastle's pitcher delivered to the plate. The baseball bounced in the dirt. The catcher blocked the ball from going to the backstop, but both runners advanced.

Full count on the batter, and the winning run stood on second. Christiana's players, coaches and spectators were on their feet.

Delcastle's coach told his pitcher to intentionally walk the batter to load the bases and set up a possible double-play. The catcher stood. The pitcher threw wide of the strike zone.

"Ball, take your base."

He did, and Christiana's next hitter stepped into the right-handed batter's box. His teammates and fans hollered for a hit. I reminded myself to stay calm. It wasn't nerves that I battled this time. It was the excitement of the moment. A dramatic last inning win was possible. As a fan, it was the greatest type of finish the game had. However, I wasn't a fan anymore. I was neutral. I had to keep my emotions in check and let the events unfold as they should.

Delcastle's pitcher delivered from the stretch. I crouched and gauged the strike zone as the baseball sped in my direction. The hitter swung and missed. A collective groan filled the air.

Next pitch came in low and hard. Christiana's hitter swung his bat like a golf club, *ting*. The baseball rocketed deep into the gap between Delcastle's left and center fielders. The boys ran hard after the ball, but couldn't catch it, and it bounced to the fence. The fans went crazy, and the game ended when the runner from second stomped on home plate. He was mobbed by his happy teammates, who then mobbed the player that had hit the ball.

I signed the scorebook and handed the used baseballs to Christiana's head coach.

"Good game, ump," he said with a wink.

"Thank you," I said.

"Good game, ump," Delcastle's coach said with a handshake.

Wow, the coach from the *losing* team paid me a compliment.

"Was this your first game?" he asked.

"Yes."

"Well, damn good job. Nice to see some new blood. You were fair and consistent. Can't ask for more."

Oh, wow, if only Joe Forrester and Coach Myers had heard that!

Jack and I walked to the parking lot. He said something, but I didn't hear him. Kelsey Delgado stood in front of me in a full length winter coat, her long black hair flowing behind her.

"Hi, Michael."

"Hi….Kelsey."

"I said so long, kid," Jack said. "I'm sure we'll work together again."

"See ya," I said, never taking my eyes off Kelsey.

"That padding makes you look like you got muscles," she said with a giggle.

I raised my arms and flexed my biceps like a weightlifter, but winced as I felt a sharp pain run up my arm. I had forgotten about the foul ball that hit me.

"You all right?" Kelsey said.

"Yeah," I said, laughing it off. "No problem. Been here long?"

"A little while. Weren't you scared out there?"

"Nah," I said, acting nonchalant. "You can't do the job if you're scared."

"That's really great, Michael."

"Hey," I said, fighting an urge to kiss her. I took a deep breath and worked up the courage, "you hungry?"

"Yeah," she said with a funny look on her face. "Why?"

"I'm heading to the mall to get something to eat. Care to join me?"

"What?" she said, looking bewildered. "You can't be serious."

I heard a loud *thud* and realized it was my heart. "Yes, I'm serious."

Delcastle's dejected players and coaches wandered by, on their way to the team bus. Kelsey waited for them to pass.

"Michael? You're a nice guy and all, but I can't be seen at the mall with you. You understand, don't you?"

I clenched my jaw and headed for my Taurus. I hoped not to cry. How would that look, an umpire in full uniform red-faced with tears? I was an authority figure. I had overseen the start and completion of an organized baseball game. I had enforced the rules and stood up to controversy among bigger boys and grown men. I had been on cloud nine.   Yet if I didn't get out of here fast, my eyes would gush like Niagara Falls.

"Don't be mad at me," Kelsey said, following me. "You know what I mean. It's not that you're a bad guy. You have to understand. I'm cursed with being popular. Yeah, not all my friends are nice, and some are real snooty, full of drama. Oh, my God, the drama can be suffocating. I wish it wasn't part of my life, but when you have friends like I do, it comes with the territory. You understand, don't you? Sometimes I'd like to tell them girls to just shut up, who cares about your stupid life, but I have to do what I have to do to stay with them. They'd be horrified if they saw me with you. No offense."

I opened the trunk of my car and tossed in my mask, cap, brush and indicator, and used all my strength to keep the flood gates from opening. I yanked off my jacket and sweatshirt.

"Please don't be mad at me."

I unhooked my chest protector and pulled it over my head and tossed it into the trunk. I put the jacket back on fast and pushed down the growing agony in my chest and throat.

"Please, Michael, I'm glad that you help me with Algebra. You're a super math geek and I hate math."

I loosened my belt and removed the ball bag.

"Michael, say something."

I worked up the courage. "Answer me this. If you can't be seen with me, why did you come out and watch me umpire?"

"I don't know," she said with a shrug. "Boys are always telling lies to impress girls. I thought yours was the craziest lie I had ever heard, so I guess I wanted to see for myself. But you really *are* an umpire."

"Yes I am," I said, gritting my teeth. "I don't lie."

"Don't be mad at me, Michael. Okay?"

I lifted my pant legs and unhooked the shin guards and tossed them into the trunk.

"You won't tell anybody about this, will you, Michael? I'd just die if my friends found out."

"Ha!" I said, sarcastic. "*Your friends*. You mean those giggling idiots who make fun of you behind your back."

She put her hands on her hips. "Don't be putting down my friends just because I won't go out with you."

I untied my steel-toed shoes and replaced them with my sneakers. I had no intention of saying anything more, but Kelsey's curiosity got the best of her.

"What do they say?"

I wanted to hurt her like she had hurt me. "They call you the Jolly Red Giant, and The Tall Squaw."

"They do not!"

I closed the trunk with more force than necessary. Kelsey flinched.

"You're a liar," she said. "You're just making that up cause you're mad at me."

I got in my car, put the key in the ignition and sped out of there. How could I have been so stupid? What had I ever seen in Kelsey Delgado?

***

I arrived home without shedding a tear and removed my jacket. The long sleeve of my sweatshirt hid the bruise to my arm and I wondered if I should roll up the sleeve and reveal the injury. No, it might upset Mom and she'd tell me to quit.

The house smelled of fried chicken. My mouth watered for what I expected was Mom's famous poultry smothered in buttermilk batter and fried to a golden brown.

"We're in here," Mom said from the dining room.

I entered. Mom and Dad sat in their usual place. They had already devoured most of the meat, mashed potatoes and green beans.

"Sorry," she said, "we couldn't wait."

I looked at them, and the food, and forgot about Kelsey.

"How'd it go?" Dad asked.

I took my seat. "Great. Even the losing coach complimented me."

"So you're not quitting?" Mom said.

I laughed. "No. Why would I quit? I found myself today."

"What do you mean?" she asked.

I answered while I filled my plate. "Well, let's face it, in school I act shy and put up walls to survive. Today, standing on that field, the person I want to be came out. I was confident, assertive. After every pitch the batter ignored, everyone looked at me for the call, and for that brief moment, I was the center of attention. I loved it."

Mom beamed. "That's great, Michael. You do look happy."

"I am."

"Did anybody argue with you, call you bad names?"

"Nothing serious."

"So you had some trouble?" Dad asked.

I waved a drumstick at him. "I handled it."

"Tell me about it," Dad said.

I did. "But in the end, the coach was really nice about it. He admitted that he hadn't taught his players about the running lane."

"Sounds like you had a great time," Dad said, but I sensed disappointment in his voice.

"I *loved* it. I can't wait for more."

After dinner, I entered the bathroom, removed my sweatshirt and finally viewed in the mirror the damage done to my bicep. I had a deep purple bruise that was sensitive to the touch. Yet I smiled. My injury was like a badge of honor. It was evidence that I had successfully umpired my first organized baseball game. I should show it to Joe Forrester and his jock friends. Maybe they'd finally give me some respect. Hey, why not show everybody?

CHAPTER 15

Come morning, I still hadn't cried about Kelsey because I was just so incredibly mad. Not at Kelsey. She couldn't help what she was, but furious at myself because I had been so stupid. I knew Kelsey sat in the cafeteria with the make-up wearing, fashion divas who erupted with hysterical laughter when they talked about somebody behind their back, or let out a scream at the mention of a cute guy, or a horrified "*ewww*" at something they disliked. I had let her exotic beauty overrule my common sense. I guess that made me like a lot of other guys, but I wouldn't let it happen again.

I should pretend to be sick and stay home. How could I go to school after such a humiliation? Then again, Kelsey had worried I'd tell somebody what happened and ruin her precious reputation. That meant she'd keep quiet. So would I. Besides, I had something else to talk about, something to brag about. From this day forward, everybody at school would look at me differently.

I stepped from my car wearing my NCCUA jacket. I stuck my chest out, hoping someone saw the insignia. I was ready to answer questions. I should get praise and respect. No more calling me nerd, dork, dweeb, wuss or geek. Call me Umpire Man.

Yet no one noticed.

I sighed, and then strutted into Glasgow.

A few classmates looked in my direction. Nobody stopped me. Nobody asked questions. They didn't care.

My excitement had disappeared by the time I reached my locker.

Austin arrived carrying his book bag. "Sorry I didn't make it to the game," he said above the noise in the hall. "How'd it go?"

"It was awesome," I said with some anger in my voice, not really meant for him. "I was damn good."

"Great. Did you deal with any irate player or coach?"

"I did," I said, and then told him what happened on the bunt play. "I came through it beautifully. I also lost interest in Kelsey."

His eyes bulged. "Impossible."

"True," I said, and then elaborated.

"That must've really hurt," he said. "Sorry."

I shrugged. "The hell with her. I got baseball."

I hung my jacket in my locker. A polo shirt revealed my deep purple bruise. I faced Austin and the passing crowd and waited for anyone to notice. Nobody did. Come on! Did I have to walk naked down these halls to get attention?

Conrad Jenkins, who was always miserable, arrived at his locker, flung it open and stuck his head inside. "Son of a bitch!" His scream echoed. He then removed his head and stared at me. "What're you looking at, wuss?"

I didn't answer.

His eyes found my bruise. "Joe Forrester get a hold of you again?"

"Oh, wow," Austin said, finally seeing it.

"Oh, you mean this?" I said, acting disinterested. "No, a foul ball got me."

"Don't you wear padding?" Austin asked.

"Yes," I replied, "but it doesn't cover the arms."

"What're you talking about?" Conrad said. "A foul ball? Baseball? Stand too close to the field?"

"No. I'm an umpire with the New Castle County Umpire Association. I called the plate yesterday at Christiana."

"*You're* an umpire?" Conrad said laughing. "No freakin' way."

"I am," I said. "I'm going to be a pro someday."

"Yeah, right? How? You're afraid of jocks."

"Not anymore."

Jason Morris, a boy three lockers down who liked to crack his knuckles, approached. "What's this I hear? *You're* an umpire?"

"I did the Delcastle, Christiana J.V. game yesterday," I said, my chest out.

"Bullshit," Jason said. "Umpires are a bunch of old farts."

"He says he got that bruise from a foul ball," Conrad said, pointing.

"More bullshit," Jason said, snapping some knuckles. Too bad he didn't break his fingers. "He got it from Joe."

"Did someone say my name?"

Crap. Joe arrived wearing his Glasgow cap on sideways and Beverly Rivers on his arm. She was the only girl I knew who had a criminal record. Drug possession, I believe. Cloaked in black, she clung to Joe as if she'd fall over otherwise.

"Hey, Joe," Jason said. "Michael says he's an umpire and that he called the Christiana J.V. game."

Joe looked me up and down for a moment, and then

burst out laughing. "Is your life so pathetic that you have to make up stories?"

"I didn't make it up."

"He didn't make it up," Austin said.

A crowd gathered. What was the old saying, be careful what you wished for. I wanted attention. Now I had it.

Joe released Beverly. She wobbled a bit, but managed to stay upright. He then put an open hand on my chest and pinned me against my locker. "I got friends at Christiana. They froze their asses off. Should I ask them if some skinny nerd umpired their game?"

"Go right ahead."

"Leave him alone, Joe," Austin said.

"You stay out of this, fag. Tell the truth."

"I am."

"Oh," Conrad said with a chuckle, "leave the dork alone."

"I'm not lying," I said. "I have a jacket in my locker from the New Castle County Umpire Association."

"That don't prove nothing," Joe said, pressing harder. "You could've bought it at any yard sale."

"I got this bruise from a foul ball."

"That don't prove nothing neither," Joe said, releasing me to inspect my arm. "But this is what you get for lying."

Joe pressed his thumb deep into my bruise. The pain put me on my knees. I wanted to scream. My eyes watered.

"No more lies," Joe said.

"I'm not lying," I said with a tear flowing down each cheek.

"Boy, you're stubborn. There's no shame in lying. Hell, I do it all the time."

The crowd laughed.

Joe released me.

I grabbed my arm, covering the bruise and waiting for the pain to subside.

"See you later, *loser*," Joe said, taking Beverly by the hand and walking away.

The crowd split up, some laughing and making comments such as, "He's so desperate for attention…What a dork, making up a story like that."

"You all right?" Austin said.

"I will be," I said, standing, "when people believe *me* instead of that muscleheaded jock."

"Did you hear what he called me?"

"I did," I said. Austin wasn't gay, but his artsy behavior and manner of dress led many to assume he was. "You have to ignore him. You know how it is. They'd rather believe what they believe instead of the truth."

"I know, but it's not right."

"What was it you said the other day? 'You'll graduate soon and never see these fools again.'"

Austin smiled. "Hallalujah."

CHAPTER 16

A week later, I had yet to umpire another game because of rain and the mud left behind. School fields
were open to the elements, so a game could get postponed even a day or two after the actual downpour. I
used the time to study what was left of my required
school work and wondered why Joe hadn't apologized. I
passed him in the hall a couple times wearing my
NCCUA jacket, and he had seen me in the cafeteria.
Hadn't his so-called friends at Christiana told him the
truth? Then again, I doubted the word sorry existed in
his Neanderthal vocabulary.

Then another week went by with no games because
of Spring Break and the Easter holiday. It was then that
I realized a transformation had taken place. The major
league baseball season started. Nothing unusual there,
but I watched the Phillies on television and caught myself rooting for the *umpires*. I didn't look at the Philly
batter and cheer for a hit. Instead I concentrated on
how the home plate umpire did his job.   I watched the

105

positioning of the base umpires when they had a play. I felt especially good when instant replay showed the umpire made the correct call on a close play. I cringed when replay proved the umpire had been wrong, but enjoyed the fact that bad calls rarely happened. My loyalties had definitely shifted. I would never have thought it possible in a million years.

***

Finally, I had a junior varsity contest at Concord High on Ebright Road, north of Wilmington. I parked and quickly put on the gear and my NCCUA jacket. The Concord High Raiders, in their white and red uniforms, were playing their rival, the blue and white uniformed Bulldogs from Brandywine High. Both teams were huddled in and around their respective, above ground dugouts. I estimated about a hundred spectators behind fencing that paralleled the left and right field foul lines. They either sat on bleachers or in their own folding chairs, some stood.

Joel Weber, a muscular and bald man, was my base partner and already present by Brandywine's third base dugout. We met both head coaches at home plate. We did the usual friendly exchange of introductions and discussed the ground rules.

The game started with a high amount of chatter from both teams, their fans and coaches. For Concord High and their supporters, however, the excitement quickly vanished as everyone in Brandywine's lineup batted in the first inning and they took a 5-0 lead. The game then progressed at that score until the bottom of the sixth. Concord rose from the dead and scored three runs. They added two more in the seventh to tie the game, forcing extra innings. In the top of the eighth inning, Brandywine got its first batter on base from a walk. The pitches had been close to the strike zone and

I overheard hostile comments from the Concord spectators.

"Come on, ump, you blind?"

"That was right there, you idiot."

"Get some glasses!"

"Get some binoculars!"

"You're missing a good game, blue!"

Brandywine's next hitter, a lefty, smacked a single to right. The runner from first base made it to third. The enthusiasm from the home fans and players disappeared. Brandywine's next hitter, another lefty, grounded sharply to first. Concord's first baseman fielded the ball and visually checked that the runner on third stayed. He then threw to second for one out and Concord's shortstop returned the ball to first for the second out. It was a well-executed double play that elated the Concord team and their supporters.

However, the inning wasn't over. Brandywine had a runner on third with two outs. Their next batter, a righty, worked a full count. He then hit a ground ball to the second baseman. It should be a routine play to end the inning, but the ball skipped between the fielder's legs and rolled into right field. The runner on third scored. Brandywine's dugout erupted in celebration.

I empathized with the second baseman. Although I had never played organized baseball, I had made enough errors in pick up games to understand his pain. His teammates remained supportive.

"Don't worry about it," they said. "We'll get it back."

Sure enough, the Baseball Gods worked it so that Concord's second baseman had a chance to atone for his error. He batted in the bottom of the eighth inning with two outs and the potential tying run on second. His teammates stood in the dugout and cheered. Concord's fans were cautious, yet hopeful.

The hitter battled to a two ball, two strike count. Then Brandywine's left handed pitcher threw a beautiful breaking pitch that cut through the strike zone and froze the kid.

I had no choice. "Strike three!"

Brandywine's players jumped in celebration and ran from the field. Concord's second baseman put his head down and dragged his bat to his dejected teammates. It had to be longest walk of the young man's life, but that was baseball. The sport challenged a person because failure at the plate was far more prevalent than success.

Joel and I left the field. The disappointed fans vented their frustration.

"How could you call that, ump? That was horrible."

"Way to ruin a good game."

Joel said, "Don't worry about that last pitch, it was right there."

"I know it was," I said with too much attitude.

"Hey, sorry," Joel said, "didn't mean to step on your toes."

I did not apologize. "No problem."

"You're a God-damn bastard," a woman said a distance behind me. I did not turn around. "My son's crying his eyes out because he failed his team. You ugly bastard!"

"Nothing like an angry mom," Joel said with a chuckle.

"No worries," I said, even though it did hurt. "It's all part of the job."

CHAPTER 17

I was on my way to Mister Tressel's classroom when my phone vibrated in my pocket. I stood away from the flow of students to take the call.

"Hi, Michael," Randy said, "I know it's Tuesday and you said you're not available, but I'm desperate to cover a varsity game at Tower Hill. Both umps called in sick."

"I'll do it." I said without hesitation. I know I should've considered Mister Tressel and the students that needed me, but I couldn't pass up the chance to umpire my first varsity game. I'd make it up to him somehow.

"Thank you, Michael. Take your pick, the plate or the bases?"

Even though umpiring home plate was more stressful and overworked my thighs, I preferred it to the bases. At the plate I was involved in every pitch and responsible for the pace of the game. I was part of the battle between pitcher and hitter. And there was something mesmerizing about watching the baseball as it shot from the pitcher's hand and came at me, the whistle sound it made as it cut through the air, and if the hitter ignored it, the loud pop the ball made when it impacted the catcher's mitt.

When working the bases, I understood why critics of baseball described the game as slow and boring. I felt displaced from the real action. Like the infielders and outfielders, I shuffled from one foot to the other waiting for the pitcher to throw. If the pitcher was slow to deliver, the game dragged and I wished my partner would speed it up. And I discovered the biggest flaw of the two umpire system. It was impossible to get into proper positioning to call a steal attempt at third base. When there was a runner on second, I stood behind the pitcher to the third base side. The runner took his lead. He sprinted on the pitch. I was two or three steps behind. I watched the catcher's throw to third. I still trailed the runner when I stopped and focused on the bag, but it was a cardinal sin to make a call while running because the action tended to bounce visually.

"I'll take the plate."

"Bless you."

Tower Hill was a private school on a 40 acre campus that was officially located at the intersection of 17th Street and Rising Sun Lane in northwest Wilmington. I parked near its athletic complex and strapped on the gear.

My base partner, Will Calder, arrived.

"A word of advice," he said, even though I hadn't asked him for any, "you have to be a bit more diplomatic with these private school kids and their parents. They think cause they got money they can get their way." He laughed. "And they usually do. There's a couple umpires in our association that got banned from ever calling a game at this school."

"Oh, it can't be that bad."

Will and I then stepped onto the best field I had seen

outside of pro ball. The grass looked like the green on a golf course. The dirt and sand portion of the field had been finely-raked. Perfect chalk lines marked both batter's boxes and foul lines. The backstop fence went dugout to dugout and protected about a hundred spectators on bleachers topped by an enclosed and occupied press box. An electronic scoreboard was lit beyond left field.

The green and white clad home team mingled around the first base dugout while the visiting Sanford team, wearing blue and gold, waited in and around the opposing dugout.

"Nervous?" Will asked.

The fancy environment, along with my first varsity experience, caused my stomach to rumble, but it was still baseball.

"Bring it on."

Will and I met the respective head coaches at home plate. They wore their school jacket and cap and were friendly enough, but I again recognized that, "You gotta be kidding, he's too young," stare.

Tower Hill's starting nine jogged to their respective positions. Infielders and outfielders had a catch while their tall and skinny right handed pitcher completed his warm up tosses.

"Coming down," I said to Tower Hill's catcher.

After the eighth practice pitch and subsequent throw to second base, I stood tall behind the catcher and put my mask on.

Sanford's first hitter approached the left handed batter's box.

The fans started clapping.

Tower Hill's pitcher stepped from the mound and looked toward the fence that paralleled the left field foul line. Like most players, I assumed he sought out his parents or girlfriend. However, I saw a man wearing a blue windbreaker who carried a clipboard. The man gave a gentle wave. The pitcher smiled. I wasn't a betting man, but I suspected the gentleman in blue was a professional baseball scout or college recruiter. If so, then this boy should have some good stuff.

The pitcher stood on the rubber. He got the sign from his catcher and started his wind up. I crouched and created my imaginary rectangle above the plate. The pitcher released the baseball near his right ear. Its laces spun horizontal like a slider and it broke so far inside and low it crashed on the top of the batter's left foot. The hitter hopped around in agony.

I removed my mask and pointed to first base. "Take your base."

"I will if I can," the batter grimaced.

Sanford's head coach arrived to check on his player. "Can you walk it off?"

The batter shook his leg a few times, winced, and then gently put weight on his injured foot. After a couple minutes, he walked with a limp, but proclaimed himself well enough to occupy first base.

Not a good omen. I had hoped my first varsity contest would be a clinic in hitting, pitching, fielding, running, throwing and completed in less than two hours. Instead, I had a hard thrower who wanted to showcase his arm by throwing breaking pitches not usually attempted until professional ball.

For the rest of the inning, Tower Hill's pitcher threw sliders, curves, even the occasional knuckle-ball, along with fast balls. He walked three and gave up four runs. The man in blue left.

At the start of the second inning, Tower Hill's head coach ordered his pitcher to throw only fast balls. He did, and I got the well played game I had hoped for.

112

***

Top of the fifth inning, Sanford High led 5-2. Their first hitter received a base on balls. While he jogged to first, and Will Calder shifted to the infield grass, Tower Hill's catcher walked to the pitcher's mound and had a whispered conversation with his battery mate.

The Sanford player bolted to second. Tower Hill's shortstop covered the base, but no throw came.

"Hey, ump," Tower Hill's coach said, "what gives? Isn't there time out?"

"No, sir," I said, removing my mask. "No time out was asked for."

"Yes, I did," the catcher said.

"He says he did," the coach said, approaching.

Will joined us.

"I'm calling time now," I said.

"So," the coach said, "you're going to leave that runner at second?"

"Yes, sir, I am."

"But the catcher had time."

"He never asked for time. I never said there was time."

The coach looked confused.

"Even if a player asks for time, there's no time out unless *I* say there is. None was asked. None was given. Now let's get on with the game."

Tower Hill's coach scratched his chin as if he hoped an idea would pop into his brain. He waved an arm and spoke to his catcher. "Make sure you get time first."

The game continued, but Tower Hill's pitcher became wild and walked the next two batters to load the bases. His coach emerged from the dugout and requested time.

"Time!" I said, putting my arms up.

"I have time out," the coach said, sarcastic. "Right?"

"Yes, sir," I said with a smile. "You do."

I let the coach and pitcher talk for a moment, and then for some reason, Will approached the meeting.

"What do *you* want?" the coach said.

"Coach," Will said, "you're outta here! You're gone!"

"What?" the coach said, getting in Will's face. "You can't throw me out of the game! For what? What did I do?"

Crap. Why did Will do that? It was the home plate umpire's job to break up conversations on the mound. I had no choice but to join the heated discussion.

"This is between him and me," the coach said. "What the hell are they doing letting children umpire, anyway?"

The players on both teams laughed, as did some spectators. I joined Will in ejecting the coach, making it my first official ejection.

Before the coach left the field, he made sure he got his point across. He never expressed a word stronger than "hell," but he released a repeated tirade of "You gotta be kidding. What the hell is this? I've never seen such lousy umpiring in my life! Where'd they find you people? You should be fired! I can't believe this." When he exhausted himself, he gave command to his assistant and then walked from the field to a standing ovation.

I got behind home plate thoroughly disgusted with my partner. "Unbelievable."

"You son-of-a-bitch!" came from a spectator.

"Dumb ass."

"Idiot!"

"The circus is in town and the clowns are wearing blue."

"Coach is right, what're they doing letting *children* umpire?"

"Stupid cowards!"

"You lousy bastards!" a woman said.

"Mom?" Tower Hill's first baseman said. "I can't believe you said that."

The laughter that followed calmed tempers, but it truly sucked that I had to stand here and listen to people scream at me for something that never should've happened. Will had no business breaking up the meeting, and even less reason to eject the coach just because the man said, "What do you want?"

"Let's go," I said, putting my mask on, "batter up."

The coach's ejection made Tower Hill a different team. They escaped the inning without a run scored against them, and then rallied to win the game 9-5. Their fans and players were happy, and I felt more secure about leaving the field.

"I'll call Randy and the A.D.," Will said.

"That's my job, *too*."

"Too?"

"Well, in case you didn't notice, *I* was the plate umpire." I pointed at myself. "*I* make the call to Randy and the Athletic Director about the ejection. Just like *I'm* the one who breaks up meetings on the mound."

"Hey, I was just trying to help you out cause it's your first varsity game."

"Did I ask for your help?"

"My, my, my, aren't we full of ourselves. Now I understand why some of the guys are calling you primadonna."

"What? I mean, so what? I take the job seriously and you should too."

"Who the hell are you to talk to me like this? You're just a kid. I got warts older than you." He pointed a finger. "I don't ever want to work with you again."

"Whatever, man," I said, waving him off. "If you don't want to do the job the way it should be done, then

I don't want to work with you either."

Why didn't I talk to Joe like this?

Will got in his car and drove away. I removed my equipment, and then telephoned Randy from the driver's seat. He agreed that Will had overstepped his authority.

"I'll clear it up with the A.D.," Randy said.

"He never wants to work with me again."

"His loss."

"Do the guys resent me? Are they calling me primadonna?"

"Take it as a compliment."

"So it's true?"

"Michael, it means you're good and these guys are just being petty. They're the same jokers who complain that I never schedule them a primo game. I don't schedule them a primo game because they don't deserve one. You keep going the way you're going and the *only* games you'll umpire will be the primo ones."

"Really?" I said, ready to burst. "Thanks."

"I had no reservations about asking you to fill in at this game. You've already proven yourself more than capable."

"But how do you know how I'm doing? You're not at the games?"

"I have my spies."

"You do? Who?"

"If I told you," he said, laughing, "I'd have to kill you."

I laughed with him, and drove home so stoked I may not sleep for days. This dream might actually come true.

CHAPTER 18

I made peace with Mister Tressel, but the Baseball Gods punished me. During a J.V. game at Mount Pleasant High School, a fastball deflected off a swinging bat and struck the top of my right foot. I must've made a thousand painful expressions behind my mask. I hobbled around and worried I had broken a bone.

The coaches for both teams asked the standard question, "You all right, ump?"

"Yeah," I said, grimacing, "I'm fine. Just give me a minute."

After the game, I stopped at Wilmington Hospital for an x-ray that revealed no fracture, but my foot had swelled up like a balloon.

Still limping a couple days later, a fastball shot off the swinging bat of a Smyrna High hitter and struck me dead-center in the mask. My head snapped back. I wobbled like a drunk until I put my hands on my knees.

"You all right, ump?" came from the dugouts.

"Yeah, it hit me in the head."

Some of the players and spectators laughed, but I found no humor in the situation.

117

Next game at Newark High, their catcher slid over to receive an outside pitch. The St. Mark's batter swung. I doubled over in agony. Even though I wore a cup, the foul ball struck me straight in the groin. I fell to one knee. My vision blurred and I worried I might pass out.

"You all right, ump?" Newark's J.V. coach said.

"Yeah," I said, cringing and blinking. "Just give me a minute."

The next day, I had the bases for a j.v game at Middletown High. Fourth inning, the Delaware Military Academy had a runner on first base. I stood behind the pitcher, between first and second base. The DMA batter hit a line drive at my head. I ducked just in time to avoid a smashed face.

Then on an off day, I felt my phone vibrate in my pocket during Social Studies. I almost wished it wasn't Randy. I had a book report for English I hadn't started, and a Calculus exam to study for.

In the hallway after class, I checked my messages and heard Randy's voice. He needed a plate umpire for a varsity game at Hodgson Vo Tech south of Newark.

"Have you found anybody yet?" I said when Randy answered.

"No," he said, frustrated. "It's not easy getting people last minute."

"All right, I'll do it."

"Bless you."

The game was routine. Hodgson beat McKean High 9-2. I survived without a scratch and hoped it meant that the Baseball Gods had been appeased.

I headed to my car.

"Hey, Dork!"

I flinched.

"Un-freakin' believable," Joe Forrester said with that up to something grin on his face. "Now I've seen everything. The dork *is* an umpire."

I opened the trunk of my car and tossed in my mask, cap, brush and indicator. I retrieved a towel and wiped sweat from my head and neck.

"I guess you didn't see me in the bleachers," Joe said.

"Obviously not," I replied, removing my chest protector. "Why are you here?"

"Hey, what's with the attitude? Be nice. I have a cousin who plays for McKean."

"How'd he do?"

"Struck out a couple times, nothing new."

"Well," I said, removing my shin guards, "nice to see you. I got to go."

"Hey, you better be nice. I could've heckled you from the bleachers, and you wouldn't have been able to do a damn thing about it. Next time, you might not be so lucky."

"Well, thank you for that."

"I still can't believe it. You really *are* an umpire. And what's even more amazing, you were good."

"Now I can't believe it. *You* paid me a compliment."

"Don't get too full of yourself. But why do this? Do you like having people make fun of you?"

"You wouldn't understand."

"Try me," he said, folding his arms across his chest.

"I need to be part of the game, Joe. Being an umpire gives me that. And you know what's even better about it than playing?"

"No, what?"

"I get to boss you jocks around."

"Only when you're wearing that uniform," he said, poking me in the chest. "In school, you're still the skinny ass nerd afraid of his own shadow."

"Not anymore, Joe," I said, standing tall. "Now, excuse me, I have to get home."

I closed the trunk and got behind the wheel. Joe tapped on the window as I put the key in the ignition.

"Yes," I said, lowering the glass.

He spat in my face, and then walked away laughing.

CHAPTER 19

Next day was Mexico Day in the cafeteria. I sat with Austin at our usual table, eating crunchy and cheesy nachos and watching my surroundings. Musclehead was at his usual place. Kelsey Delgado sat among the popular girls, although lately she had been eating around the fringe of the group. To my astonishment, she looked at me, got up with her lunch tray in hand and headed toward me.

She said hello to Austin and then asked me, "Can I sit with you?"

I broke out in a sweat. Had she truly come to sit with me or had somebody put her up to it as a joke? My anger showed. "I don't know. Can you?"

Kelsey put her tray down and sat. Her actions caused a few classmates to gasp in horror.

"Hi, Michael."

"Hi," I said, cautious.

"Should I leave?" Austin said.

"No," I replied.

"Sorry I was so mean to you."

I wasn't impressed. "Okay, you're sorry."

"I mean it, seriously."

"All right. Thank you."

"You probably don't know, but Joe's telling everybody, to use his words, what a sucky umpire you are."

"Really?" I said, sarcastic. "Anything else?"

"That you're too scared of the players and coaches to call a fair game, and that you called his cousin out on pitches that missed the strike zone by a mile."

"Unbelievable," I said with a sigh. "He talked to me after the game and told me I was good."

"Why would he lie?"

"Oh, the hell with him. I'm a *good* umpire, Kelsey. Players and coaches tell me I am after every game. I'm already doing varsity. The other day, I had a pitcher for Newark happy to see me. Yet everybody believes Joe instead of coming out to see for themselves."

"I saw for myself. You *are* good."

"Thanks," I said, wanting to forget that occasion. "I wish I could land one good punch against Musclehead's pointy chin. Just one good shot that would send him into a deep sleep for a long time."

"Musclehead," she said with a chuckle. "I like that."

"Well, thank you for telling me."

"Yeah, well, you told me what people were saying behind my back. And it was true. So I thought I should do the same."

"I didn't want to tell you, but you made me so mad."

"I know. It was my fault. You really are a nice guy, Michael. And you're honest, brutally honest, but that's okay. I really appreciate your help with algebra. I got a C on my last test and I'm getting better grades on my homework."

"That's good."

"So you like tall girls?" she asked with a smile.

"I better go," Austin said, standing. "Bye Kelsey. I'll

see you in English class, Michael."

"Okay, see ya."

Austin left.

I looked at Kelsey. I shouldn't get my hopes up that she'd actually want to date me, yet I was ready to leap from my chair. Then again, she could also be setting me up for a practical joke.

"Yeah," I said, "I like tall girls. But that's not the only reason I like you."

She flashed her gorgeous smile and I melted. "Well, I'm not saying we'll become boyfriend and girlfriend, but nobody's asked me to the prom."

Holy crap!

"So what do you think, Michael?"

I would've given my right arm to take her to the prom, but she was still Kelsey Delgado, the same girl who found the idea of us together in public repulsive. "What would your friends think if I took you to the prom?"

"I don't care."

"Be honest, Kelsey. Do you *really* want to go with me?"

She squirmed. She stopped looking me in the eye. She sounded pitiful when she said, "I want to go with you."

"I'm sorry, Kelsey, I don't believe you."

"Nobody's asked me, Michael. I'm going to be home prom night."

"So am I."

"Yeah, but I shouldn't be."

"Oh, and I should?"

"I didn't say that!"

I shook my head. "Sorry, Kelsey."

"Fine. Be that way."

Kelsey stood. She collected her tray and returned to

her previous seat.

Damn it, why did I have to be so moral? Why not take her to the prom? At least I'd drive her in my car, walk into the Newark Country Club with her on my arm and everybody would see us together. I'd dance with her, hold her--*feel* her. She'd smell great and might even wear a low-cut dress that showed off her shoulders and most of her chest. I'd be peeking and salivating all night. Anything could happen. But *noooo*, I had to be a *nice* guy.

Joe Forrester arrived with cheerleader Susan Neely on his arm. "There's the dork who thinks he's an umpire. Take a good look."

"Oh, Joe, you're terrible."

"He doesn't date either. Right, Michael? You'll be spending prom night with your baseball cards and your favorite five-fingered lady."

Susan, and students within earshot, laughed.

"Hey," Joe said, "I got an idea. Susan, why don't you help Michael lose his virginity?"

"Oh, no," Susan said, giggling, "he's too ugly."

A heartier laugh rose from my classmates. I wanted to crawl into a hole. I guess it was too much to ask for some respect among my peers. Even being an umpire, something I thought they'd consider cool, only gave them another reason to tease me.

"Sorry," Joe said, "At least I tried. Do you want me to talk to Kelsey for you?"

"Go to hell," I said.

Everybody gasped.

"What did you say?" Joe said, releasing Susan and standing over me.

I stood, no longer shaking in his presence. "I said go to hell. That's where liars like you belong."

Joe looked me up and down. I waited to be knocked out. Instead, he chuckled and waved a hand. "Ah, you're not worth the trouble. Come on Susan. See ya later, *loser.*"

Classmates laughed again. *Come on Graduation*!

CHAPTER 20

Mask off, I used the back of my hand to wipe sweat from my forehead while Concord's varsity coach held a conference on the mound with his pitcher and infielders. Concord led 9-7 over the home team, Middletown, in the bottom of the seventh inning. Middletown had runners on first and second with one out. Their players stood excited in their dugout. The fifty or so spectators made more noise than they had the entire game.

I broke up the meeting, and then gave the thumbs up signal to my base partner, Nate Buford, who stood behind the pitcher. He replied in kind.

As if on cue, Middletown's next batter hit a pop up between first and second base. I stepped out from behind the plate and put my right fist in the air. "Infield Fly! Infield Fly! Batter's out!"

By rule, the batter was automatically out and runners advanced at their own risk. The rule existed so an infielder wouldn't intentionally drop the ball and have the potential for a double or triple play.

Either the sun got in the second baseman's eyes or he just misjudged the flight of the ball because at the last split second he moved to his right and the ball bounced off the heel of his glove and landed on the ground. Middletown's runner on second took off. Concord's second baseman picked up the ball and rushed a throw that went over the head of his teammate at third. The ball ricocheted off the eave of Concord's dugout and rolled in foul territory by left field. Middletown's runner from second rounded third and scored. Their runner from first arrived at third and had every intention of staying there, but Concord's leftfielder hurried a throw home. The ball bounced short of the plate and skipped between the catcher's legs. Middletown's runner at third scored to tie the game. His teammates and coaches mobbed him when he reached the dugout. The fans were screaming and banging their feet on the bleachers.

Two outs, game tied.

Concord's catcher picked up the baseball against the backstop and threw hard to third.

What? Why? What's going on? *Another base runner*!

The ball sailed wide of the bag and into left field. The runner scored. Middletown's players, coaches and spectators went crazy. Concord's players walked off the field with their heads down.

"No, no, no!" I said, mask off and waving my arms like a maniac. "Game's *not* over! That run does *not* count. The batter's out! Infield fly! Get back here!"

I got hoarse repeating myself until I recognized a baffled expression of, "What?" on everyone's faces.

Concord's coach applauded and chased his players back onto the field. "That's right, ump, you're right."

"What do you mean the game's not over?" Middletown's coach said.

"There were runners on first and second with one out," I said. "Your batter hit a pop up. I called infield fly. Batter's out. Yet your player never left the field. I guess when he saw the ball drop, he thought he was safe

127

and kept running. But he's out. His run does *not* count. We have *two* outs, the bases empty and a tie game."

"Are you kidding me," Middletown's coach said. "I never heard you call infield fly!"

"I did, sir."

"You did not!"

"Yes, he did, Jeff," Concord's coach said. "Teach your boys the rules. That kid confused everybody."

"This is highway robbery," Middletown's coach said. "We won the game. You never called no God-damn infield fly."

"We called infield fly," Nate Buford said, joining us.

"Now you're just covering for each other," Middletown's coach said. "I never heard no infield fly."

"Whether you heard it or not," I said in a firm voice, "it was called. Now, let's get on with the game."

Middletown's coach stared at me for a long moment. Then he stomped his foot like a toddler. "Son of a bitch."

The game resumed, and Middletown won it in the bottom of the eighth when a sacrifice fly sent a runner home from third.

"Good thing we won," Middletown's coach said, "or I'd report you."

What a freakin' a-hole.

Randy telephoned later while I watched the Phillies-Braves game on the basement television. "I got a complaint about you that had to be stupidest one ever made. Apparently, it's your fault that the player didn't know the infield fly rule and ran around the bases and got everybody excited."

"Unbelievable," I said. "I should laugh about it, but it's pretty sad."

"You ready to quit yet?"

"No."

"Good. I spoke with the Concord coach and got a good idea of what happened. He had nothing but good things to say about how you handled the situation. So I've decided to give you more varsity games. Maybe I'll assign you some tournament games, but no promises."

I bolted from the sofa. My eyes watered. "Really?"

"Like I said, no promises. I'll check into it. I have a lot of senior umpires that might cause a stink. Tournament assignments are by seniority, as well as ability."

"Oh, wow, if I did tournament games that must set some kind of record for a rookie umpire. Does it?"

"Probably. I don't know for sure."

"Doing more varsity games would be *sooo* cool."

"I'll email you a revised schedule in a few minutes."

"Okay," I said, full of enthusiasm until a negative thought popped into my head. "I'm not cheating somebody out of a job by taking more varsity games, am I? I don't want to cause anymore trouble."

"Oh, no. I have some older guys that have been asking me to cut back. Plus we've had a lot of rain outs, and one postponement because the team bus broke down on the way to the game. So we're quite busy."

"Okay. Thank you. I won't let you down."

"I know you won't."

I ended the call and just wanted to bust. What more proof did I need? So I ran upstairs to my room, sat at my computer and logged onto the Matt Fogel Umpire School website. I completed and printed the registration form, wrote a check for the deposit, stuffed an envelope, addressed it, and put it with my school books so I'd remember to mail it in the morning.

Crap. I had left the Phillies game on. I hurried downstairs. Dad waited for me next to the door that led to the cellar. I got ready for his "electric bill" lecture.

"How many times have I told you to turn off the t.v.

129

when you're not watching it? Electricity isn't cheap. When you're living on your own and paying your own bills, you'll know what I'm talking about."

Mom entered from the kitchen, carrying two Bloody Mary's. She handed Dad one and they sat on the living room sofa. I couldn't contain my excitement.

"Mom, Dad, I know what I'm going to do with my life."

"Great," Dad said, sipping his drink.

"I'm going to be a professional baseball umpire."

"What?" Dad said, bewildered.

"I just enrolled in the Matt Fogel Umpire School," I said. "I need to attend it to get hired into pro ball. It's in Daytona Beach, and classes are in January."

"Michael," Mom said, "what're you talking about? You want to umpire as a *career*?"

"Yes," I said, practically jumping out of my skin. "I'm good at it, really good. Randy's already changing my schedule to give me more varsity games. He even said I might do tournament games."

"Oh, no," Dad said, shaking his head, "this was only going to be a part-time job. You're going to college."

"I can do *both*."

"How?" Mom asked.

"Umpire school takes place *between* semesters."

"Michael," Dad said, "you can't be serious. I mean, this is even crazier than trying to play. How many major league umpires are there?"

I hesitated to answer because I knew what his reaction would be.

"Michael," he said, "how many?"

"Sixty-eight."

"Sixty-eight! Are you out of your mind?"

"Michael," Mom said, "you have such a bright future ahead. Do you want to throw all that away?"

"Major league umpires earn six-figure salaries," I said, defensive.

"That's in the majors," Dad said as expected. "Which we already know is near impossible to achieve."

"Look," I said, "if I get hired as an umpire, I'll be in the minor leagues for awhile. I'll take college courses in the fall, umpire in the spring and summer. I'll get my degree."

"So you have this all figured out?" Dad said.

"I do."

Mom and Dad looked at each other and appeared desperate to counter my plan.

"We're not paying for this," Dad said, probably hoping that would win the argument in his favor.

"I'm not asking you to," I said with pride. "Between what I earn umpiring and what I expect to make this summer at Lums Pond, I'll have enough."

"How much is tuition?" Dad asked.

"Three-thousand for the five-week course."

Dad whistled. "Plus expenses. Are you driving or flying?"

"Driving."

"Add the cost of gas and tolls. And what about your car? It already has over a hundred-thousand miles on it."

More like a hundred-ten thousand. I too worried about the old rust-bucket. Before I started umpiring, I had only driven the Taurus back and forth to school and around Newark. Now, I covered an entire county.

"Michael," Dad said, "do you realize how lucky you are? I'd kill to have your brains and opportunities."

"I know, Dad. Trust me, I know. But I'm so damn happy on the field. I was made for this. Yeah, I get yelled out sometimes, but deep down, everybody respects me and appreciates what I do. They *like* me. I am accepted. I have to take a shot at this. If I fail, then so be it, but I have to try."

"You've never been away from home," Mom said, eyes wet. "How can you go to Florida by yourself?"

"I have to leave the nest some time."

"I don't get it," Dad said. "This is just replacing one crazy dream with another. I had no problem taking you to Little League tryouts because every American boy should play baseball. Then I watched you cry your eyes out when none of the coaches picked you. Even so, you insisted on going back every year. Then you kept trying out for the high school team. It's as if you have no grasp on reality."

"I can't help it, Dad. I love baseball. I want to be a part of it. I don't have this feeling with anything else."

"Why do you love it?" Mom asked.

"Oh, I don't know, it's not something I can put into words."

"You can do better than that," Dad said. "You'll have to do better than that to convince me."

Wow, he seriously wanted to talk about it. "All right. It's the only team sport where the defense controls the ball and there's no time clock. And probably best of all, it's a game for optimists. I mean, more often than not the batter fails to get a hit, so there's plenty to be pessimistic about. Yet between every pitch, every at-bat, there's always hope. The players and fans all believe the next pitch will be smacked for a base hit, or a home run. And even if it isn't, everybody believes it'll happen on the pitch after that. If you're rooting for the team in the field, you believe a strike out is coming, even if the worst pitcher in the league is on the mound. The game just has so many positive things about it. I can't help but love it. I want to be a part of it for the rest of my life. These past few weeks have been so fantastic. I want this feeling to continue."

Mom and Dad stared at each other for what seemed like several minutes, waiting for the other to blink. I wondered if they were going to tell me to move out.

"All right," Dad said. "But we're not helping you financially, even if you're just a dollar short. This is all on you."

I embraced them. "Thank you, thank you, that's all I ask."

CHAPTER 21

Although Randy revised my schedule to include more varsity match ups, he left me as the lone umpire for a game at George Reed Middle School in New Castle. Top of the fifth inning, George Reed trailed Gunning Bedford 4-3, and the visiting team had a runner on first with one out.

Reed's pitcher delivered from the stretch. I crouched over the catcher's right shoulder. The baseball ran inside on the left-handed batter, about waist high. *Ting*.

My instincts told me the ball should be down the first base line. The batter stumbled backwards and blocked my view. By the time he regained his balance, dropped his bat and ran, the baseball was scooped up in right field on the foul side of the line.

Holy crap. What should I call? Did the ball bounce past first base on the fair or foul side of the bag? Or did the ball stay in the air and land on the foul side of the outfield line? What should I do?

Reed's players had gone full speed. Bedford's base runners had too. They now occupied second and third. Their actions told me the ball must've been fair, but I prepared for a tidal wave of screaming from Reed's coach, their players and spectators, all claiming foul ball. What defense had I?

Yet the Reed players and fans were quiet. Reed's coach remained in the dugout. He clapped his hands. "Come on, guys. Let's shake it off."

I got lucky, and released a big sigh of relief. Maybe I should play the lottery.

Bedford's next batter, on a one-one count, hit a ground ball that should've been turned into a double-play, but the baseball went between the legs of Reed's second baseman. The batter reached first, while the runner from third scored and the runner on second took third. Reed's coach requested time and I granted it.

When play resumed, Bedford's hitter worked a two-two count. Next pitch, the runner on first took off. *Ting.*

The ball stuck in the catcher's mitt. He made no throw to second. He stood, turned around and looked at me through his mask. "Don't he go back to first?"

"Hey, ump," Reed's coach said, "that's a foul tip."

"Time," I said, removing my mask. "It was a caught foul tip."

"Yeah," the coach said, "so the runner goes back to first."

"No, sir. A foul tip caught is a live ball."

"What?" the coach said. He came closer. "It's a foul ball. That runner returns to first."

"No, sir. A caught foul tip is no different than a swing and miss."

"Now, wait a minute," the coach said, his tone rising. "I had runners on first and second in a game last week and we pulled off a double steal. My batter foul tipped the ball. The umpire sent both runners back. We ended up getting no runs and lost by one."

"A caught foul tip is no different than a swing and

miss. Runners advance at their own risk."

"No, no, no!" he said, turning red. "You're wrong! That runner needs to go back to first."

"I'm sorry, sir. He stays on second."

"But that's not what happened last week!"

"I can't comment on what happened last week."

"Oh, you've got to be kidding me?" the coach said, throwing up his hands. "This is pure….*garbage*. I'm playing this game under protest. You're wrong. That runner goes back to first."

"Write your protest in the scorebook and I'll sign."

"You're damn right you'll sign. And I'll be happy to prove you wrong."

Gunning Bedford won the game 8-5. As expected, Randy called that evening. I spoke to him in my bedroom while I studied for my Calculus final.

"Heard you had some trouble today," Randy said.

"Nothing I couldn't handle."

"True. The protest was dismissed."

"What about the umpire who made the wrong call last week?"

"Yeah, I just spoke to him. It's unfortunate, but these things happen. We're not professionals. We do our best. But the coach should know the rule too. Then he would've protested *last week's* call."

"I wish I could call the coach and tell him, 'I told you so,' but I guess I'll just enjoy this little victory in silence."

"For us umpires," Randy said with a chuckle, "that's as good as it gets."

CHAPTER 22

In late-May, I had the plate for a varsity game at John Dickinson High School, south of Wilmington. Top of the sixth, Dickinson led their rival McKean High 8-7. McKean's first batter hit a single to left.

Dickinson's coach emerged from the first base dugout with an open scorebook in his hands. "Time, ump. I need to speak to you."

"Time!" I said.

"Number 8," the coach said, referring to the runner on first base, "batted out of order. Number 6 was scheduled to lead off."

My partner, Jim Smithers, approached.

"What's the hold up?" McKean's coach said, joining the conference.

"We have a dispute about the batting order," I said. "He claims number 6 should've led off."

"Yes," Dickinson's coach said, "Number 8 is scheduled to bat second."

"Jordy," McKean's coach said toward his dugout.

Jordy was a student. He ran from the dugout, scorebook in hand.

McKean's coach grabbed it from him and looked it over. "Did you tell Eric to lead off?"

"No," Jordy said. "He did it on his own."

"Come on, Jordy," the coach said, slapping the book. "It's your job to keep this stuff straight."

"So," I said, "you agree your team batted out of order?"

"It appears so," McKean's coach said.

"Ok," I said to both coaches, "then the batter who was supposed to hit, number 6, is out and the single doesn't count. The second batter, the player standing on first, is up to bat."

"What?" McKean's coach said. "That's not right. The guy on first is out and we continue from his spot."

"No, sir," I said. "The batter who was supposed to hit is out, and the lineup continues as it normally would."

"That's not right," McKean's coach said. "Is it?"

"Hey," Dickinson's coach said, "it sounds like the kid knows what he's doing."

Don't call me kid.

"What do you say?" McKean's coach asked my partner.

"The call's *correct*," I said.

"Hey," McKean's coach said to my partner, "tell your friend here he's wrong. The batter that hit is out, and the next guy is up."

Jim Smithers stepped toward third base and tugged on my elbow. I shrugged him off.

"We have batting out of order," I said, "one out and the base hit doesn't count." I pointed at the player who stood on first base. "You, you're up."

"That's it?" McKean's coach said.

"That's it," I said. "Return to your dugout."

"I'm playing the rest of this game under protest,"

McKean's coach said.

"So noted."

It took a few minutes, but the coaches returned to their dugouts. Jim Smithers stood behind first base with a frown on his face and his arms folded across his chest.

Let him be mad. I had a job to do and couldn't worry about hurt feelings.

McKean High failed to score. Dickinson High added five runs in the bottom of the sixth inning and won the game 13-7.

As I left the field with Jim, McKean's coach blocked our path. "You'll be hearing from me."

I said nothing and stepped around him.

"Tough game," Jim said in the parking lot.

"Not really."

"I didn't appreciate what you did when I tried to have a private word with you."

"Well," I said opening my car's trunk, "I didn't like what you did."

"And what was that?"

"You pulled me aside right in front of the coaches, players, *everybody*. Do you have any idea how that looks, what message it sends? It gives the impression that I need help from somebody *older*. I know the rules. No doubt in my mind. And you should know them by heart too."

"I had heard you were a primadonna."

"Primadonna has nothing to do with it. It's *perception*. Because I'm young, I've had to work extra hard to build up a good reputation. When my own partner makes it look like I don't know what I'm doing, it just destroys everything."

"Christ, man, calm down. It's just high school."

"I don't care if it's a pick-up game played on the moon. I'll do the best job I can, not for me, but for the players. These guys work hard to get here. They deserve umpires who work just as hard."

Jim stared for a long time. I guess to size me up. I wasn't sure if he was going to punch me or apologize. Fortunately, he did the latter. "Fair enough. I'm sorry."

"Apology accepted," I said, and we shook hands.

Jim wished me good night and headed to his car. I started to remove my gear.

A man in a Dickinson High tee-shirt introduced himself. "Brandon Clemons. I'm the A.D. I couldn't help but overhear. I want to thank you for your commitment to these boys."

"You're welcome."

"You call a good game. Are you new?"

"It's my first year."

"Well, again, good job. Do you have aspirations beyond school ball?"

"Yes, sir. I hope to turn pro someday."

"I kinda guessed that. My brother umpires in the Carolina League. I see him whenever he comes to Wilmington for a Blue Rocks game. He loves it. He started out like you, doing high school games. Then he went to the Fogel school."

"That's where I'm going in January."

"Well," he said, shaking my hand, "best of luck to you." Then he winked. "And you're right on that batting out of order."

"Thank you, sir. I appreciate it."

***

At home, I undressed and showered. I put on fresh clothes and shared a quiet spaghetti dinner with my parents. Afterwards, I sat at my desk and studied for an upcoming history final. I heard a strong knock on the door that had to be Dad.

"Come in."

140

He did, and sat on the edge of my bed.

"So what's up?" I said.

"You were awfully quiet at dinner. Ever since you started umpiring, you've come home like a house afire, full of enthusiasm. You can't wait to tell us everything, even when it's bad. Today, nothing."

"I had another issue with my partner," I said with a sigh. "We had batting out of order. I enforced the rule correctly, but McKean's coach wasn't sure, and I guess my partner wasn't sure either. So he grabbed me by the arm right in front of everybody to have a private talk. I didn't need to talk. I called it right, so I shrugged him off."

"You called it right. That's all that matters."

"Yeah, I know, but I shouldn't upset these guys. I have to work with them."

"Michael, you're pursuing a career where the odds of success are extraordinary. You have to be better than the best to get recognized. Try and get along with your partners, but don't compromise your standards. The second you do that, you lose."

"I know, Dad, but they're calling me primadonna."

"So? Would you rather be called lousy, or average?"

"No."

"Michael, this is no different than your issues at school. The other kids don't understand you. Not because you're weird, but because you're a leader. You won't compromise who you are just to fit in."

"So I'll be alone all my life?"

"No. Trust me, when you get to college, everything will be different. Your intelligence will be respected. You'll make lots of friends. So don't worry about it."

"Thanks, Dad," I said with a smile. I really did have great parents. Of course, I couldn't tell them that. I wouldn't want them to get a swelled head.

Dad patted me on the shoulder and left. My phone vibrated in my pocket.

"I dismissed the protest," Randy said. "And I spoke to Jim. He said you gave him the third degree, but that you were right."

"Well," I said, sarcastic, "that was big of him."

"You're right, though. Perception is a large part of the job. But I must say, you continue to get accolades. Dickinson's coach and A. D. both called to tell me how impressed they were by how you handled yourself."

"Thanks, but I keep causing trouble with my partners."

"Michael, listen to me, you're the best damn rookie umpire we've had. I mean that sincerely. You do a super job. You're a walking rule book, but more importantly, you're fair and impartial, you interact well with the players and coaches. You work hard, you have a great attitude. I wish I had a whole staff like you."

"Thank you," I said, choking up. "I needed that."

"But I do have a bit of bad news."

"What?"

"I've looked at the tournament schedule and the number of veteran umpires that want to work it."

I heard the "but" in Randy's voice before he said it.

"But," he continued, "even with four umpires per game, I don't see how I can fit you in. Hope you understand."

"It's okay," I lied. "I have a ton of finals next week."

"Take pride in your accomplishment. In your rookie season, you went from middle school and J.V. games to varsity. Nobody else has done that. Summer leagues are starting soon. I'll have plenty of work for you."

"Bring it on."

PART II
TOUCHING THE BASES

CHAPTER 23

My summer job at Lums Pond State Park began on the Saturday of Memorial Day weekend. Located off Howell School Road in Bear, the park encompassed 1790 acres, 200 of which consisted of the largest fresh-water pond in Delaware. The St. George's Creek had been dammed in the early 1800's to provide water for the locks of the Chesapeake and Delaware Canal. No longer needed for that purpose, Lums Pond had opened to the public in 1963. It offered boating, camping, fishing, ball fields, picnic pavilions and woodland trails for hiking, biking and horseback riding. No swimming. Dad said swimming had been permitted when he was a boy. The former beach was visible from my job location at the boat rental office, but it had been taken over by wild grass.

I entered the Boat Rental Office wearing the park's official brown polo shirt, matching shorts and sandals. Referred to as "the shack," the office was a single-story, brown-painted and non-insulated building with exterior shutters on three sides. I put my bagged lunch in a small refrigerator under the counter and got reacquainted with my boss.

"Hard to believe," I said, "another summer already."

"Yeah," June Hunter said, sarcastic, "time flies when you're having fun." She appeared more masculine than feminine, with the hint of a moustache. The past year must've been extra rough. Her pale face had dark circles around bloodshot eyes and more wrinkles than I remembered. She had a coarse speaking voice from smoking, and the stench from the cigarettes remained on her person despite heavy perfume. "This is Cole Bannister."

I shook hands with a guy who must've dyed his hair because I've never seen tomato-red hair.

"I know you from somewhere" he said, pointing a bony finger to the ceiling. "Just can't remember where."

"Do you go to Glasgow?" I said.

"No, Middletown."

"Allison Mansford," June said.

I shook hands with a short and busty girl with hazel eyes behind glasses. She wore the state park uniform, with the polo shirt buttons unfastened.

"Can I have my hand back?" she said with an attitude.

"Oh, sorry."

Cole snickered.

"Michael," June said to Cole and Allison, "is a full time summer employee on your staggered schedule, so you'll see a lot of him."

Cole nodded. Allison returned to the cash register to complete her money count for the morning.

"So Michael," June said, "You graduate soon, right?"

"A week from today."

"Then UD in the fall?"

"And umpire school in January."

"What school?"

145

"Professional baseball umpire school. I umpired school ball this spring. I start summer leagues on Wednesday. Then come January, I'll be at the Matt Fogel Umpire School in Florida trying to get a job in the pros."

"Really? I thought you'd go into engineering or something."

"I still might."

"Won't umpiring conflict with this job?"

"No. I already forwarded my work schedule to the guy who assigns the games."

"That's it," Cole said, his eye wide. "I played first base for Middletown. You umpired a couple of our games."

"Well," I said, joking, "don't hold that against me."

"No, no," Cole said, "you were better than most."

"Thanks, I think."

"All right," June said, clapping her hands, "hate to break this up, but let's get ready for business."

Although Allison and Cole were new hires, they were acquainted with the working routine because their service began on May first. The rental office operated weekends only from May first to Memorial Day, then every day until Labor Day, followed by weekends only until the end of September.

Cole and I opened the shutters to let in natural light. We then stepped outside. Rowboats, canoes, kayaks and pedal boats were arranged in a line from the shack to a concrete boat launch and dock.

"Since you've worked here before," Cole said, removing his phone from a pocket. "I guess I don't need to train you."

"No," I said. "Just get their receipt and give them the boat they rented."

"That's it. So you like being an umpire?"

"Love it."

"I couldn't do it. People screaming at me and calling me names. Did you eject anybody?"

"A couple."

"How can you stand it?"

"It's not so bad.   Most of the crap I hear is worn out expressions that umpires have heard for years. 'Come on, ump, you blind? Get some glasses! Get some binoculars! Call it the same for both teams. You're missing a good game, blue.' In reality, arguments and ejections are rare."

"It don't seem rare."

"That's because of t.v. Arguments and ejections are always shown on the highlights."

"I hear that, but I could never do it. Did you ever hear something really funny, but couldn't laugh and let them know it was funny?"

"A few. Like, 'Weren't you the lookout on the Titanic? Can I pet your seeing-eye dog? I've seen potatoes with better eyes."

"I guess someday," Cole said, laughing, "you'll be famous and on T.V. I can tell people I worked with that dude."

"I don't think it's a good thing for an umpire to become famous. That usually means he screwed up."

"I hear that. Got a girlfriend?"

"No."

"You mean umpiring all those games didn't get you some?"

"No," I said, remembering Kelsey. "Umpires are hated."

"Hey," he said, leaning into me, "you like Allison?"

"I don't know. I just met her."

"Yeah, well, let me tell you, she's a whiner. Don't seem to like nobody. But if you want to make a play for

147

her, go right ahead. I ain't interested." Cole's phone buzzed. He read a text message. A moment later, the tip of his thumbs tapped away on a tiny keyboard. He no sooner sent the message than he received another. "Just can't keep the babes away."

"Mister Popular," I said.

He grinned. "You got it." Then Cole whispered, "Hey, she's looking at you."

I turned. A man with a little girl holding his hand stood at the shack. Allison and I locked eyes for a second while she reached across the counter to accept the man's money and driver's license. The license was kept to make sure the customer returned the park's property.

"Go for it, dude."

"I don't know."

"Don't like big girls?"

"It's not that," I said. "I've only been here ten minutes. Give me a chance."

The man and his daughter made their way to us, each wearing a life jacket.

"You take the first one," Cole said.

"Hello," I said to them. "Welcome to Lums Pond."

The girl smiled. The man handed me his receipt. I searched the inventory of two-person canoes for number 3, the digit painted on the bow. I then dragged it with its pair of plastic paddles to the water's edge and kicked off my sandals. The man and his daughter stepped into the canoe and took a seat, the man preparing to row. I pushed them away from shore and got about ankle deep in the water.

"See you in an hour," I said.

I slipped on my sandals and returned to Cole.

"I think you're scared of girls," he said.

Here it comes, the teasing. Did I have a flashing tattoo on my forehead that announced pick on me, I was an easy target.

"I just met her. Give me a chance. Besides, if she's a big whiner like you said, I might not like her."

"So what? I hear she's a slut. Dresses like one too. You don't have to like her."

"I'll think about it."

Cole clucked like a chicken and walked away laughing, receiving and sending more text messages.

CHAPTER 24

It was the most unbearable, crappiest holiday weekend ever. I wanted to pull every dyed hair out of Cole's head. He spent more time texting and phoning than helping customers. When he talked to me, he pestered me about Allison. Did I ask her out yet? Why not? What was I waiting for? And he made that annoying clucking noise.

We called for a park ranger twice. The first time involved three teenage boys who each rented a kayak and then held their own naval battle. They rammed into each other in an attempt to tip one another over and jousted with their oars. Two boys lost their oar. June held onto the oldest boy's driver's license and told them they had to pay for the lost equipment. The three cussed her out until two rangers arrived and threatened the boys with arrest.

The second time was pretty funny. This guy kept his paddleboat for ninety minutes on a one-hour rental. June told Allison to charge the man for the second hour. He refused to pay. June refused to return his license. The man stormed off and drove home, forgetting that June had his license. She gave it to the rangers. The state police had no trouble tracking the man down and charging him with skipping out on the bill and driving without a license.

***

With my shift finally over on Memorial Day Monday, I walked to the parking lot. Allison was present. She had her back to me and shifted from one foot to the other and stared toward the park's entrance.

"Do you need a ride?" I asked.

Allison folded her arms across her chest. "No. My mom should be along."

"Did you call her?"

Allison moaned. "I don't *have* a cell phone, and neither does my mom. She's just late getting out of work."

"Where does she work? I can call."

"She's a cook at Shady Pines Nursing Home," Allison said. "Don't bother. She's on her way. She would've called the shack if she'd be really late."

"Are you all right?" I said.

She huffed. "Of course I'm all right. Why would you ask such a stupid question?"

"You seem angry," I said. "You've looked mad all weekend. Is it the job?"

Allison shrugged. "Beats working fast food."

"Have you done that?"

"Yeah, can't you tell?"

"I don't know what you mean."

"Don't be stupid," she said.

"I'm not."

"Fast food is why I'm fat. I ate it at work and took it home."

"You're not fat."

Allison laughed. "Then you're blind."

I changed the uncomfortable subject. "What high school do you go to?"

"McDonnaugh," Allison said, a little nicer. "I'll be a junior."

"Any plans for college?"

She chuckled. "My plans are to be rich and famous."

"And how are you going to accomplish that?"

"Marry a rich guy. Do you know any?"

"No. Try hanging out at the DuPont Country Club."

"Good idea."

An awkward silence took over. I pulled my keys from my pocket. "Well, goodnight."

I took a couple steps toward my car.

"I like baseball," Allison said. "The Phillies have some cute players."

I faced her. "Is that the only reason you like baseball?"

"What other reason is there? When do you umpire next?"

"Wednesday," I said. "At Midway. It's on Lander Hill Road."

"I know where it is. I had a boyfriend who played there."

She *had* a boyfriend.

"What time's the game?" Allison asked.

"Six," I replied. "I have the bases. Come on out and see me."

"I don't have a ride."

"I can drive you. I'll be going there right from work."

She looked me up and down. "I don't think so."

I felt the sting of rejection. "Okay, then. Why did you ask?"

"Just curious."

"You know," I said, "you have beautiful eyes behind those glasses. Are you near-sighted or far-sighted?"

Allison hugged herself. "You actually noticed my

152

eyes?" She turned away. "What color are they?"

I spoke with confidence. "Green."

She faced me and dropped her arms to her side. "Okay."

"I meant no disrespect."

"Don't worry about it," Allison said. "Cole wouldn't know the color of my eyes. He's a pig."

A gray Chevy Caprice with rust spots on its dented hood approached.

"My mom's here," Allison said.

Her mother had the driver's side window down, not only because of the heat but she puffed on a cigarette. Her strawberry-blonde hair was in disarray. Her heavyset body wore a white smock over a flowery dress and she seemed to be pinned between the seat and steering wheel.

Allison did not introduce me.

Her mother gave me a half-hearted smile.

Allison got in the car on the passenger side. Her mother flicked the cigarette butt onto the parking lot, and then gave a half-hearted wave before she stepped on the gas.

***

Hallelujah, back to baseball. The Midway Athletic Complex in New Castle had outdoor tennis and basketball courts, a soccer and football field, one tee-ball and Little League field, a softball diamond and two full-sized baseball fields. Each baseball field had lights, an electronic scoreboard, perimeter fence, a pair of above ground, cinder block dugouts, a set of aluminum bleachers and a concession stand topped by a small press box.

"Pretty impressive," I said to my plate partner, Clarence Owens.

"Only in appearance," Clarence said while he suited

153

up at his car. "The quality isn't as good as high school."

A short while later, he and I met the opposing coaches at home plate. We had charge of a Babe Ruth game between the Collins Lumber Blue Jays and the Crescent Drug Store Pirates. Ballplayers on both teams were walking billboards, advertising their sponsor on the back of their jerseys. I recognized some of the faces from school ball. A few of them waved at me.

After ground rules, I noticed a girl in a tank top and white shorts leaning against the chain link fence next to the Blue Jay's first base dugout. She waved.

"Wow," I said, half stunned.

"Girlfriend?" Clarence asked.

"No. Somebody I work with."

"Well, if I was her father I'd kick her ass for going out in public like that."

"I don't know if she has a dad."

I took my position behind first base. Allison smiled. Had she really come here to see me? How did she get here? Why didn't she say she was coming?

A man in the press box broadcasted the batting order for Collins Lumber. His voice echoed from the field speakers. Then he said, "Today's umpires are Clarence Owens behind the plate and Michael Briggs at the bases."

Wow, my name echoed across a baseball field for the first time. I better get used to it. It'll be echoing across major league ball parks soon enough.

"Michael," Allison said, waving at me to approach.

"I can't."

She frowned. "A friend dropped me off. Can you give me a ride home?"

What? This was really odd. She had barely spoken to me all weekend, declined my offer to drive her here, and now she wanted me to take her home? Didn't she have any friends that could help her out? Why me?

"Michael, can you?"

"Yeah," I said just to quiet her, "I'll give you a ride."

The lead-off hitter for Collins Lumber stepped into the right handed batter's box and took a couple practice swings. I stared down the first base line and had a nice four-deep profile of the batter, the stooped catcher, a masked Clarence and spectators in the bleachers behind the tall backstop.

"Play ball," Clarence said.

Crescent Drug Store's pitcher went into his wind-up. The baseball was delivered and less than a second later passed shoulder-high on the batter and smacked into the catcher's mitt.

"Ball," Clarence said.

I looked at Allison out the corner of my eye. Yeah, she was a little heavy and revealed a lot of skin, but she did have a pretty face. The glasses made her look smart.

I noticed other boys staring at her, whispering comments to a friend, and then laughing. Did I really want to get involved with a girl who got so little respect? Why did she go out in public like that?

"Ball two," Clarence said after the next pitch.

Oh, crap. I had better watch the game.

"Strike!"

Next pitch, the batter hit a ground ball to Crescent Drug Stores' shortstop. I moved into position while the fielder scooped up the baseball in his glove and made a strong throw to first. I focused on the bag and heard the ball impact leather long before the batter's foot arrived. I released a dramatic and loud "Out!"

"I think they heard you in California," the first base coach said.

Idiot, there had been no reason to over-react to such a routine play. Showing off for Allison?

155

The next batter for Collins Lumber hit a ground ball deep in the hole between shortstop and third. The shortstop backhanded the ball and made a strong throw across the diamond, barely nipping the runner at the base. This time the play deserved a dramatic and loud, "Out!"

The next batter for Collins Lumber hit a fly ball to left field that was caught. Their nine players jogged from the field, replaced by nine players for Collins Lumber. While their pitcher warmed up, I met with Allison.

"Awesome," she said, her eyes shining behind the glasses. "You know what's even more awesome?"

"No," I said, playing along, "what?"

"It's so awesome to see somebody I know doing something so different. My friends are working in stores or asking people if they want fries with that."

"And I make more money than they do, and in less time." Now that was really bragging. Did I have to say that? She might be interested in me for more than just money.

"Really?"

"Yeah," I went on, unable to stop myself, "I get thirty-five dollars for this game."

"Wow," she said, her eyes wide. "You're the richest boy I know."

"Well," I said, faking modesty, "I'm not really *that* rich."

"What're you doing with the money?"

"Saving for umpire school."

"That's right. Don't you ever have a little fun?"

"Sure," I said as the pitcher completed his warm up. "I have to go."

I returned to my position behind first base. Clarence stared at me through his mask. I hoped he didn't mind that I talked to Allison.   It had been between innings, after all, so he should be cool with it. I had had lots of partners who stepped away from the field between innings to talk to somebody, or puff down a cigarette.

The remainder of the game progressed at a nice pace, with Collin's Lumber winning 11-2. I had looked at Allison a few times, but did not visit her again.

"I'll meet you in the parking lot," I yelled to her.

I joined Clarence by home plate and we headed for our cars.

"Good game, sir," he said, wiping his sweaty brow with the back of a hand. "Did you make a date yet?"

"I guess we will at my car," I said with a nervous chuckle. "She needs a ride home."

"Oh," he said with a laugh, "the damsel in distress."

"What do you mean?"

"Since I'm the suspicious type, I'd say she planned it this way."

"You think so?"

"I do. Be careful. A minute of fun can make for a lifetime of regret."

"Oh, I'll be careful. I have plans."

"Good," Clarence said. We shook hands. "See you around."

Allison met me. "You were just awesome out there. You got every call right, too, even that one in the sixth inning that that player bitched about."

"Yeah," I said, acting macho, "it was close, but the ball beat him." I popped open my car's trunk long enough to toss in my cap and indicator. I then unlocked the passenger side door and held it open. Allison looked, but didn't move. "You said you needed a ride home, right?"

"Oh, sorry, I ain't never had nobody hold the door open for me."

Allison got in, the first girl to sit in my car. *And what*

a girl! I looked down and had an excellent view of her deep cleavage and mostly naked breasts. I tried not to stare, but couldn't help it. They were right there, in all their humongous glory.

Wow, I sounded like other boys who whistled and made crude comments at girls. Joe Forrester and his jock friends kept a score sheet rating a girls' hotness. Any female, especially in the cafeteria, risked hearing a remark about their bodies that was followed by a number from one to ten, one being so-so in appearance and ten being super hot. Most girls resented it, some did not, soaking it up and strutting like models. However, Joe and his friends also yelled out negative numbers for someone they found unattractive. The amount of hurt these girls felt was evident on their faces.

Allison buckled herself in. I closed the door and hurried to the driver's seat.

"Really nice car," she said. "Had it long?"

"A couple years," I said, starting the ignition and shifting into drive. "It used to be my grandfather's. His eyes went bad and the state took his license. My dad convinced him to sell me the car for a hundred dollars."

"Oh, you're so lucky. I wish something like that would happen to me. I don't know how I'm ever going to have enough money for a car. Whatever I make, Mom takes as rent. She doesn't seem to realize I need money to go out with my friends. Not that I have a lot of friends, just a few, but they still want to go out and do stuff. I know Mom needs money to pay the bills and all, and I'd be homeless and starving without her, but I just wish she'd let me keep my own money."

"Have you talked to her about it?"

"Yeah, but she says we're poor and I need to contribute my share. Oh, I just get so jealous, you know. Some girls in my school are *sooo* spoiled. They have cars.

They have the latest phones, fancy clothes and the most expensive perfume and accessories. And then they pick on me because I don't have these things, like I'm abnormal. Girls can be so mean, you know. There's a few in my school I'd like to beat up, but then I'd probably act just like them if I had parents that spoiled me."

Wow, for a girl who hardly said a word to me she sure was making up for it now. "Where do you live?"

"Smyrna."

"You live in Smyrna?" I said, irritated. It wasn't a short drive.

"North of town. It's not *that* far."

"It's at least twenty miles."

"No it isn't. I'll show you. So when's your next game?"

"Tomorrow at Banning Park," I said, heading south on Route 1.

"I ain't never been there. I guess you do a lot of driving. Do you get gas money?"

"No."

"Too bad."

"So why couldn't this friend give you a ride home?"

"Her name's Jessie. She has a boyfriend that plays for Tastytreats. What a crazy name for a baseball team, right? But that's who sponsors them. He's no good. Her parents hate him. Anyway, they have to meet in secret and he mostly hangs out at Midway. Her parents think she's with me at the mall, which was partly true, but she dumped me here for him. I mean, I understand the boyfriend thing, but it was pretty mean of her to use me like that."

"Good thing I was here to give you a ride, then."

"Oh, I told her a boy I worked with would be here. That's when she got all excited and we made up the story about going to the mall."

159

I wasn't sure if I should feel complimented, insulted or used. "So you didn't really come out to see *me*."

"Oh, I don't know. I *was* curious, and I'd like to see your game tomorrow. Can I ride with you?"

Oh, wow, she wanted to be with me. "Okay."

"Awesome."

"I'm kinda hungry. Will your mom have dinner for you?"

"I fend for myself most of the time. I'm pretty independent. Sometimes I wish I wasn't. I know most teenagers want their parents off their back, but I wish my mom would show some guidance once in a while, help me with decisions. She taught me independence, but what else."

"You need to talk to her."

"It's not easy. She's always *busy*."

"Would it be all right then, if we stopped somewhere?"

"Sure."

I drove across the Delaware-Chesapeake Canal and entered Middletown. I then pulled into the drive-through lane at Hamburger Junction and bought us each a combo meal of a burger, fries and soda. I parked with the sunset in view.

"This is why I'm fat," she said, unwrapping her burger loaded with cheese, lettuce, tomato, ketchup and mustard.

I put my burger down, suddenly not hungry. "I'm sorry. I forgot. I shouldn't have stopped here."

"Oh, no, no. I'm just venting. I'm happy you stopped here. Thank you."

"Okay," I said with little enthusiasm. "Again, you're not fat."

"You're a rare, non-judgmental person. People are always judging me on first sight. I try not to do that, but probably do it too, like I hate the supermodel wannabes. I tell them to stop binging and purging. But of course they come back with fatty, fat, fat, ugly, disgusting. I've never been skinny, wouldn't know what that's like. So for the longest time I hid behind baggy clothes."

Allison raised the burger to her mouth. A thick blob of ketchup dripped and landed in her cleavage. The red condiment then flowed like lava between her mounds. "Oh, damn."

I stared. I couldn't help it, and wanted to lick it off.

"Can I have a napkin," Allison said, irritated.

I retrieved one from the paper bag the meal came in and watched her wipe her chest clean.

"Get a good look?" she said. "What's the big deal, anyway? They're just boobs. I'm sure you've seen plenty of them in magazines and movies, the internet. Maybe even for real?"

"Sorry, but you are showing a lot."

"That's because boys call me hot when I dress like this. Otherwise, they call me fat. Better to be called hot than fat, so no baggy clothes."

"I guess there's some logic to that."

"There was this one boy, Justin Keller, who teased me constantly. He walked around like he owned the school, but I think he's missing some brain cells. He stole my backpack a few times. He punched me in the arm a couple times. Everybody said he did it because he liked me. I thought that type of behavior went out in elementary school, but turns out, they were right. We went on a date, just to the mall and a movie. We kissed. Then one of his friends teased him for liking fat girls so he denied the date ever happened. Can you believe it? He pretended nothing happened! He yelled at me in front of everybody in the cafeteria, saying I imagined it, and called me slut. I wanted to kill him. So, you don't think I'm fat?"

"No."

"Do you think I'm hot?"

"Of course."

"Do you like me?"

I wasn't sure. She talked a lot, and might be full of drama, but I wasn't about to toss away the first girl to show any interest in me. "I like you."

"Good."

When we finished eating, I started the car, turned on the headlights and followed Allison's directions. As we neared Smyrna, she put a hand on my knee and gave me a squeeze. I flinched and almost drove off the road.

"Hey, what's the matter?" she said. "Ain't never had a girl touch you before?"

"No," I lied and tried to act cool. "You just startled me, that's all."

Allison left her hand in place until we entered Bentfield Trailer Park. "I just die every time I come here."

Street lamps, some not working, provided a dim light on older cars and pick-up trucks parked along street curbs or in the narrow driveways to single and doublewide trailers. Some homes had rust stains, fallen siding, or awnings above front doors that appeared ready to collapse. Men, women and children of all shapes and sizes loitered.

"I'm sorry," Allison said.

"Sorry for what?"

"Where I live."

"Stop, it's not your fault."

"This is it."

I parked in the street, left the engine running, opened my door and hurried to the passenger side.

Allison opened her door and stepped out. "Oh, were you going to get the door for me?"

"I was."

"Awesome," she said with a kiss to my cheek.

Wow, just like that I got my first kiss from a girl I wasn't related to. It wasn't earth-shattering, just on the cheek, but definitely noteworthy.

"How 'bout a kiss goodnight?" she said at her doorway. She closed her eyes and puckered her lips.

I hesitated. This was happening way too fast. I hadn't kissed any woman on the lips since I kissed my mom as a little boy.

"What's the matter?" she said, opening her eyes and pouting. "You said you liked me."

"Nothing's the matter."

"Then kiss me goodnight."

Oh, wow, I better get this right or she'd probably laugh at me and tell her friends what a lousy kisser I was. But what type of kiss? Just touch lips? Open mouth or closed? Tongue? What was she expecting? Close my eyes or leave them open?

I had no choice except to go for it. I tilted my head and hoped we wouldn't bump noses. Our lips touched. I tasted ketchup, but also a gentle warmth that tingled my senses.

"Very nice," Allison said with a smile.

She liked it! Play it cool. "Yes, it was."

"See you tomorrow."

She entered her doublewide. With its windows open, I heard her mother inside. "Why didn't you invite the boy in?"

"Oh, Mom, he needs to get home."

Yes. I need to get home and under the shower.

CHAPTER 25

I hardly slept. I couldn't believe I actually had a girl-friend. How did that happen? I wasn't even looking for one. I had been happy to work my summer job, umpire baseball and look forward to college and umpire school. I must be dreaming. Yet how did I feel about Allison? She certainly wasn't Kelsey Delgado.

However, Kelsey proved to be hot on the outside and cold on the inside. Allison had a cute face. She looked smart with those glasses on, yet I had a feeling she didn't do well in school. And man could she talk, mostly about nothing, but I had to give her a chance.

Should I tell Austin? How would my relationship with Allison affect my full-time job and those I worked with? Would I be distracted? Might I get fired? Oh, there were too many variables.

***

Come morning, I sped to Lums Pond about a half hour before I had to and parked in an empty lot. The shack was closed, no one about. I passed the boats and walked to the concrete dock and leaned on its metal railing. Sunlight reflected off the water and a couple mallards floated by. The former beach was to my left. I imagined it as Dad had told me, with a couple lifeguard stands, men, women and children in bathing attire, either relaxing on the sand, on top of blankets or beneath umbrellas, while others swam in the water.

I enjoyed the quiet and tranquil scenery for several minutes before I heard a noise behind me. I turned and saw Allison, dressed for work and lunch in hand.

"Hey, you," she said with a smile. She kissed me on the lips. My heart raced. "You like me, don't you?"

I feigned indifference. "Maybe."

She pressed against me and kissed me again. "Yes, you do."

"Are you trying to convince me?"

"Yes."

"This is going to interfere with our jobs."

"You worry too much," she said, backing off. "I'm mostly in the shack and you're out here with the boats. Just relax."

"I'll try."

Allison leaned closer. I sensed she wanted me to wrap my arms around her, but I resisted. I worried that June and Cole might arrive and catch us.

"Allison," I said. "it was really nice of you to come out and see me umpire. My closest friend and my parents haven't done that."

"That's mean. Why not?"

"Well, Austin doesn't like baseball. My parents are busy working."

"Sounds more like excuses."

"It's all right," I said, "I might feel more nervous if they were around."

"Good morning," June said.

165

I flinched.

"You two are awfully early," she said.

"Just woke up early," I said.

"What about you?" June asked Allison.

"Same thing," she replied.

"That's your story?" June said.

"And we're sticking to it," Allison replied.

For the next couple hours I understood why companies had rules against employees dating fellow employees. I couldn't concentrate. I peeked into the shack whenever the opportunity presented itself. Allison acted coy, but she puckered her lips at me when she felt no one was watching.

At noon, Allison and I took our lunch break together. She collected her bagged meal from the refrigerator. I had forgotten mine. We headed for a nearby bench.

June, however, intercepted us. "What am I going to do with you two?" she said. She sounded angry, but her smile was gentle. "Please don't make me have to fire you."

"What're you talking about?" I said.

"Seriously?" June said, sarcastic. "You have no idea what I'm talking about."

I knew my face was red without having to check a mirror.

"Just do your jobs," June said. "I'm too old for this nonsense. Understand?"

"Understood," I said.

"Yes," Allison said, "I understand."

June nodded her head. "Good."

She wasn't the only one to notice the flirtations. Cole teased me for liking "big girls," and he wanted me to provide in detail any sexual encounter we might have. He even asked for nude photographs of Allison.

"Leave me alone," I said.

Cole clucked like a chicken.

***

After work, Allison and I walked to my car. I held the passenger door open for her. Before getting in, Allison removed her sweaty Lums Pond shirt to reveal a white tank top. My eyes almost popped from their sockets. We kissed.

"This is so awesome," she said, once I sat in the driver's seat.

I started the engine and drove toward Newport for my game at Banning Park.

"You got any brothers and sisters?" Allison asked.

"No, only child."

"Were you a mistake?"

"A mistake? No. Mom had a real hard time carrying me, so they decided not to risk her health."

"Well, at least you got a mom and dad. My daddy ran off when I was nine. Jenny, this girl at school, her dad died of cancer last year and got buried at Riverview Cemetery. It was the first funeral I went to. It's sad, but at least she knows where her daddy is."

"Wow, how can somebody just run off and leave their family?"

"I don't know. All's I remember is them fighting and fighting. At least I don't have to deal with that anymore. Do you use social media? I use it a lot. I keep hoping maybe Dad will see my profile and get in touch with me. So do you network?"

"No."

"Why not?"

"I tried it, but kept getting unfriended."

"Well," Allison chuckled, "I'm not unfriending you."

"So," I said with a grin, "I'm just a *friend*?"

"More," she said with a smile. "Better than any friend I have in school.   I mean, I'm so confused about

167

what a real friend is. These people who say they're my friend, I don't know if they really are. They can be back-stabbing and two-faced. They'll talk about me behind my back and get some sick entertainment out of it. I wouldn't call that a true friend. Would you?"

"No."

"You got any friends like that?"

"Other than Austin, I don't have any friends."

"How long's he been your friend?"

"Since middle school. We met in English class. I knew who Steinbeck and Dickens were, so he started hanging out with me. We don't have much else in common except that we get picked on for being smart and can't get a girlfriend."

"Well," she said with a grin, "now you have a girl friend. So, might he be upset or jealous."

"He's a good guy, so I think he'll be happy for me."

"Have you told him about me?"

"Not yet."

"Why not?"

"I haven't talked to him," I said, which was the truth. Then I lied. "He's away right now."

"Well, he sounds like a good friend. Not a fake friend. Fake friends aren't worth your time. The worst was Katy Daniels. I thought she was my best friend for-ever. She hung out with me, showed up at my house. We shared everything. I mean, *everything*. Then she got mad at me because I looked at the same boy she did. She spread all sorts of lying rumors about me so he'd like her instead of me. Well, real friends don't do that, so I punched her in the face. Got suspended for it. Turns out the boy didn't like either one of us, so it was all for nothing. But you and me, whatever happens, whatever we say to each other, stays between us?"

"Absolutely," I said, wondering if I was a fake friend.

I mean, what was my true motivation for hanging out with Allison? Was I with her only because she was the first girl to show interest in me and I hoped to see her naked? Did I really like her?

***

Banning Park was a county-owned property. It had two small ponds, baseball and softball fields, a couple soccer fields, a bike path, tennis courts, a playground, several pavilions for picnics and barbecues, and a wooded area for hiking.

"This is so awesome," Allison said, watching me strap on the gear by Field 1. "Look at all these people. And those players are kinda cute. I wish I played a sport."

"Why don't you?"

"I'm fat, remember?"

"Stop saying that. You can play a sport if you want to."

"I thought about trying out for field hockey, running around in those little skirts. Some fashion divas at school think they're hideous. I didn't try out because I was trying to impress Billy Cantor. I didn't want him to get the wrong idea. I mean, it's a common rumor that girls who play sports are Lesbos. It was stupid."

"Yes, that was stupid."

"Plus, you got to understand, I hate gym class. Playing sports is just an extension of gym class. I hated the other girls seeing my body, and I was always wishing I had *her* body. I had one gym teacher, when we did stretching exercises, tell me 'it's okay if your hands can't reach the floor.' She never realized how hurt I was."

"Yeah, I wasn't too fond of gym class either."

"Then I got a boyfriend and thought my body's not

169

so bad after all. Oh, I was such an idiot. He was only after one thing."

I felt guilty and wondered if he got it.

"But it's like we're brainwashed to think we're nobody until we get a boyfriend. Like we have no value. It's so stupid. Getting a boyfriend didn't solve anything, it only brought on more stress. Does he really like me? Why is he talking to other girls? What's he telling his friends? I mean, really, who cares? Anyway, I'm glad you don't have a lot of drama. You're so focused on what you want to do. I like that."

I said nothing, feeling lower than low and wondering if I should break up with her right now. Instead, I took her hand and escorted her to the field.

"Good luck," she said with a kiss. She sat on the lowest level of the bleachers. I noticed a familiar person seated on the top row. He wore the same white dress shirt I had seen on him this morning, but no tie, so his collar lay open.

Oh, crap. Now, he shows up?

Dad left his seat and walked right past Allison as if she wasn't there, and stood in front of me. He tapped my shoulder pads. "You look buffed. Been working out?"

"Not funny, Dad. I'm glad you finally came to a game." *But why did it have to be this one?*

"Don't rub it in," Dad said. Then he whispered, "So who's the girl?"

"Allison, we work together."

"You must be doing more than working together."

"I met her Memorial Day weekend," I said, irritated. "We started hanging out. That's all there is to it."

"Really? Your mom and I thought something was going on by the way you acted this morning."

"So that's the real reason you're here, to spy on me?"

"No," Dad said, shuffling uneasy on his feet. "I came to watch you umpire."

Liar. "Dad, I don't need a chaperone."

"I don't know. She looks rather….trashy."

Even though I agreed, I couldn't let him talk about her like that. "Dad, go home."

"Don't talk to me like that. Have you invited her to your graduation party?"

"No."

"Well, I wouldn't. She doesn't look like the type I'd introduce to the family."

"Dad," I said, gritting my teeth, "stop it. There's nothing wrong with Allison. If I want to invite her to my graduation, I will."

"I don't know, Michael. You're not making sense lately. You're throwing away your future for this umpiring thing, and now you're with some trailer trash."

I walked away. Otherwise, I might've punched him. I had always suspected Dad was a snob. He just proved it. Maybe I should invite Allison to my graduation just to see the look on his face.

On the field, I met my partner, George Stein, and the coaches for Stellar Auto and Wilmington Metal. After our conference at home plate, I glanced at the bleachers. Dad had returned to the top row, Allison remained on the bottom. Rather symbolic of my father's thinking. Would he lower himself to introduce himself to Allison?

The pitcher for Stellar Auto completed his warm up throws. The first hitter for Wilmington Metal approached home plate. I put my mask on, stood behind the catcher and hollered, "Play!"

I had become accustomed to being watched. Fans, players and coaches looked at me for a call after every pitch the batter ignored. However, with Dad watching,

I felt under a microscope. What was he thinking? What opinions were forming? What would he tell Mom? What kind of reception would I get when I arrived home? I had to get my mind off of him and concentrate on the game. A close contest would help.

That wasn't to be. Wilmington Metal won 15 to 4. There had been no energy on the field, no enthusiasm among the fans. The coaches and players appeared to go through the motions and seemed relieved when the game ended.

I looked at the bleachers. Dad had gone. Allison stood waiting for me with her arms folded across her chest and a frown on her face.

"Was that your dad?" she asked, irritated.

"It was."

"Why didn't you introduce me? Are you embarrassed by me? Don't want your daddy to see you with a dumb fat girl?"

"What? Wait. No!"

"That was pretty rude, Michael. I was sitting right here."

"You need to calm down, and not be so self-conscious. I wasn't thinking any such thing. He yelled at me because I hadn't mentioned you before. You know, all of sudden, he sees me kiss a girl. So he wasn't in a good mood."

She stared at me for a long moment, sorting through my lie to make sense of it. Did I believe it myself? Her arms unfolded. "Yes, Michael, you should've told him. Why didn't you?"

"I don't know," I said, heading to my car. "We just met. I didn't really have a chance. Why didn't you introduce me to your mom? Then I dropped you off at your house. You could've asked me in for a minute. I even heard your mom through the window ask you to invite me in."

Allison didn't respond until I opened my car's trunk and started to remove my gear. Her eyes were wet, her voice strained. "I told you why. I'm just so embarrassed by where I live. I know I shouldn't care. Any real friend won't care where I live. But everybody judges. It's a crappy neighborhood. My house is a trailer. It's falling apart. It looks even worse on the inside. There's a big crack in the back window that's been there for a couple years. There's junk piled in the extra bedroom. The walls and ceiling are dirty from mom's smoking, the crappy furniture smells like smoke. Our carpet in the living room is so stained I can't bear to look at it. The whole place is filthy. Why would I want to invite you in to see that?"

I took a deep breath and changed the subject. "Do you want to come to my graduation and party Saturday?"

"Really?" she said, removing her glasses and wiping her eyes. "I'll have to ask June for the day off. Maybe she can get Rachel from the gift shop to cover for me."

"Yeah," I said, removing the chest protector, "she'll do that for you. Then I can introduce you to everybody, not just my dad."

Allison jumped up and wrapped her arms around my neck and gave me a good squeeze.

"Oh," I said, "I'm all sweaty."

"I don't care," she said, followed by a long kiss.

CHAPTER 26

I drove Allison home. This time she remained seated until I opened her door.

"You're so awesome," she said when she got out. She threw her arms around me and kissed me. "So very awesome."

I squeezed her tight, feeling her body pressed against me, only releasing her when somebody whistled. The door to the trailer opened.

"Allison," her mom hollered from the doorway, "stop tonguing that boy and get your ass in here."

"Mom!"

Good God.

Her mom came down a couple steps from the doorway. "Name's Laura."

I shook her hand and told her my name.

"So this is the genius who umpires baseball games," Laura said. "Allison says you got your shit together, whatever that means."

"Mom, please."

"Oh, stop," Laura said. "I'm not hurting you. Michael, you'll have to come over for dinner sometime.

You got any food allergies?"

"None that I know of."

"Well, don't worry, I won't poison you. I got no problem with boys coming to see my Allison, as long as they behave. She needs to get out and socialize and not spend so much time in her room."

"Mom, stop."

"Always claims to be bored. Spends too much time watching movies, searching the internet for God knows what. If she'd only put that much effort into doing her schoolwork."

"Dear God, Mom, must you? He invited me to his graduation Saturday."

"Don't you have to work?" Laura said.

"I can get somebody to cover for me."

"I don't know. We need the money. But since it's a special occasion, I guess it's all right. We'll have to find you something nice to wear. Would you like to come in for a minute?"

"Oh, Mom, he needs to get going."

"Yeah," I said, uncomfortable.

"Oh, all right," Laura said. "Give him another kiss and then get your ass in the house."

"Mom!"

Laura laughed and went inside. The door stayed open.

"See you," Allison said.

We kissed, and I waited until she closed the door behind her. I heard her mother again through an open window. "Don't let this one get away."

This one? How many boyfriends has Allison gone through? What kind of boyfriends, for that matter?

I drove home. Dad must've told Mom about Allison and what he thought of her, so this could get ugly.

I entered the house. Mom and Dad weren't around. I

then heard conversation coming from the backyard. I walked through the kitchen, slid open the glass door and found my parents stretched out on patio lounge chairs, next to our round table with its center umbrella. The lid to the black grill was up. A couple burned hot dogs and burgers waited.

"Hi, Michael," Mom said. She had a frown on her face that told me she had heard about Allison. "How was your day?"

"Fine."

"Did you have a good game?"

"You hungry?" Dad said, interrupting. "Help yourself."

Paper plates, rolls and condiments waited on the table. I opened a roll, put it on a plate, and then used a spatula to lift a burger from the grill. I felt my parents' eyes on my back the whole time and wished they'd say something so we could get through this awkward moment.

"If you don't mind," I said, facing them, "I'm going to eat this in the basement so I can watch the rest of the Phillies game."

"Fine," Mom said.

I headed for the glass door. I gave them plenty of time to say something. When they didn't, I did. "Oh, by the way, I invited Allison to my graduation and party."

"Oh, no you didn't," Dad said.

"Yes," I said, facing them, "I did."

"I told you not to."

"Well, I did anyway."

"Michael," Mom said, "do you really like this girl?"

"I don't know. We're just hanging out. I'll see what happens."

"Grandchildren is what'll happen," Dad said. "Do you want to ruin your life?"

I almost threw my hamburger at him. "I'm not going to get her pregnant."

"I don't know," Dad said. "I was eighteen once. A girl shows off that much skin, how can you control yourself?"

"Is she really that…*provocative*?" Mom asked.

"She wore the tightest, smallest shorts you've ever seen," Dad said, "pinched up into her crotch. And just a piece of fabric wrapped around the lower part of her boobs. I'm surprised they didn't pop out. I tell you this girl can't have any self respect, and must have very low self-esteem to dress like that. She's drawing attention to herself, and not healthy attention."

"Thank you Dr. Freud," I said, irritated.

"Don't get smart with me," Dad said. "I forbid you to see her."

"Forbid?" I said, laughing.

"Allen," Mom said. It was serious whenever Mom called Dad by his name. "Calm down."

Dad released a deep sigh. "I just want the best for you, son. Do you have anything in common with this girl?"

I shrugged.

"Michael," Mom said, "I hope you see her as a person and not just someone you hope to get lucky with."

Mom saying "lucky" made me laugh, especially since my parents and I never had the "birds and bees" discussion. When I was eight and curious about where babies came from, Mom said that after two people got married God put a baby in the woman's stomach. This was a weird statement coming from someone who wasn't religious. I mean, we never went to church, except for weddings or funerals. I asked why God hadn't put another baby in Mom's stomach so I'd have a brother or sister. That had made her cry. Dad told me the reason years later. Yet they had left sex education up to school, classmates, television and my own research.

"Trust me, Mom, Dad, I won't ruin my life. I have plans."

There was a long silence. Mom and Dad looked at each other.

Mom spoke. "That was very nice of you to invite Allison. Right, hon?"

Dad hesitated. He didn't look too happy about it, but nodded.

"Good," I said. "And thank you."

CHAPTER 27

Graduation Day, I knocked on Allison's front door wearing black dress pants and shoes and a white short-sleeve shirt already stained with perspiration. Fortunately, the ceremony would be held in air conditioned comfort at the University of Delaware's Bob Carpenter Sports/Convocation Center, a 5,000 seat basketball and concert arena virtually across the street from my house.

Her door opened. I breathed a giant sigh of relief because Allison wore a peach-colored, sleeveless dress that covered her chest and fell below her knees, and had a tie belt. She had put her hair up and applied a touch of cosmetics.

"You look really nice," I said.

"Where's your outfit?" she asked after we kissed.

"My outfit?"

"Whatever it's called. That long dress thing."

"Oh, it's on the backseat. Is your mom home?"

"No," she said, rolling her eyes. "Thank God, she had to work. Are you nervous?"

"I'll be glad when it's over. Are you nervous about meeting my family?"

179

"Not really," she said with a shrug. "They'll either like me or they won't."

"They'll like you," I said with my fingers crossed.

A half-hour later, we arrived at the David M. Nelson Athletic Complex, home to the University of Delaware's football stadium, field hockey, baseball, softball, soccer fields and The Bob Carpenter Center.

Well-dressed men, women and children filed through "The Bob's" main entrance. Graduates, boys in red and girls in white, used a side entrance. I assisted Allison from my car and then slipped on the gown.

"You look awesome in red," she said. "I hope I graduate. My grades ain't so good. Even if I do graduate, I doubt I'll be going to college. It's so much tougher, from what I hear."

"You have to stop thinking that way. I'll bet you're smarter than you know."

Allison smiled, but said nothing.

My cell phone vibrated in my pocket. It was Austin. I gave him a rough estimate of my location.

"I can't wait to meet him," Allison said.

I laughed uneasy. "I can't wait for you to meet him either."

Austin arrived, wearing his gown and holding his mortarboard. His eyes focused on Allison and his face displayed an inquisitive expression.

I introduced Allison only by name.

She got indignant. "That's it?"

"What else is there?" I said.

She put her hands on her hips. "How about, this is Allison, my *girlfriend*."

"What?" Austin said. "When did this happen?"

"I don't believe this," Allison said. "You still didn't tell him?"

"I didn't have a chance," I said, pensive.

"You've had a week to tell him," Allison said.

She folded her arms across her chest, so did Austin. The two of them glared at me as if I had committed a crime. I anticipated a lecture, but my cell phone saved me.

"It's Dad," I said. "They're waiting outside the entrance."

"Good thing," Allison said.

I grabbed my mortarboard and the three of us walked to the main entrance. On the sidewalk by the ticket windows, Allison met Mom and Dad, my paternal grandparents, five uncles and their wives, four nieces and three nephews.

"She's a darling girl," Mom whispered, with a gentle slap against Dad's arm.

I sighed, relieved. What a difference clothes make.

"You sit next to me," Granddaddy William said to Allison.

"Behave," Grandma Julia said.

"Well, we have to go," I said. "See you afterwards."

"Aren't you forgetting something?" Allison said.

"What?"

"Well," she said, pouting, "if you don't know, I'm not telling you."

"Kiss her, stupid," Granddaddy William said.

I gave her a quick peck on the lips. My family released a chorus of, "Awe."

"I shouldn't have to tell you," Allison said.

"Sorry."

Austin and I walked to the side entrance.

"She's not too happy with you," he said. "And neither am I."

"I know, I know. I'm sorry."

"Why didn't you tell me about her?"

"I don't know," I said, defensive. "It all happened so

fast. I didn't think she liked me, and then she just showed up at one of my games. I only invited her to my graduation to get back at Dad for calling her trashy."

"She seems nice."

"Today, yes," I said as we stopped by the side entrance. Other graduates passed us and entered the building. "You should see how she dresses the rest of the time."

"Really? Shows a lot?"

"I'll say."

Austin laughed. "And you're hoping to see more. *That's* the only reason you're with her?"

"Maybe."

"If sex is all you're after, then you should break up with her. You'll just end up hurting her."

"I know," I said, whining. "I don't know what to do. One minute I like her, and then the next I don't. She can talk and talk, but she's also very nice. I'm so confused."

"Did she come after you?" Austin said.

"Yes."

"How did that feel?"

"Weird, but in a nice way. I guess that's why I'm not breaking up with her. I've never had a girl chase me. I guess I want to hold onto that feeling as long as I can."

Austin shook his head. "Like I said, you're just going to hurt her."

I tried to joke. "Who would've thought that Michael Briggs would be a heartbreaker."

Austin wasn't amused. "I don't think Allison will be laughing."

I tired of the subject, mostly because Austin was right. I put on my mortarboard. "Let's get this over with."

Austin and I entered The Bob and joined about two-hundred graduates in a spacious concourse. Most of them waited in small groups, talking, laughing, texting or talking on their phones. Austin and I kept to ourselves, observing the drama.

"I'm not going to miss anything about high school," Austin said. "I just want to get onto the next stage of my life."

"Didn't you like any of your teachers?"

"Miss Hodge was pretty cute. I liked her a lot."

"Yes, but I mean as teachers. Didn't any of them leave a good impression?"

"No," Austin said, shaking his head. "Not really."

"Hey, loser!"

Joe Forrester approached.

"Wow," I said, sarcastic, "miracles *do* happen."

"What do you mean?" Joe asked.

"*You* graduated."

"Be careful there," Joe said with a poke to my chest.

"You know what's great about today?" I said.

"What?"

"It's the last time I have to see you."

"Feelings mutual, dude. I'm only sorry I won't have anymore chances to watch you make an ass out of yourself on the baseball field. Hey, I got an idea, come down to Virginia and try out? I could use a good laugh."

"You'll be crying," Austin said.

"How's that?" Joe said, perplexed.

"You'll be crying," Austin replied, "when Michael's in pro ball and you're not."

Joe laughed. "Never in a million years." He then saw a couple buddies. "Goodbye, *loser*. Or should I say *losers*."

"You'll be the loser," Austin whispered.

"Thanks," I said.

"For what?"

183

"For saying what you said. I hope it comes true."

"It will."

Mrs. Dennison, a social studies teacher, spoke through a megaphone and ordered us to line up for the processional. "Remember," her voice echoed, "from rehearsal who's in front of you and who's behind."

"I'll see you later," Austin said, and left for his place in line.

At noon, my fellow graduates and I entered the back of the arena. About a thousand people stood and applauded. Glasgow's band played *Pomp and Circumstance*. The music and clapping continued as we filled row after row of chairs on a brown carpet that covered the basketball court.

At my seat, I picked up a copy of the Commencement Program and scanned the audience for my family and Allison. No luck.

On stage, school district officials and our principal, Doctor Jeffrey Ogden, sat in front of a black backdrop and an American and Delaware State flag. When Jimmy Warren, the last graduate, took his seat the band stopped playing. Everyone sat and our principal rose. He moved to a lectern at center stage and spoke into a microphone.

"Welcome. Welcome one and all." He talked about how proud he was of the graduates and congratulated us on our accomplishment. He then had everyone stand for the playing of the national anthem.

Afterwards, Principal Ogden introduced Valerie Pomeroy, our Valedictorian. Her presence at the podium caused some snickering among my fellow graduates. Valerie acted prim and proper, but rumor had it she had been quite slutty at the prom. Her speech about how bright our futures would be borrowed song lyrics and lines from popular movies, such as the Joker in Batman:

Wait till they get a load of me.

"And that's what we should all say," Valerie went on, "when we go out into the world. Look at me. I'm here to make a difference."

If she hoped to bring the house down, she failed. I yawned and joined the casual applause.

Principal Ogden returned to the lectern. "Thank you, Valarie. It's time for the Presentation of Diplomas."

The graduating class stood and formed a line off stage left. I wouldn't have to wait long. Only eight people were ahead of me. So one by one, Principal Ogden announced our names into the microphone. Then a young man or woman crossed the stage and accepted their rolled up diploma tied with a red ribbon. Hands were shook, congratulations expressed, photos taken, and then the graduate filed off stage right and back to their seat. As the moment drew near for my turn, I just hoped I wouldn't trip and fall and get laughed at.

"Michael Briggs," Principal Ogden said.

My name blasted from speakers. Light applause.

"You did it!" Granddaddy William shouted. His outburst echoed in the arena and caused mild laughter. I grinned, and found my family and Allison near the top row of seats off stage right.

"Congratulations, Mister Briggs," Principal Ogden said as we shook hands.

"Thank you," I said, grabbing my diploma. "It was fun."

Crap. Did I really say it was fun? How stupid. I returned to my seat and waited out the ceremony.

When Joe Forrester's name was called, a barbaric roar went up from the graduating jocks, along with the non-graduating jocks who sat together. Joe hurried to the stage. He grabbed his diploma from Principal Ogden, turned to the crowd, raised his arms over his head and released a loud, "Yeah!" The jocks cheered and then made ape sounds like a wild band of gorillas, much to the delight of the crowd.

When Austin Jenkins got on stage, he walked slowly, soaking in the moment. His face broke into a wide smile when he grabbed his diploma.

In fact, each of my fellow graduates had their own style of acceptance. There were some who wanted to complete the task as quickly as possible. There were others who strolled as if they had all day. Some looked bored. A few girls cried. Still others took hold of their diploma and held it like gold.

After Jimmy Warren received his diploma and returned to his chair, Principal Ogden pronounced our class. We cheered, removed our mortarboards and tossed them high into the air. A few struck the underside of a large electronic scoreboard that hung over center court before they rained down on us.

CHAPTER 28

An hour later, and wearing casual clothes, my family, Austin and Allison gathered in my backyard for my graduation party. Dad had rented a large white canopy in case it rained. He and my uncles had assembled it to cover three long folding tables and their chairs. Another table by the back door had a pile of wrapped gifts. Tiki torches had been set around the yard's perimeter to provide light should the festivities continue after nightfall. I seriously doubted that would happen, not with old people and young kids in attendance.

Dad wore a body apron and served as barbecue chef. He cooked hamburgers and hot dogs on our gas grill. There was also potato salad, macaroni salad, a tray of fruit and one of vegetables, and buffalo chicken wings. Four coolers were stuffed with ice, canned sodas, beer and plastic bottles of water. A devil's food cake with vanilla icing had "Congratulations Michael" written in red and was kept inside because of the heat.

I received hearty congratulations. I fulfilled requests to explain my future plans. I never saw so many dumbfounded facial expressions as I did when I told them I'd be attending a professional baseball umpire school in January. A couple uncles thought me brave to try it, but nobody seemed confident I'd actually achieve a spot in pro ball. "Good thing you have options," was the general feeling. I guess older folks didn't believe in dreams, or supporting dreams. Why was that?

Conversation also revolved around me and Allison. "How does it feel to have a girlfriend?" was the general question. My Aunt Mary put her foot in her mouth by saying, "I never thought it would happen."

What had she meant by that?

Poor Austin, he seemed out of place. Now that I had a girlfriend, he was the odd man out. He ate and drank and sat with me, but he squirmed whenever Allison held my hand or put a hand on my knee. After a couple hours he used the excuse, "I have to get home and pack." His parents were treating him to five days at Disney World, but the flight didn't leave until tomorrow afternoon.

I walked Austin to his car. "I'm sorry you're uncomfortable."

"I'm not uncomfortable," he said.

"Don't lie to me."

He nodded, and then surprised me with a hug. "I'm happy for you, Michael, really." Then he released me. "I'll see you around."

"Have a great time at Disney."

"I will. Hope you like my gift."

"I'm sure I will."

Austin got into his Camry and drove away. I returned to the party.

"Bored yet?" I asked Allison.

"No. I'm having a good time hanging out with my boyfriend on his big day."

Boyfriend, it was still hard to believe.

188

***

Allison and I mingled for awhile, and then ended up joining Granddaddy William and Grandma Julia at one of the tables. Granddad had a beer in hand. He had removed his shirt and sat comfortably in a muscle tee-shirt that revealed too much of his hairy shoulders and arms.

"You got a fine young lady there," he said. "How do you feel about this umpire thing?"

"I think it's awesome," Allison said.

"Good attitude," Granddaddy William said. "It's always nice to have a woman's support. So Allison, are you off to college?"

"I just finished my junior year."

"But you still have an idea if you're going or not."

"I hope to," Allison said, her face turning red.

"Well," Granddaddy William said, "you need to change that hope to into a definite yes. Michael, that's your job."

"Yes, Granddad," I said. Allison appeared uncomfortable, so I took her by the hand. "Let's get a hot dog."

"Okay," she said, sounding relieved.

We excused ourselves and got a hot dog from Dad. We found a couple chairs and sat away from the crowd.

"They don't think I'm smart enough for you," Allison said, ignoring her food.

"Oh," I said. "Granddad was just talking."

"Not just him, *all* of them. They talk to me like I'm an idiot. Your dad definitely hates me. Your mom's nice, but I don't think she wants me around. Did you see the look your granddad gave me when I said I *hope to* go to college?"

"No," I lied.

"My grades are awful. And we ain't got no money for

college. And what's so important about college anyway? If you're going to be a doctor, I can see how it has value, but what if I just want to be a bank teller? Do you really need college for that? And college is no guarantee of success. There are plenty of college failures, and successful people who didn't go to college, or so I've heard."

"I can help you get your grades up."

"How? You're *going* to college."

"Yeah, right across the street. I can tutor you."

"Why? They're right. I ain't smart."

"You're not stupid."

"How can I change? I mean, you're awesome in the way you can do your umpiring and still graduate with honors. It shows how really focused you are. I'm not like that. I'm too scatterbrained. How do I get smart?"

"You can start by not saying *ain't* anymore."

"Do I say it a lot?"

"Enough that it's noticeable. And don't worry about not having money for college. There are student loans, grants and scholarships you can apply for."

"You really want to help me?"

"Of course, but you have to be serious about it. In my opinion, the only difference between smart kids and the rest is effort. Stick with it, don't be lazy."

Allison leaned into me. I put an arm around her shoulders. My family saw us and said, "Ahhh."

"Okay," she said.

Bellies full, I unwrapped presents in front of a captive audience. Each gift had a greeting card with *Congratulations Grad*. I received a pair of Phillies tickets, a Phillies sweatshirt, and a Phillies white uniform top with my last name embroidered above a number one, and gift cards to the University of Delaware bookstore.

Austin's gift left me speechless. It was a scale model

of Shibe Park, later known as Connie Mack Stadium, once home to the Philadelphia Athletics and the Phillies. It measured eighteen inches wide and ten inches high, authentically painted to reveal its brick exterior, blue seats and the green and brown of the playing field.

"What a great gift," Mom said.

I found my voice. "Wow, it must've cost a small fortune."

Mom and Dad held back their gift so that they could present last. Dad hurried into the house and returned with a brown-wrapped, rectangular item about two feet by three feet and a few inches thick.

"From your mom and me," he said.

I removed the paper to reveal a glass-protected and gold-framed print. The painting's foreground depicted three black-suited umpires who looked up at a darkening sky. The home plate umpire held his outside chest protector and mask in one hand and extended the other palm side up to catch a raindrop. In the background, a scoreboard showed Pittsburgh leading Brooklyn 1-0 in the bottom of the sixth inning. Behind the umpires, the manager for Brooklyn grinned and pointed a finger skyward. The Pittsburgh manager grimaced.

I assumed the Brooklyn manager, because they were losing, hoped for a rain out so the game wouldn't count. It was a humorous and well done piece, but a baseball game was official after four and a half innings if the home team led. Even if the umpires stopped the game, Pittsburgh won.

"I love it," I said. "I really do."

"There's a card attached," Dad said.

The art gallery had taped an envelope to the back of the print. Inside was a card that provided background on the original painting. The artist had been Norman Rockwell. "Game Called Because of Rain" had appeared as *The Saturday Evening Post* cover on April 23, 1949.

"I'm still not crazy about your career choice," Dad said. "But the other day at Banning Park, I saw not a boy, but a grown man, confident and poised. Your mom and I are very proud of you."

"Here, here," the other adults said, some downing beer.

Mom cried.

Wow, Dad called me a man, confident and poised. I got a lump in my throat and had difficulty just saying, "Thank you. Thank you all."

CHAPTER 29

By July, thanks to my two jobs that kept me outdoors, I had the darkest farmers' tan of my life, firm abs and great stamina. On days when I did not umpire, I didn't know what to do with myself. My body had become accustomed to a certain amount of exertion, and when it didn't get it, I roamed around nervously. I almost begged Randy to schedule me a game every day.

My time at Lums Pond, however, was a test of social endurance. When Cole wasn't phoning or texting, he bragged about his sexual conquests and begged for intimate details about me and Allison. When I didn't give any, he clucked like a chicken and called me, "wuss, gay." I still imagined pulling every red hair out of his head. June worried I'd get Allison pregnant. Fat chance of that, Allison never let me touch second base, and she had some impressive bases!

I admit that that surprised me. Allison dressed like a slut, but didn't act like one. At least how I thought a slut would act. She enjoyed watching me umpire. We held hands and kissed in public, but never made out. I took her to dinner and the movies a few times. We hung out at the mall, yet she made sure my hands never wandered where she didn't want them to go.

She was also lazy. I gave Allison my copies of *The Great Gatsby* and *To Kill A Mockingbird* so she'd be ahead on the reading assignments she'd get in her senior year, but she put them down after a couple chapters. I tried to teach her math and chemistry. After a half hour, she got tired and complained that it was summer, a time to have fun and not worry about school work. She said *awesome* too much, and still used *ain't*.

Umpiring became a welcomed reprieve, where I felt relaxed and in control.

***

Top of the fourth inning at Midway, there was no score when River Plumbing's lead off hitter sent a hard ground ball between Wilmington Dental's shortstop and third baseman for a single. My base partner, the gray-haired Alex Stanton, moved to the infield.

River Plumbing's coach stood in the third base coach's box and clapped. "We're getting to him, we're getting to him."

I glanced at the bleachers. Allison's scantily-clad body had drawn the attention of two boys who had moved themselves from a lower seat to the row above her. They glanced over Allison's shoulders, obviously peeking at her cleavage. They playfully laughed and pushed one another, and then took another peek.

I clenched my jaw and released a frustrated sigh. I wanted to say something, but it would have to wait until after the game.

The next batter for River Plumbing approached the plate. He looked to his third base coach for the signs. The man touched the bill of his cap, both shoulders, tip of his nose, his chin and then his belt. Somewhere in that dance should be an order to bunt.

As Wilmington Dental's pitcher delivered, their first and third baseman crept closer to the plate. The hitter squared to bunt, but pulled the bat back and let the pitch shoot past him shoulder high.

"Ball," I said, and set my indicator.

River Plumbing's hitter stepped from the batter's box and again looked to his coach for the signs. On the pitch, the batter squared to bunt. *Ting.* The ball shot past my head and hit the backstop.

"Foul ball," I said shouting, arms raised.

Next pitch, the batter faked a bunt and swung. *Ting.* The baseball rocketed past a ducking pitcher and bounced into center field. I moved half way between home and third and kept an eye on the runner from first. Alex stayed with the batter.

Wilmington Dental's centerfielder scooped up the ball in his glove. River Plumbing's runner from first turned the corner at second and continued.

"No!" his coach screamed.

Wilmington Dental's centerfielder threw the ball to his third baseman. The infielder caught it in plenty of time to tag the runner before the runner even had a chance to slide.

"Out."

The face on River Plumbing's coach turned red, his jaw clenched and his hands formed a tight fist. "Why did you do that? What were you thinking? What player in his right mind takes third in that situation? Everything was right in front of you."

The player walked away.

"Don't turn your back on me when I'm talking to you."

"Go to hell."

A collective gasp came from players and spectators.

"What did you say?"

"I said," the player got within inches of the coach's face, "go…to…hell."

An eerie quiet came over the field. I half expected either the player or coach would throw a punch. I wondered if I should do anything, but there wasn't anything *to* do. The rule book didn't cover this situation.

The boy brushed past his coach and walked to the third base dugout and sat on the bench. His teammates gave him plenty of room.

"Hogan," the coach said to the dugout, "you're in for Justin."

I assumed Justin was the "go to hell" boy. I waited for him to erupt and complain about being replaced. He didn't.

River Plumbing's next two batters grounded out to Wilmington Dental's second baseman to end the inning. I removed my mask and stood along the third base line.

"You know," River Plumbing's coach said, stopping next to me, "between the parents who think they can do a better job, and their arrogant brats, I wonder why I do this. I'm a volunteer for Christ's sake. I don't get paid for this."

"You love baseball," was my lame answer.

"I did," he said with a deep sigh. "Now I'm not so sure."

Wow, a coach looked to an umpire for sympathy.

***

Bottom of the seventh inning, Wilmington Dental got a player to second base on a double. It was followed by a two out single to right field that drove in the lone run for a thrilling 1-0 victory. The team celebrated around home plate.

"That was fun," Alex said as he and I headed for our

cars. It makes up for all the 15-3 games. What did the River Plumbing coach say to you?"

"You should've seen his face," I said as Allison joined us. "He looked like his best friend had died."

"In my day," Alex said, sounding like Granddaddy William, "I had coaches who would've decked me for back-talking, and my parents would've approved. Hell, my dad would've taken the belt to me when I got home."

"Really?" Allison said.

"You better believe it," Alex said, and then excused himself. "Nice working with you, kid."

"I wish they'd stop calling me kid."

"That was an awesome game," Allison said behind my car. "Weren't you nervous?"

"Nervous about what?"

"That the game was so close."

"No, I can't let the score affect me."

"So you feel the same whether the game's 1-0 or 20-0?"

"I have to," I replied, opening the trunk. "I can't display any emotion because then I might get swept up by it and do something unfair."

"That must be hard."

"Not really. I don't care who wins or loses, and that's the attitude I have to have to remain neutral."

"I couldn't do it," Allison said, "especially after that player cussed at his coach. If I were the umpire, anytime that boy came to bat for the rest of the season, I'd call every pitch a strike, no matter where it was. Don't you feel that way about certain players?"

"I might *think it*," I said, removing my gear, "but I'd never *do it*."

"*That's* why you're so awesome."

I lost it. I couldn't help it. "Can you *please* try to say

something else. Use another word?"

"What do you mean?"

"Say something other than awesome once in a while, that's all. It'll expand your vocabulary."

She put her hands on her hips. "You always got to bitch about something, don't you? You don't like the way I talk. I don't have my face stuck in a book."

"Well," I said, wiping perspiration from my face and neck with a small towel. "Would you prefer that I never tell you what bothers me?"

"I know the way I dress doesn't bother you."

"Actually," I said, looking her over, "it does. You say I'm your boyfriend, yet you keep dressing like this, drawing a lot of attention to yourself. Why do you do that if we're together?"

She shrugged.

I did a sarcastic shrug. "That's all you got?"

"Well, what do you want from me?"

"An honest answer. Why do you keep dressing like this if I'm your boyfriend?"

"Don't you like showing me off? Don't you like looking at what I got?"

I grit my teeth. "If I can't have it, then what's the point in you showing me what you got?"

Allison's eyes went wide behind her glasses and her mouth fell open. Soon her eyes were leaking. "I thought you were different, but no. You're no different than any other boy."

"You said it yourself. You dress this way because you'd rather have boys call you hot than fat. So don't blame me. It's your own fault."

"I also dress this way because it's summer, it's hot. I want to be comfortable."

I waved a hand. "Whatever."

"I'm not ready for that, Michael. I made that mistake

before. I wanted to be sure about you, that you really liked me for me."

I took a deep breath and realized she was right to be cautious. I'd been asking myself all along if I really liked her. "Sorry. It's been really nice having you come to my games and watch me umpire. I enjoy your company. It's just that maybe…."

"What're you saying? You don't *really* like me?"

My silence answered her question.

"Are you breaking up with me?"

"I'm sorry," I said, finding the courage I should've had sooner. "I never had a girl like me, who liked hanging out with me."

"So," she said, looking seriously wounded, "you've wanted to break up with me for awhile now?"

I nodded.

She said nothing for a long moment. Her eyes watered. Then she released some real venom. "You're just another *fake friend*."

"Allison," I said, feeling two inches tall.

"No, it's true. You're no different than Jessie ditching me at Midway, or Janet and Kelly ditching me at the mall. Suddenly I'm not welcomed anywhere! What kind of friend does that? *Fake friends*! I'm surrounded by fake friends. I can't trust anybody. I can't believe anything anybody says. Why me? What have I've done to be treated like this?"

"I'm sorry."

"Don't say another word. Just take me home."

Not another word was spoken until I parked in front of her house.

"Goodbye," Allison said, opening her door and stepping out.

"Goodbye? You mean, goodnight. I'll see you to-morrow."

"Maybe," she said, and slammed the door.

Maybe?

***

I hardly slept because of the break up with Allison and her "maybe." What had she meant by that? My imagination went so far as to wonder if she'd kill herself. I pictured police at my door, showing me her suicide note, where she blamed me for ruining her life and leaving her no option. The thought freaked me out so bad I almost called her to make sure she was still alive.

Come morning, I almost called in sick because it would be pretty awkward working with Allison, but I chose to man up and deal with it. I'd be cordial to Allison, nothing more. If she hated me, I'd just have to accept it.

When I arrived at the shack, June was at the register with Rachel Anderson, a part-timer. Where's Allison? I broke into an instant sweat, my heart pounded.

"You and me gotta talk," June said. She turned to Rachel. "Are you all right opening on your own?"

"No problem," she said.

June led me outside, lit up a cigarette and coughed. "Allison quit."

"Oh, good," I said, relieved.

"What do you mean good?"

"Nothing. I'm sorry to hear that."

"What's going on?" Cole said, arriving.

"She called last night and said she wasn't coming back," June said. "When I asked her why, she said talk to you. Did something happen between you two?"

"Nothing happened."

"Yeah," Cole said with a laugh, "that's the problem. *Nothing* happened."

"What?" June said.

"Mind your own business," I said. "It's not my fault

she quit. That's her decision."

"Damn it," June said, whispering. "Allison was a good worker. Rachel's dumber than a box of hammers."

"Yeah," Cole said with a laugh, "but Rachel's an improvement. I might make a play for her myself."

"Oh, no," June said, pointing her cigarette at Cole. "No more romances. I'm not dealing with this crap another minute. I'm too old. Stupid ass kids." She went behind a tree to calm down with her cigarette.

"You're so gay," Cole said.

"Shut up."

I walked to the dock.

"Call her?" Cole said, laughing. "Get her back."

I didn't want her back, but man, did I screw up. I always tried to do the right thing, to not rock the boat or hurt anybody, because I knew how it felt to be hurt. But this was inexcusable. I never had any real feelings for Allison, other than lust.

I had also been curious. I mean, why did she like me when other girls didn't? Why couldn't I like her in return? Why did I let her hang around? I should've broken up with her the first day. We weren't anything alike.

Austin was right. And I knew it would come to this. So until Allison's dying day, she'd swear eternal hatred for Michael Lawrence Briggs, and I had to live with that.

CHAPTER 30

An hour before twilight on the Fourth of July, Austin and I walked across Route 4 and joined about 30,000 people between the University of Delaware's football stadium and South College Avenue. Everyone had dressed comfortably. Some carried folding chairs or rolled up blankets in preparation of viewing fireworks. Many had already camped out a location on a grass field that served as a parking lot on game day.

Canopies had been erected by individual retailers promoting their stores. There were charity organizations seeking donations, artisans who made and sold arts and craft items, such as woodworking and jewelry. One busy promoter sold glow in the dark sticks and play swords. Artists hawked their prints, paintings and sculptures. Photographers solicited business and offered prints of Newark's historic buildings and other locales. Authors sold and autographed their books. A live band on a temporary stage filled the air with current hits.

"Too bad you didn't see her naked," Austin said.

"Oh, not you too," I said.

"Come on, admit it. You wanted to."

"Well, of course. But you know I couldn't without hating myself. I couldn't treat her like a thing."

"Everybody else our age has hook ups and they never even learn the girl's name."

"Everybody?" I asked, sarcastic.

"Well, I hear it's like that in college. Everybody's free from their parents and they do whatever they want. With all the partying I hear about, it's a wonder anybody studies."

"I don't think Vermont is known as a partying school," I said. "Congratulations on getting into their writing program. You going for a Masters?"

"Yes. Master of Fine Arts."

"Then a famous writer," I said.

"And you a famous baseball umpire."

"We'll see," I said. "And thanks again for my graduation present. You really didn't have to spend that much."

"It wasn't that much," Austin said. "But you're welcome again."

Austin and I came upon the food vendors. We salivated at a popcorn and cotton candy seller, spice promoter, hot dog, hamburger and sausage stand, and ice creamery. We settled for a couple slices of pizza and a soft drink, and then sat and ate in the shade of a tree near the stadium's main entrance.

"Hey! It is you."

A teenage boy in a muscle shirt and his male companion approached. They wore black baseball caps with a gold letter N on the crown--Newark High School.

"I told you it was him," the boy said to his friend. Then he addressed me. "You're an umpire, aren't you?"

"I am," I said, standing. "But don't hold that against me."

"Oh, no, you were good," the boy said.   He put his

203

hand out. "I'm Lamar. This is Rick. We played varsity for Newark. You called a couple of our games."

I shook their hands, introduced myself and Austin.

"Excellent," Lamar said. "You were really good. Just thought you should know that. I mean, you don't look much older than me, but you were the best umpire we had all season."

"Thank you," I said, my chest rising. "That's nice to hear."

"Are you umpin' summer ball?" Lamar asked.

"Babe Ruth."

"We play for Post 14, American Legion," Lamar said.

"They don't usually let rookie umpires do American Legion."

"That doesn't make sense. You did varsity."

"There's more veteran umpires available in the summer," I said.

Lamar nodded. "Ok. Well, I hope you get a chance to do one of our games. We've had some real lame-o's."

Rick made a face and became animated. "Some of them are so blind. One cost us a game last week. He wasn't even paying attention. I stole second. He was too busy daydreaming or something. I had the bag easy. He had to ask his partner for help. Of course that old geezer was too far away to see anything, but he called me out. Oh, you should've heard the screaming."

"I can imagine," I said.

"Well," Lamar said with another handshake, "it was nice seeing you. I hope you can do one of our games."

"We'll see," I said with the shrug.

After Lamar and Rick left, Austin looked at me with an expression I could only describe as reverence.

"What?" I said.

"So," Austin said, "I guess you *are* good."

"I've been telling you that."

"Yeah, but who believes you?"

Austin and I finished our meal just as darkness fell. We then sat among the crowd. Children with glow sticks provided an eerie green light as they walked about or settled with their families.

"Won't be long now," Austin said.

A few minutes later, fireworks erupted over the two football practice fields next to the north end of the stadium. The series of explosions and spider web of colors drew the usual ah's from the crowd.

The fireworks lasted twenty minutes. They were followed by a traffic jam of cars that tried to exit simultaneously. Austin and I moved faster than the automobiles and we were soon outside my house, standing by Austin's car along the street curb.

"See ya," I said.

"Michael?"

"Yeah."

"Do you think I'll ever get a girlfriend? I mean, a girl that really likes me?"

"Of course you will."

Austin nodded, but didn't appear convinced.

"Look, don't worry about it. There's more to life than whether or not we have a girlfriend. We're chasing our dreams. Right now, *that's* more important. The other thing will happen when it happens. It'll probably happen when we're not even looking for it."

"Yeah, but at least you've kissed a girl. I'm off to college and haven't even done that."

"Big deal."

"Easy for you to say."

"It wasn't right, Austin." Then I grinned. "But maybe when I umpire, I'll have a girl in every town."

"Oh, right," Austin said, laughing. "Keep dreaming."

CHAPTER 31

The following Saturday, I had the day off from Lums Pond. I wouldn't have to listen to Cole, or watch him on his phone avoiding customers. However, I was scheduled to umpire an afternoon game at my alma-mater. Wow, I used the term alma-mater. Only old guys at Homecoming said that.

Unfortunately, record heat had been predicted and for once, the weatherman got it right. My scheduled partner, Mark Longer, would lose a few pounds burdened by the weight of the protective gear.

I parked next to the field where I had failed on four occasions to earn a spot on the school team. What an idiot I had been. No wonder Coach Myers got tired of me and Joe Forrester had found it hysterical. Then again, it took that failure to lead me to umpire.

Two coaches for the Fraternal Order of Police raked the dirt portion of the infield. Their maroon tee-shirts were soaked in sweat. The players on both teams sat in the shade of their respective dugouts. I counted only eight people sweltering on the small bleachers.

Two minutes to game time, Mark had yet to show. My phone vibrated in my pocket. It was Randy.

"This can't be good," I said.

"It isn't. Mark's claiming his car overheated. I don't have a replacement."

"For Mark or his car," I said, trying to joke.

Randy chuckled. "Instead of one and half pay, I'll give you double."

"That helps a little."

"Take it easy out there. I don't want to visit you in the hospital."

I cussed Mark and the Baseball Gods and strapped on the gear.

A Camry pulled up. Austin got out, wearing shorts, a tee shirt and sandals.

"Wow," I said. "You finally came out to watch me."

"Yeah, don't rub it in. But my God, it's too hot to play."

"And I have to work the game alone, my partner isn't coming."

"Can't you cancel it?"

"No."

"I might not be able to stay too long."

"I don't blame you."

Gear on, I grabbed a small cooler stuffed with ice and four bottles of cherry-flavored sports drink that I had brought for the game. Teams supplied water and were nice enough to share with umpires, but it never hurt to bring my own liquid relief.

I stepped onto the field by third base, near the Lion's Club dugout. Austin volunteered to watch my cooler.

I met three FOP coaches and the one for the Lion's Club at home plate.

"Can't we cancel the game?" the Lion's coach said.

"You know we need to get it in," a FOP coach said.

207

"Why?" the Lion's coach said. "It's not like they're going to the playoffs."

"Well," the FOP coach said, "somebody needs to get a win."

"What?" I said.

"Rookie division," the FOP coach said. "Neither team has won a game."

"Are you serious?" I said.

"It hasn't been pretty," the Lion's coach said.

Oh great, the hottest day of the century and the two worst teams in the Newark Babe Ruth League. The Baseball Gods were going to get even with me for hurting Allison.

"Where's your partner?" another FOP coach asked.

"Not coming."

Each coach released an uneasy laugh.

"Sucks to be you," The Lion's coach said.

"Let's get it over as fast as possible," a FOP coach said. "I have a date tonight."

"I have to work at six," another said.

Like the coaches, I hoped for a quick game, but throughout the first inning both pitchers struggled to find the strike zone, even when I expanded it without being ridiculous. There were a combined nine walks and three fielding errors and the inning took almost an hour to complete.

I stood by The Lion's Club dugout and gulped my sports drink. Sweat covered my body. My chest protector and shin guards felt heavier than usual and retained heat.

"I don't know much about baseball," Austin said, "but is it always this bad?"

"No," I said after removing the drink from my mouth. "This is a damn disaster. We should be in the third or fourth inning by now."

"It's so boring. I don't know how you can stand it."

"You picked the wrong game to come to. Go on home."

"No. I'll stick it out a little longer."

The second inning wasn't much better. Because the pitchers were wild, the batters just stood at the plate and waited to get a walk. I silently screamed at them to swing the bat.

"I haven't taken an official count," I said to Austin after the inning, "but I must've already crouched behind the catcher and called ball or strike more often than I did for an entire game. At this rate, I'll be hoarse and my legs will be like wet spaghetti."

"I'm worried you'll get heat stroke."

"Pray for rain."

Each team used new pitchers for the third inning. I didn't think it possible, but their skill level was even worse. A number of baseballs bounced short of the plate. The catchers blocked most of them. Some shot by and struck me on the foot or leg. It got so bad that I flinched on any low pitch from sheer anticipation of getting hit.

After the inning, the coaches apologized many times for their players.

"You're doing a great job," one FOP coach said. "All things considered."

Austin couldn't take anymore and left. I envied him.

I cussed the Baseball Gods again because had this been a weekday game that started at six, nightfall would end this misery. My only hope lay in the ten run rule, which took effect after the fourth inning. The Lion's Club led 15-9. As they came to bat, I prayed that they'd score four runs and FOP score none. Unfortunately, and I shouldn't have expected otherwise, The Lion's Club scored only one run in the top of the fourth inning for a 16-9 lead.

Bottom of the fourth, my body reeked. People could probably smell me in the next county. I ignored uniform dress code and lifted my shirttail out for ventilation. I pulled the chest protector away from my soaked tee-shirt to help cool my skin. My thighs screamed. Water seeped from every pore of my body, yet I couldn't keep my mouth wet. I had already finished two bottles of the four in my cooler and my system begged for more.

The first two batters for FOP hit infield pop ups that, to my surprise, were caught. Their third batter walked. On the next pitch, he sprinted to second. The ball passed shoulder-high on the hitter.

"Ball."

I removed my mask and ran from behind the plate and around the batter. The Lion's Club catcher threw to second. I stopped. The shortstop caught the ball chest high over second base. I focused on the bag. The fielder tagged the runner's knee as he slid feet first. The runner's foot was already against the base.

Now seriously, I *saw* it that way. Yet my right fist went up. "Out!"

"What?" came from FOP's dugout. "You gotta be kidding! He was under the tag, ump! Come on, I know you want to get this game over with, but that's ridiculous. How can you call that?"

Mask off, I stood along the third base line and wondered why I had made such a horrible call. I *knew* it was horrible. I had seen the runner reach the base. My brain said safe. Yet my mouth and right arm betrayed me. How could that have happened? I should tell Randy. I deserved to be punished. Did the association suspend umpires? They fired them. Or did I warrant no pay for this game?

Then to make matters worse, FOP scored three runs

in the fifth and two more in the sixth. They trailed by a run as the bottom of the seventh inning started. A tie game would force extra innings. The Baseball Gods were determined to punish me for my bad call.

The first hitter for FOP hit a single to right field. The second hitter received a walk. *Oh, crap.* However, I had another option. Let FOP score, not one run but *two.* That would end this nightmare in their favor and avoid extra innings.

FOP's next batter worked a full count. Then he hit a sharp ground ball to The Lion's Club shortstop. I ran onto the infield between the plate and pitcher. The shortstop fielded the ball, threw to second for one out, and then the second baseman threw to first to complete the double play. It had been the only double play of the game, and judging from the players' celebration, the only double play they pulled off all season.

"Watch him at third!" The Lion's Club coach yelled.

Dear God, please keep him from scoring.

FOP's next hitter, I called ball one, ball two, ball three. Next pitch, I crouched behind the catcher and created my imaginary rectangle. The baseball spun at me, about shoulder high on the batter.

Baseball axiom dictated that a player never swing at a 3-0 pitch. As bad as the game had been, I shouldn't have been surprised when the batter did just that, on what would've been ball four. *Ting.* He hit a lazy pop up over third base. I removed my mask, stepped from behind the plate and hoped for the best.

"What're you doing swinging at a 3-0 pitch?" FOP's third base coach moaned.

The third baseman caught the ball and The Lion's Club celebrated their first victory. I breathed a gigantic sigh of relief, and then returned the used baseballs to one of the FOP coaches.

"Thanks a lot ump," he said in an angry tone. "You cost us the game."

"What?" I said, not believing my ears.

"That call at second stopped us from getting a run that inning and changed the momentum of the game."

"You're kidding, right? It wasn't the fifty walks and thirty errors, and swinging at 3-0 pitches that lost the game?"

My response shut him up, but I shouldn't have said it. The one thing all umpires knew was that the players made far more mistakes than an umpire. We knew that, but it wasn't polite to point it out.

I left the field muttering every four-letter cuss word I could think of, swearing at my partner for not showing, the heat for draining my body, and the Baseball Gods for giving me the game from hell.

I checked the time on my phone. It was 5:30. The seven-inning game had taken *four-and-a-half hours* to play.

CHAPTER 32

A week later, my phone vibrated just as my shift ended at Lums Pond.

"Sorry," Randy said, "I know it's last minute, but can you do the bases at Banning Park?"

I was half way there before I realized I hadn't asked Randy for any information about the game and he hadn't provided any. Then to confuse matters, there were teams warming up on two different fields. I recognized Mid-Atlantic Realtors and Correlli's Pizza on Field 1. They played in the New Castle Babe Ruth League. Field 2 had older boys in professional-looking uniforms that had patches with military insignias on the sleeve of their jerseys.

American Legion! I wish I had that game.

I walked to Field 1 and watched the Babe Ruth teams warm up. A couple umpires arrived. I had worked with the one in full gear at Tower Hill High School. We had argued over his decision to eject their coach.

"Well, well, well," Will Calder said, "it's the Primadonna. Kenny, this is the kid who doesn't make any mistakes."

Kenny looked me up and down. "Leave the kid alone."

"What're you doing here?" Will said.

"Randy said he needed a base ump."

"I got the bases," Kenny said.

"Yeah," Will said, "this game's covered."

"Well, then," I grinned with great satisfaction, "*I* must have the American Legion game. See ya."

I laughed. I couldn't help it. The jealous look on Will's face was priceless.

"We haven't worked together," James Wilson said when I met him on the field. "But I'm in charge. It's my game to run. I expect nothing less than a hundred percent effort. These boys are good. They're serious. Be on top of your game."

"Bring it on."

James and I met the coaches for Cranston Post 14 and Elsmere Post 18 at home plate.

"Aren't you a little young?" Elsmere's coach said.

"No, sir," I said. "I'll be nineteen in the fall."

"I've got children older than you, and I wouldn't trust them to umpire."

"Come on, J.J.," the coach for Cranston said, "leave the kid alone."

Stop calling me kid!

After ground rules, I walked to my position behind first base. Cranston's starting nine took the field.

"Hey, ump," two players said as they jogged by, "good to see you."

"Hey, guys," I said, mystified.

One player stopped at the shortstop position, the other took left field. I tried to recall who they were and how they knew me. Then again, I shouldn't care.

Cranston's pitcher completed his warm up throws. James called play and the game got underway.   It took just an inning to realize how superior American Legion baseball was to Babe Ruth, even high school. For starters, the first inning took only ten minutes. Both pitchers had a quick delivery and hit the strike zone. Batters swung with authority. Anyone who got on base took sizeable leads and threatened to steal on every pitch. Their speed was electrifying. Infielders covered a wide range of territory, scooped up grounders with relative ease and threw baseballs to first that were a blur. There was a double play executed from second to first with professional-like skill. Outfielders caught everything in the air. Coaches, players on the bench, and spectators seated around the field were loud and into the game. The entire atmosphere was incredible and I loved every second of it.

***

Top of the seventh inning, Cranston led 3-1. Should they hold the advantage, they wouldn't bat in the bottom of the seventh and this wonderful experience would be over. I almost hoped for Elsmere to tie the game. However, they went down one, two, three. I started to leave. Nobody else did. There was no victory celebration by Cranston. A couple of their players grabbed a bat while their teammates took to their bench. Elsmere players jogged onto the field. James stood with his mask off along the third base line. Had I miscounted the number of innings?

The first base coach for Elsmere arrived.

"What inning is this?" I asked.

"Bottom of the seventh."

Why would Cranston bat in the bottom of the seventh if they were winning 3-1? There could be only one explanation. American Legion played 9 innings, just like the pros!   I almost jumped up and down like a child on Christmas morning.

215

***

Cranston held onto their lead and won the game. The nine innings were played in two hours. I had some close calls, but no arguments, so it served as a great ice breaker to this level of competition. The coaches on both teams shook my hand and congratulated me on a nice game.

Elsmere's coach added, "I'm sorry I gave you a hard time about your age. You did a good job."

"Thank you, sir," I said, almost hugging him. I couldn't help it. I had never enjoyed myself so much on a baseball field.

The two players that had greeted me at the start of the game approached.

"Good game, ump," one said. "I'm glad they let you do American Legion."

"Hey," I said, the light coming on in my memory. "I'm sorry but I forgot your names."

"I'm Lamar. This is Rick."

"Yeah, I remember, Fourth of July. You guys play a good game."

"Thanks," Lamar said. "Are we on your schedule again?"

"No, but you never know. I got this game last minute."

"Well," Lamar said, "see you around."

"Yeah," Rick said, "see ya."

"Good job," James Wilson said as we walked to our cars.

"Wow," I said, "that was *in-cred-i-ble*."

"Yeah, once you get a taste of this level, it's hard to go back to Babe Ruth."

"I know what you mean."

"You're a good kid. I was a little worried because of your age, but you were better than most of my partners.

216

A lot of times I feel I have to babysit them. I didn't feel that way with you. You were always in position and made firm decisions. It was a pleasure working with you, kid."

"Thank you," I said as we shook hands. He had called me kid too, but on this occasion, I didn't mind.

CHAPTER 33

I concluded my first year with the New Castle County Umpire Association during the final Wednesday of July. As with school ball, I'd be excluded from the upcoming tournaments because Randy had enough older umpires to work the games. I swallowed my disappointment, but my final contest had post season implications as the winner qualified for the Babe Ruth playoffs.

The game also marked my first appearance at Midway since my break-up with Allison. I couldn't help but remember how she had shown up at that initial game, and then got me to drive her home. I really didn't miss Allison. I just felt her absence driving to and from games because the passenger seat of my car was vacant. No one watched me from the bleachers. No one told me how "awesome" I was. Yet these reasons weren't enough to second-guess my decision, and my parents were happy.

Prior to the first pitch, Aaron Snead, decked out in full gear, looked at a darkening horizon. "I see any lightning, I'm stopping the game.   I can't leave my kids orphans."

No one had mentioned that part of an umpire's job was weather forecasting. I had no degree in meteorology, yet coaches, players and spectators expected me to decide if a game continued or got postponed because of rain. Their favorite question was, "Do you think we'll get it in?" How should I know?

Harry's Drug Store and Randal Trucking played four and a half scoreless innings of intense baseball. Prior to the bottom of the fifth, black clouds thickened overhead. The Midway field lights came on. The wind picked up. A couple hot dog wrappers blew across the infield. Some of the spectators abandoned the bleachers for their cars.

Aaron stood away from the plate while the pitcher for Harry's Drug Store warmed up. He looked at me and pointed upward. I nodded. Chances were excellent I'd experience my first suspended game.

The lead-off hitter for Randal Trucking flew out to center field. Their next batter, on a 1-2 count, lined the ball between the left and center fielders. Their players, coaches and fans cheered as the batter rounded first and headed for second. I ran parallel with him on the infield grass.

The centerfielder picked up the baseball against the fence. The batter rounded second and headed for third. The centerfielder threw the ball to his shortstop in short left field. The shortstop threw the ball to third. The runner slid head first.

"Safe!"

We had the first scoring threat of the game, and I smelled rain.

The next batter for Randal Trucking, on a 1-1 count, hit a deep fly ball to centerfield that was caught. The runner on third took off and touched home plate. Randal Trucking led 1-0. Their players and fans were jubilant.

Bases empty, I jogged to my position behind first base.

The coach for Randal Trucking grabbed his next batter by the arm and whispered something I couldn't believe. "Hurry up and strike out. We gotta end the inning to make it an official game."

The boy nodded. As he stood in the right-handed batter's box, a huge bolt of lightning ripped across the sky.

I flinched. The hair on my arms stood up. A boom of thunder followed.

Aaron stepped from behind the plate and waved his arms. "Clear the field! Clear the field! Game suspended!"

Spectators scurried to their cars. Players on both teams collected their bats and gloves. Another flash of lightning and rumble of thunder added urgency to their cause.

I jogged to Aaron.

The coach for Randal Trucking charged past me and confronted Aaron. "Wait! You can't! Let him finish his at-bat!"

"I'm suspending the game," Aaron said. "We'll wait it out."

"Oh, don't give me that," the coach said. Veins bulged on his neck. "You know damn well this field won't be playable after this passes. We'll have to resume tomorrow."

"Then so be it."

I felt a couple rain drops on my face.

"You can't end it *now*!" the coach said. He held up a finger. "Just one more out, damn it! My batter's going to strike out anyway. Just three pitches!"

"Come on, Coach," Aaron said, "it's for everyone's safety."

"The storm's still a distance away!"

As if on cue, another flash of lightning lit the sky, with almost simultaneous thunder. The storm clouds opened and we stood in a deluge.

"We're done here," Aaron said, water dripping from the brim of his cap.

Aaron had been polite and reasonable, the coach ridiculous. Yet that didn't stop the coach from throwing a punch at Aaron's head. To Aaron's credit, he dodged the blow. The coach slipped and fell into what had become mud. He got up. I wrapped my arms around his waist and held on.

"I'm gonna kill you, you son of a bitch!" the coach said.

Aaron stayed out of the man's reach. I couldn't hold much longer. Players and coaches from both teams, and some league officials who had watched the incident from the press box, ran onto the field.

"Let me at him, damnit!" the coach said. "I'll kill him!"

"Jack, Jack!" others yelled against the noise of the rain. A couple men helped me restrain him. "Calm down, man. What's wrong with you?"

Jack slipped and fell again. I went down with him. My right arm got pinned under his weight. Pain shot up from my hand. I freed myself, grimacing and holding my injured hand.

"You all right?" Aaron asked.

"I think so," I said, flexing my wrist and moving my fingers. "How about you?"

"Fine."

I didn't believe him.

"Get away from me," Jack said, sitting. "Leave me

221

alone."

Everyone backed off.

Midway's president, a soaked little man named Martin Collier, asked if we were okay.

"I'm good," I said, although my wrist hurt.

"I'm *fine*," Aaron said. "The game's suspended until tomorrow."

Martin turned to Jack. "What's wrong with you?" He looked at Aaron. "Do you want to call the police and press charges?"

Aaron, drenched, looked down at the coach. "I should, but I won't."

"Well, Jack," Martin said, "you're done. We can't have this type of behavior."

The coach looked up. His eyes were bloodshot. I wasn't sure if he was crying or if it was all raindrops on his long face. He extended a hand to Aaron. "Sorry."

Aaron hesitated, and then shook the man's hand. He even helped Jack to his feet.

"Clear the field," Martin said.

Everyone did.

When I got home to my room, I put on dry clothes and telephoned Randy. He failed to answer, so I left a message. He called back a short while later while I watched the Phillies on television play Arizona.

"Jose Martinez will do the plate tomorrow," Randy said.

"Why not Aaron?"

"He doesn't want to. He quit."

"What? The season's over."

"Yeah, well, he says he needs to spend more time with his kids. I know that's somewhat true, but he's had enough. Having a fist thrown at him was the final straw."

"It *was* pretty stupid."

"Yeah, hate to get on my soapbox, but this is why we're having trouble recruiting and keeping good people. Nobody wants to deal with this crap, and they shouldn't have to. And I spoke to Mister Collier. He apologized again for the coach's behavior and pointed out that the man's going through a divorce."

"That's still no excuse."

"Agreed. And again, thank you for all your excellent work this year. You'll definitely work the tournaments next year."

Weird, but I hadn't told Randy about my plans to attend umpire school. I mean, I bragged to everyone else. I guess I didn't tell him because he was my current employer and I didn't want to reveal the fact that I was looking for another job. Crazy maybe, but that was the only explanation I could think of.

"I look forward to it," I said.

PART III

ON DECK

CHAPTER 34

Austin left for Vermont in mid-August to study literature and writing. Knowing him, he'd land a big New York agent his freshman year and probably write a best selling novel before his sophomore year. I wished him all the best in front of my house and watched him drive away.

I started college a few days later. From a physical point of view, attending the University of Delaware was no big deal because I had seen the campus all my life. It was just another school in the neighborhood, so entering its classrooms felt no different than when I had matriculated from McVey Elementary to Kirk Middle School to Glasgow High.

I then endured one final weekend at Lums Pond. I said goodbye to June when my shift ended on Labor Day. I thanked her for being a good boss during my three summers of employment. She wished me well, and then startled me with a hug.

"See you in the big leagues," she said.

225

Cole still had his tomato-red hair. Despite many temptations, I hadn't ripped it from his scalp. We were cordial in our goodbyes, nothing more.

***

As the fall semester progressed, I got acclimated to college life and wondered why public school couldn't emulate higher education. I liked my classes. I met students from across the country and around the world who took their academics seriously and they didn't tease me for being smart. I was one of them, and I made a few friends. Yeah, they enjoyed partying in their time off, but they had goals. They had optimism, ideas, enthusiasm, different viewpoints and hope. My professors were published authors. They were approachable. I got to know them on a first name basis. And of course, I noticed the co-eds. How could I not? They were everywhere, and *gorgeous*.

By Christmas break, I hardly slept and ate less than normal. I couldn't sit still. I paced. I studied the baseball rule book over and over. I checked and double-checked everything I needed for Florida, such as clothing for cold and warm weather, an iron and board to keep my umpire shirts and pants looking their best, shoe-shining supplies to keep my umpire shoes their blackest, a suit for the graduation banquet, and I labeled all my umpire equipment and baseball glove. Still, it felt as if I had forgotten something.

Austin came home for the holidays. He had gained weight and bragged about a girlfriend he now had named Cindy. He showed me her picture on his phone. The picture wasn't the greatest. I mostly saw a large pair of glasses and a head of black hair.

"She looks nice," I said.

"Yeah," he said, "and she's a *junior*. And," he whispered, "we did it."

226

"Really?"

"Yeah, again and again. I didn't want to leave."

"I'm happy for you," I said with suppressed envy.

On Christmas Day, Mom, Dad and I shared gifts and hot chocolate before visiting relatives in the afternoon. The holiday had always been a special time, only *me* time, when I didn't mind not having a brother or sister. Older now, and anxious to get to Florida, I saw the day as an obstacle, something to get through on my way to New Year's Eve and departure.

So when the morning of December 31 finally arrived, I woke before dawn and packed my car's trunk. I didn't drink coffee, but I started the coffee-maker in the kitchen hoping the smell of fresh brew would wake my parents. If they didn't rise soon, I'd leave anyway. Didn't they know my future waited?

My ploy worked. Mom, Dad and I were soon shivering next to my Taurus.

"Please be careful," Mom said as we embraced. "Email us every night. If you need anything, call."

"I will," I said. "Don't worry. I'll be fine."

"Of course you will," Dad said.

"It's such a long drive," Mom said. "Are you sure you're up to it?"

"I'd drive to California if I had to."

I shook hands with Dad and hugged Mom, and then got into my car. I started the engine, shifted into drive, gave my parents one last wave and then pressed on the gas. "Yeeha!"

Finally, I was on my way. I merged onto Interstate 95 south and said a temporary goodbye to Delaware. I had never been south of Washington D.C. I had never driven alone passed Baltimore. So after two hours on the highway, I surpassed my personal limits when I crossed the Potomac River and entered Virginia. There were signs for Arlington National Cemetery and George Washington's Mount Vernon estate. Maybe I'd visit them on my way home. For now, only bathroom breaks, hunger, gasoline for my car, and the need to sleep would halt my driving.

***

That evening, I called Mom from a hotel room in Florence, South Carolina.

"Wow," she said. "You made it *that* far? Great."

"Yeah, saw my first palmetto."

"Your first what?"

"Palmetto. It's like a small palm tree."

"Oh, okay. Your dad says hi. Get a good night's sleep."

That was impossible. When I closed my eyes it felt as if I was still driving, and the sheer anticipation of what lay ahead kept my body anxious. I rose at dawn on pure adrenalin, showered and dressed and continued south.

I arrived at Daytona Beach on a cool and overcast afternoon and located the six-story La Planta Hotel on Seaside Boulevard. The pastel-colored, ocean-side resort looked weather beaten and old compared to some of the taller chain hotels nearby.

I parked in its multi-level garage, and then wheeled my suitcase to the first floor lobby. The hotel's interior had a 1920's black and white art deco style, with period chairs and sofas near a large fireplace. Behind the check-in counter, a young lady wearing a black business suit greeted me. Her name tag announced Kate.

I introduced myself. "I'm checking in for the umpire school."

"You're one of the early ones," she said, checking her computer screen. She completed her process and then handed me an electronic key. "Room 604, ocean side."

"Great! Has my roommate arrived?"

She again looked at the monitor. "No."

"Do you know his name?"

"Robert Strauss."

"Hope he's a good guy. Never shared a room before. Wouldn't want some colossal jerk."

Kate looked at me weird, probably shouldn't have said jerk. Then she pointed at an open doorway off the lobby. "You're checked in at the hotel, but check in for the school is in our Conference Center tomorrow at 3. Good luck."

I thanked her and then peeked inside the dimly-lit Conference Center. There were rows of tables and at least a hundred chairs that faced a low stage. For some reason, I hadn't expected so many aspiring umpires. I thought, because the profession was so hated, just about fifty or so guys would show up. Oh, well, bring it on.

I took the elevator to the top floor and entered my room. I dropped the suitcase on one of the two beds, and then spread apart the floor to ceiling curtains. Daylight filled the room and hurt my eyes until they adjusted. Sliding glass doors separated me from a balcony that overlooked a boardwalk, a white sandy beach and a gray ocean that stretched to a cloudy horizon. It was far from the bikini weather Florida loved to advertise. Then again, it *was* January.

I slid the door open and a cold, stiff wind almost knocked me down. I shivered and stepped outside. I blinked and did a double take.

There were cars on the beach! Slow-moving two way automobile traffic!

CHAPTER 35

The next afternoon, my roommate still hadn't shown when I stepped from the elevator and into a crowded and noisy lobby. Other than Kate behind the counter, everybody present was male. They came in all shapes and sizes, and from different ethnic groups and races. Most appeared to be around my age, but I noticed some gray hair, a few receding hairlines and a couple bald guys. Everyone dressed casual.

Three tables had been set up just inside the doorway to the Conference Center, each with a sign taped to the front, either A to L, M to R, or S to Z. A young lady and an athletic-looking dude sat behind each table. They wore blue tee-shirts that displayed a black umpire's mask and the name *Fogel* printed above the mask and *Umpire School* printed beneath.

I stood in line at the first table. A chubby guy stood in front of me and introduced himself as Ken Dillard.

I told him my name as we shook hands.

"Where you from?"

"Delaware?"

"Where's that?"

"It's between…."

"Just yanking your chain," he said, laughing. "I know where it is. I'm from Jersey. It took me all of five minutes to drive through your state on my way down here."

"Really?" I said, sarcastic. "It took you *that* long?"

"Great," he said with a chuckle, "a sense of humor. I like that. However, we shouldn't become friends. I mean, this is a competition, right?"

"It looks like more than a hundred-fifty guys."

"And I hear there's just fifteen job openings. Brutal."

"Well, one of those jobs has my name on it."

"Good attitude."

Ken's turn came at the table. He gave his name to the brunette. She searched for his registration on her laptop. Her partner handed Ken a blue cap with a short brim, a Fogel Umpire School tee-shirt and Major League Baseball Rule Book.

"Be back at 5 for the opening meeting," the brunette said.

"See you later," Ken said.

I announced my name to the brunette. "Do you work for the school?"

"No," she said. "We're interns, so it's free labor." She checked me in and I received the same supplies as Ken. "Be back at five."

As I left the Conference Center, I glanced over my shoulder to take one last look at the brunette and bumped shoulders with someone in passing.

"Oh," I said, without looking, "excuse me."

"No problem."

I stopped in my tracks. Had my ears played a trick on me? The voice sounded female. I turned around and in the first line stood a thin person with short black hair, long legs in blue jeans and two bumps under a red sweater. Cat-like green eyes glanced at me.

Wow, a woman umpire. Why not? There had been a handful of female umpires in the history of professional baseball. None, however, had gotten farther than calling a major league spring training game.

I thought about introducing myself and talking to her because I admired her courage. The odds of a man making it to the major leagues were extraordinary. What must the odds be for a woman? Now that was a math problem!

I noticed a wedding ring, and with the hustle and bustle of check-in, I decided to wait for another, less hectic opportunity to talk to her.

***

I arrived twenty minutes early for the opening meeting. Seating was arranged in alphabetical order, with name tags placed on the tables. I plopped down in the first row, virtually in the middle, with the stage and lectern in front of me. I met Nathan Crow of Las Vegas, Nevada. The other adjacent chair was still empty. The name tag read, Elizabeth Bridger. Elizabeth? That must be the woman I saw earlier.

Thirteen chairs on stage were gradually taken over by older, clean shaven men wearing suits and ties. I recognized Matt Fogel from the website and three other men from T.V. as major league umpires.

With five minutes to go, Elizabeth Bridger occupied the chair on my left.

"Hello," I said to the familiar face. I extended a hand and introduced myself.

"Elizabeth Bridger, Boulder, Colorado." We shook hands. "But you can call me Beth. Excited?"

"Absolutely. I can't wait to get started."

"How old are you, if you don't mind my asking. You

look like you're in high school."

"I'm nineteen. I just finished my first semester at the University of Delaware."

"How far is that from home?"

"Across the street."

"Really?" she said, laughing. "Most kids want to go to college as far from home as possible."

"Yeah, but I wake up in my own bed and bike to class. So it has its advantages. And Mom and Dad don't have to pay for a dorm."

"I grew up in Ohio and attended the University of Colorado. I fell in love with the mountains and my husband and never left. Got a girlfriend?"

"No," I said.

"Too shy?"

I shrugged, and must've turned red.

"Sorry, didn't mean to embarrass you. Have you withdrawn from college?"

"Oh, no. I'm here between semesters. How were you able to get away?"

"I *was* the girl's gym teacher at Continental Middle School. I had pretty much resigned myself to doing that for a living, and umpiring softball part time. I love umpiring. So when I got laid off, I thought I might try this."

"And your husband's okay with it?"

"He couldn't be more supportive."

I smiled, and noticed how men around us looked twice at Beth to confirm her sex. Most reactions were favorable. A few laughed and pointed. Beth, to her credit, said nothing and focused on the stage.

Matt Fogel, a tall and barrel-chested man who appeared to have no neck, stepped up to the lectern. He had a round face, wide smile and a crew cut. He tapped on the microphone. The pounding sound echoed across the room and quieted everyone.

"Hello," Matt said in a booming voice. "And welcome to the Matt Fogel Umpire School. I'm Matt Fogel."

The class and I applauded.

"So," Matt said, "you want to be a professional baseball umpire? I'm sure your families are preparing your commitment papers right now."

Some light laughter.

"Did you hear about the time the devil challenged God to a baseball game?" Matt continued. "God smiled and replied, 'you don't stand a chance. I have Babe Ruth, Lou Gehrig, Mickey Mantle and plenty more greats to chose from.' The devil smiled and said, 'yeah, but I have all the umpires."

A bigger laugh came from the audience.

"Welcome to a profession where you're expected to be perfect," Matt said. "If you appear on Sportscenter, or any other highlight show, it's *not* a good thing. You screwed up and the entire sports world will know about it. It's not a glamorous living. It's not for the faint of heart, and it's damn difficult for the family man. You're away from home a good chunk of the time. You'll struggle for years in the minors, with low pay, crappy hotels and food, and accumulate serious debt. But for those of you who want it, for those of you who want to travel and do something different with your life and don't mind sacrifice, it's a great life. You'll meet fascinating people, from ordinary fans to celebrities. But to achieve it, your journey starts here."

The class applauded.

Matt introduced the men to his right, and then his left. They stood as their name was called. Along with the three major league umpires, there were four retired, and five that worked in various minor leagues. All had graduated from the Matt Fogel Umpire School.

"Damn," Beth said in a whisper. "Sneaky little devil."

"What?"

"The short guy on stage with the white hair, Wes Clinton?"

I looked at the row of men. "What about him?"

"He shuttled some of us from the airport. He said very little beyond giving his name as Wes. He never said he was an instructor."

"Oh, okay, so you've met already."

"You don't understand. He overheard everything we said. And I didn't think anything of it when we asked him where to find the best bars in town."

"I'm sure you're okay. A drink isn't going to hurt."

She breathed deep. "I hope you're right."

Wow, that was pretty sneaky to plant a spy as the shuttle driver. Good thing I drove myself. Why had they done that, character check?

"I and my fellow instructors," Matt said, "are about to give you five intense weeks of classroom and field work. I know there's a beach nearby, but it's January, so don't expect too many hot babes strolling the sand showing off what their mama gave them. There's also some pretty nice strip clubs in town…or so I'm told."

Light laughter.

"But if that's why you came to Florida," Matt continued, "quit now. This is no vacation. You're pursuing a rare and wonderful career. It's hard, demanding, and tough on your body. But there isn't a day goes by that I don't miss it. Being a major league umpire is part of an elite club. It's special. And you must give it the respect it deserves. When we evaluate you, we're not just looking at proper mechanics, a good eye, sound judgment, proper positioning, a thorough knowledge of the rules, but we're also looking at character. I won't graduate anybody who hasn't got integrity, ethics, and a strong sense of fair play. You're here for the game. If you're here for yourself, we'll find that out."

Everyone applauded.

"Our schedule is six days a week," Matt said. "We start here at 8:30 a.m. for classroom instruction. I warn you now, don't be late. We close the doors on time and won't open them until class is over. Know the rule book inside and out, as well as how to apply the rules. Our written exams are not multiple guess. You'll be given a two, three, maybe even a four part scenario that you'll have to break down and write the correct ruling. You need a seventy-five percent average on the exams to pass the course. However, nobody, and I mean *nobody*, will be hired for the pros unless they finish with an average test score *above* 90 percent."

The audience reacted with soft whistles, gentle sighs and expressions like, "Sweet Jesus."

"Bring it on," I said.

"Also," Matt continued, "if you have trouble hearing me or seeing the screen once we start using it, by all means, move to the front of the class. Then quit the course immediately. You picked the wrong profession."

Matt and the other instructors laughed. It took a moment for the rest of us to understand the joke.

"Oh, I get it," Beth said.

"At 10:30 we report to the fields," Matt continued. "There's a period of exercise to get you loosened up. We do drills to teach proper stance, voice control and proper positioning for every possible situation. Field training includes a wide range of both plate and base technique for the two man system. We only teach the two man system because that's what the minor leagues use. You'll each get intense one on one mentoring in a batting cage with a pitching machine. You'll be instructed on the proper wearing of equipment. We'll teach the correct method to handle angry players, coaches and managers. If your ears are sensitive to the F word, you might as well leave now. You'll hear it from skippers and players more than any other word. It'll be used as a noun, verb, adjective, and it'll be a major part of their tirade about your ancestry, your mother, your sister, and whatever else they put into the mix."

The audience and I laughed.

"For the first couple weeks," Matt went on, "the afternoons will involve umpiring pick-up games with your fellow students on each of our six fields. Each day a schedule will be posted in the locker room at our facility, letting you know who will umpire, at what field and what inning. You will umpire one full inning, maybe not everyday, but close to it. When you're not umpiring, you'll watch your classmates or play in a game, that's why you were asked to bring a glove. These games are not for you to show off your athleticism. If you had talent, you'd be pursuing a multi-million dollar contract. These games are for the umpires. We end the day around 4 p.m. Then starting the third week, our day will be longer because you'll umpire actual college and high school games that start at 3:30."

The audience clapped.

"Let me assure you," Matt said, "you *will* mess up. Each and every one of you will make mistakes. So you better be thick skinned because we'll be on you like drill sergeants and watching you like Big Brother. But for now, put on your name tags and let's get to know each other. A temporary bar has been set up in the lobby. Enjoy, and good luck."

Everyone applauded, stood, and then mingled in the lobby. After names and handshakes were exchanged, the main question was, "Where you from?"

A gray-haired man from Minnesota asked Beth, "Why would a woman want to do this?"

She countered with, "Why would an old man want to do this?"

"Oh," he said, laughing, "it's not for me. I'm President of the Birch Lake Little League. I hope to take whatever I learn here and teach it to our volunteer umps."

"So I won't be competing against you," I said.

"No, son, you don't have to worry about me."

He wished us good luck and disappeared into the crowd. Matt Fogel appeared with a drink in hand. Beth and I gave our names and hometown.

"Oh yes, the First State," Matt said to me. "We've had a few students from there. You're either a Phillies fan or an Orioles fan."

"Phillies," I replied.

"Then you're from northern Delaware."

"I am."

"People from southern Delaware tend to root for the Orioles."

"That's correct, sir."

"Call me Matt," he said, and then turned to Beth. "You're the only woman this year. If you encounter any issues with anybody, let me know. You have my word you'll be evaluated on merit."

"I know," Beth said. "Thank you."

Matt patted us on the shoulder and departed into the crowd.

"That was nice of him," I said.

"Yes it was," Beth said. "Are you on the meal plan?"

"I am."

"Well, I'm hungry. Do you want to join me for dinner?"

"Good idea."

238

The hotel restaurant was an ordinary looking place, with booths and tables and a front counter for single diners. It served buffet style. Students from the umpire school presented their meal voucher to the cashier in place of cash.

Beth loaded up on salad. I couldn't resist the pot roast, gravy and mashed potatoes. We ate and shared small talk about our families, our lives and hometown and situations we had encountered when we umpired.

"With my gear on," Beth said with a chuckle, "most people don't realize I'm female until I speak."

She laughed it off, but I sensed a little sadness. "How long have you been married?"

"Three years," Beth said, grinning. "I've known Danny for five. We met in college. I was on the softball team. He wrote for the school paper and interviewed me after I threw a no-hitter against Colorado State. When he found out I loved to go camping, hiking, used power tools, could fix a car and talk about sports, he practically proposed on the spot." She laughed. "He's a rare find. Not too many men want to be seen with a masculine looking woman. People make so many judgments about me when they see me. Danny didn't do that."

"Good for him."

"Yeah. He was so refreshing after all the crap I dealt with growing up. Even my mom hurt me by constantly trying to put me in a dress. Dad was great, though. He's the one who taught me to use power tools and camp. He said he'd rather his daughter stand on her own two feet and take care of herself than anything else. I'll always love him for that."

"Well, you have to be who you are."

"That's the truth. Besides, I envied boys. They were able to have so much more fun, playing sports, climbing trees, getting dirty, racing cars. I never wanted any of that prissy stuff. One day my brother Timmy let me tag along with him to a neighborhood baseball game. The other boys were shocked. 'You brought a *girl*?' But after I showed them I could hit and pitch better than they could, they all wanted me on their team."

"And now you've come to umpire school to show us all how it's done," I said.

"Exactly," she said with a smile. "And win a job."

"Good luck," I said, raising my glass of iced tea.

***

Robert Strauss still hadn't appeared when I returned to my room. I sat at the table with my laptop and sent an email to Austin and my parents. I summarized the opening meeting and expressed my enthusiasm for the upcoming five weeks. Then wearing briefs, I turned off the lights and got into the bed nearest the sliding glass doors. I wasn't asleep long when a noise woke me.

The door opened. Light from the hallway entered the room and created a tall and husky silhouette of whoever came in. He dragged a suitcase.

"Hello," I said, a little nervous.

"Relax, man," he said, closing the door. "I'm your roommate."

"Oh," I said, a little upset, "nice of you to show up."

"Robert Strauss," he said, standing over me with his hand out. "I'm from Boston. Sorry to introduce myself at this hour, but I saw no reason to come to bed until I was ready to sleep."

"Michael Briggs," I said, shaking his hand. He had a mean grip. "Were you at the meeting?"

"Yeah. Been here all day. Like I said, no cause to come to bed until I'm ready to sleep. Me and some of the guys checked out the local scene. Matt was right. There are some nice strip clubs around here.   Maybe we can go together next time.”

“I don't think so. I'm on a pretty tight budget.”

“All work and no play, eh?”

“For the next five weeks, yes.”

“Okay, but fair warning, I'm taking one of the jobs. This is my second time here. I know the routine. I know what they're looking for, and what's expected. So don't get in my way.”

“Aye, aye, Captain,” I said with a mock salute.

“Very funny. Are you sure you're in the right place?”

“What do you mean?”

“Clown College is in Palmetto, Florida.”

“Ha, ha.”

Robert laughed on his way to the bathroom. He came out a couple minutes later wearing boxer shorts and flopped face down on his bed.

“Goodnight,” I said.

He snored.

I wondered if I could move to another room. Then again, if Robert liked to party, he might not be around long.

CHAPTER 36

The next morning, I entered the Conference Center carrying a spiral notebook, pencil and the baseball rule book. Beth was already seated.

"Good morning," she said when I sat. "Sleep well?"

"No," I said, sarcastic. "I met my roommate, Robert Strauss from *Bass-ton*, around two in the morning. He snores like a freight train. I'm surprised there's still paint on the walls."

Beth laughed.

"It's not funny."

"Sorry," she said. "Not to rub it in, but I don't have a roommate."

"Well, *yeah*, for obvious reasons."

At 8:30, a couple of interns closed the doors. I noticed a few empty chairs. Matt stood at the lectern and called the class to order. He had replaced his suit and tie for blue jeans, a red sweater and an unzipped Matt Fogel Umpire School blue windbreaker. His instructors were also dressed casual and they roamed the perimeter.

"Hope you all slept well," Matt said.

Beth chuckled.

I playfully elbowed her.

Matt gestured to a male intern in the back of the room. The young man stood next to a video projector. He pressed a wall switch and a large screen came down from the ceiling and over the stage. Another intern switched off most of the lights.

"Please remove a piece of paper from your notebooks and write your name at the top," Matt said. "Then place your notebooks and rulebooks on the floor."

A loud, almost simultaneous rip of paper echoed in the room.

"Every morning," Matt continued, "you'll be given a sticky baseball situation that you must provide a full answer for in five minutes. These are on top of the weekly exams and pop quizzes. Anyone caught cheating will be expelled. Afterwards, we'll go over the scenario and discuss various rules and their interpretations. We'll watch actual footage from games and discuss what had happened. Then we'll hop on busses, or you can drive your own car, over to the facility for field work. We break for an hour lunch around one. For those of you on the lunch plan, meals will be provided on site from a couple mobile caterers. All right, let's begin."

The intern switched on the projector.

"You have five minutes," Matt said, and left the stage.

Runner on first, no outs, two strikes on the batter. On the next pitch, the runner attempts to steal second. The batter swings at the pitch, misses, but the pitch was inside and hits the batter in the stomach and lands in fair territory. The runner on first sees the ball on the ground and heads for third. The catcher retrieves the ball and throws the runner out at third. The batter, because he was hit by the pitch, walks down to first base. What is the proper ruling?

Like a polynomial, I separated each segment of the

problem. *Two strikes on the batter. The batter swung and missed.* BATTER STRUCK OUT! Therefore, he cannot have first base. However, a batter hit by a pitch created a DEAD BALL SITUATION. The runner had to return to first.

I wrote my answer, folded the paper and waited. Out the corner of my eye, Beth tapped her fingertips against her thumb as if counting, still pondering the scenario in her head.

At five minutes, Matt called time and the question disappeared from the screen.

"Damn," Beth said.

"Pass your papers to the right," Matt said from the lectern. The class did, and they were collected by a couple interns.

"Did you answer it?" Beth asked.

"I did. Did you?"

"You know I didn't."

"Sorry."

"What're you sorry about? It's not your fault I panicked."

Once the papers were collected, Matt gave the answer. "The batter struck out, runner returns to first. I hope you all got that." Some students moaned. "I don't like the sound of that. Let's review some actual game situations."

I got ready to watch a serious film about incidences that had happened during a game. Instead, the footage was a montage of bloopers showing umpires in both minor and major leagues falling while running, tripping over bats, getting struck in the groin by a foul ball, or direct hits against the mask, all timed to the beat of Tchaikovsky's 1812 Overture.

Everyone was in hysterics.

The video then switched to a series of hostile managers and players screaming within inches of an umpire's face, managers who kicked dirt onto umpires' shoes, managers who picked up bases and threw them, players who entered the dug out and tossed bats and helmets onto the field, and one manager who ripped off his shirt and hurled it at the home plate umpire.

The funny video relieved the tension that the initial exam had created, but it didn't last long. The lights came on. Matt ordered us to, "Open the Bible. I mean, the Major League Baseball Rule Book." Class began for real.

CHAPTER 37

I drove my car with Beth in the passenger seat and followed the school's buses to the Daytona Speedway Baseball Facility. The backside of the racetrack where the Daytona 500 occurred each February was adjacent to six fenced-in ball fields with lights. Each well-groomed diamond had an opposing pair of cinder-blocked dugouts with an adjacent section of bleachers behind four-foot high fencing. There was a boarded up concession stand, but an open locker room next to three batting cages.

Beth and I joined the crowd of students who entered the locker room to check the schedule, a copy of which had been hung on four separate bulletin boards.

"Wow," I said to Beth, "I have the plate for the first inning on Field 3."

"I have the bases for the sixth on Field 2."

The Umpiring Schedule was accompanied by 12 smaller pieces of paper that contained a large letter at the top and eleven names underneath.

"I'm with Group D," I said.

"Group K," Beth replied.

A short while later, Beth and I joined the entire class for calisthenics on Field 1. All students wore the Matt Fogel Umpire School baseball cap along with their own sweatshirts or windbreakers. I showed off my NCCUA jacket. We had also been instructed to bring our mask.

Matt stood in front of us with a megaphone. "Let's form up. Get more than an arm's length from your neighbor, front to back and side to side."

"Let's go," one instructor said, walking behind us. "This ain't no picnic!"

I extended my arms. Beth reached out and touched my fingertips.

"Not quite far enough," she said, stepping farther away.

"Better," Matt said. "For now, put your masks on the ground." We did. "Now I realize most of you see big, fat umpires when you watch a major league game. Well, let me tell you we earned that fat. We deserve to wear it proudly. But until you reach the majors, you had better be in shape. Minor leagues only use two umpires. You must hustle and cover the entire field. So to warm up, each day we'll do a series of exercises."

We were ordered to stretch our bodies by reaching to the sky and then touching toes. That was followed by twenty-five jumping jacks, ten push ups, and then we ran in place for thirty seconds.

"Rest," Matt said.

I put my hands on my hips and sucked air.

"Don't tell me you're tired," Beth said. "That was nothing."

I stuck my tongue out. She laughed.

"Now we'll do *umpire calisthenics*," Matt said. "I'm sure you're wondering what that means. Well, here at the school, to be judged fairly, we want all of you to use the same signaling for safe, out and strikes, especially strike three. I know all of you probably have some dramatic style for strike three, but don't use it here. Save it for when you're out on the circuit. All strike calls must be done the same way, same voice and same mechanics.

"Let's begin with safe," Matt continued, and his instructors demonstrated, "begin with your hands on your knees and head up." We got into position. "Then stand and put your arms straight out in front of you. Spread them wide and level with your shoulders. Belt out in a strong voice, safe! Let's begin."

The class moved and spoke in unison. "Safe!"

"That was pretty cool," I said.

"No talking," an instructor yelled.

I cringed.

"Louder," Matt said.

The class repeated the safe signal and voiced the call.

"Keep those arms straight," an instructor yelled. "No bending at the elbow."

We performed it again.

"Louder!" Matt and the instructors said.

We went again.

"I can't hear you!" Matt said.

"Have I joined the army?" I said.

"Almost," Beth replied.

"No talking!"

The class performed the safe task a dozen times.

"All right," Matt said, "for out and strike calls, start with your hands on your knees."

We did.

"While you stand," he continued, "extend your right arm out from your side and then bend upward at the elbow at a ninety-degree angle. Close the fist and say, *out!*"

Along with the instructors, fists were raised in unison and a simultaneous "Out" echoed all across the complex.

"Come on," Matt said, "you can do better than that."

We repeated the exercise fifteen times, and then Matt mixed it up. "Safe, strike, out, strike, safe, out....."

Meanwhile, the instructors roamed throughout the rows.

"Look straight," one said behind me. "Stand tall."

I wasn't certain if he aimed his direction at me or not, but I obeyed.

"I can't hear you!" another said.

"You sound like a bunch of wimps!"

"I want military precision," Matt said. "Body language is just as important as everything else, maybe more so. *Present* yourself!"

I couldn't believe how much huffing and puffing I did just from calling strike, safe and out and moving my body accordingly.

"Stop," Matt said, and we did.

"I should've gotten into better shape," I said, breathing hard.

"Should've, would've and could've," Beth said, only slightly winded.

"All right," Matt said, "put your masks on."

We then received instruction on the proper way to remove our mask without knocking off our cap. The method was no different than what Randy had said during my training at William Penn High School. Had Randy attended the Fogel Umpire School? If he had, then crap. I had missed a great opportunity to learn about the training ahead of time.

Now, I hadn't knocked my cap off during the entire season. I hadn't even thought about it. Yet under the watchful eye of Matt and his instructors, I became aware of it and moved slower than normal.

"Do it again and again," Matt said, "and faster."

The class practiced removing our mask for fifteen minutes. A few caps fell to the grass. Some got tangled in the elastic straps and stayed with the mask. Other students struck the underside of the cap's brim, but the cap stayed on their head.

"Appearance is important," Matt said. "For those of you who lost your hat, practice, practice, practice in your room tonight. I don't want to see any topless heads tomorrow.

"All right," Matt continued, "put your mask on the ground." We did. "You will do a lot of running between the infield and outfield and covering all the bases. So to prepare for that, I want four laps around the field right now. No slackers!"

I jogged with my classmates, and was soon breathing hard again.

"I wasn't expecting this at all," someone said.

"Let's go Delaware," Ken Dillard said, passing me.

"I'll be a son of a bitch," Robert Strauss said. He didn't know I jogged behind him. "The dyke's out front."

A couple guys near him laughed.

"Hey," I said, running up to him, "her name's Elizabeth."

"You know her? I guess you would."

"What does that mean?"

"You figure it out, scarecrow?"

"Dumb ass," I said under my breath.

After laps, the class returned to the infield. We were allowed a few minutes to catch our breath. I did so with my hands on my hips. Other students had their hands on their knees.

"You need to run on the beach," Beth said. "Best thing to build up stamina."

"Thanks, coach," I said sarcastic. "I'll do that."

CHAPTER 38

Each instructor gathered around Matt with a clip-board in hand. They then took turns announcing what group reported where.

Morris Tandy, a muscular, thick-necked man who umpired Triple-A Pacific Coast League, said, "Group D! Batting Cage 2."

I joined Morris and ten other guys outside a fence that surrounded a dirt area about a hundred feet in length and twenty feet wide. It contained a pitching machine set sixty feet from a home plate.

"Hey, Delaware," Ken Dillard said. "We keep running into each other."

Morris Tandy took attendance, only pausing when he reached my name. "I'm from West Chester P.A. So we're practically neighbors."

"Have you trained students from Delaware?"

"Oh, quite a few. None of them made it to the majors."

"Then I'll be the first."

"You think so," Morris said with a grin. "You'll have to get passed me. Terence Sauer, Little Rock, Arkansas."

"Here, sir," the man said. "I don't have any experience, so fair warning."

"No warning needed," Morris said. "We teach everybody like they don't have experience."

Morris completed roll call, and then opened the rear gate to Cage 2. A male intern arrived with a catcher's mitt and two industrial-sized buckets, one stuffed with baseballs and the other empty. He placed the full bucket at the base of the pitching machine, a device on a tripod that had two slanted, tire-like objects on top. He placed the empty bucket next to home plate.

"You stand in like a right handed batter," Morris said to Jose Ramirez of San Antonio, Texas. Sam Pleasant of Garden City, Kansas played catcher.

Morris got behind Sam and demonstrated proper positioning for a right handed batter. "When the pitch is delivered, crouch over the catcher's left shoulder and get a clear view of the strike zone. Rest your forearms on your thighs. I'm sure you've seen umpires put their hands on their knees, or even balance themselves with one hand on the back of the catcher. I see that and I'll slap you. When you crouch down, I want to see legs wide and forearms on your thighs."

"Show me your stance," he said to me.

He and I switched places.

"The pitcher delivers," Morris said. "Get down."

I crouched behind Sam and over his left shoulder.

"You're a little low," Morris said. "Keep your chin level with the top of the catcher's head, and don't arch your back so much." He got behind me and pulled on my shoulders. "Put your feet farther apart."

I obeyed.

"Good," he said. Then he stood beside me and gave me a gentle push. I stood firm. "Remember, you'll be crouching around three hundred times a game, maybe more if the game goes extra innings, so proper balance will save your legs." He folded his arms across his chest and looked so stern I wanted to laugh, but didn't dare. "Not bad. Let's call some pitches."

The intern switched on the pitching machine. The two wheels on top spun.

"Let one rip," Morris said to the intern.

The young man fed a baseball into the device. I crouched and created my imaginary strike zone above the plate and in line with the top of Jose's knees and the middle of his chest.

Thumph.

The ball ejected from between the spinning wheels and came at me. It crossed the plate, waist high on Jose and smacked into Sam's mitt.

I stood with a raised fist. "Strike!"

"Good form," Morris said, "but more authority in your voice."

"Yes, sir."

"Belt it out from the diaphragm like an opera singer," he said, releasing a loud and firm, "Strike!"

"Yes, sir."

"And," he said to all, "the speed on the machine is set at seventy-five miles an hour. If you can't call pitches at that speed, you might as well go home now, because believe me, that's nothing. Truth is, the fastest speed you'll ever see will be in the minors. Everybody throws hard. It's the breaking ball that separates the minors from the majors. If a pitcher can throw a breaking ball for strikes, he'll make it to the show. If a batter can hit the breaking ball, he'll make it as well. Fastball hitters and pitchers wash out in the minors."

"I can vouch for that," Terence Sauer said. "I couldn't hit a curve to save my life."

"Ex-player, eh," Morris said.

253

"Yes, sir. In the Red's organization."

"Ex-players make the worst umpires."

"Why is that?" Terence asked.

"Because they have to think."

We laughed.

"Then I got some work to do," Terence said with a wink. "Don't I?"

"Yes, you do," Morris grinned. "Now back to what I was saying about the breaking ball. The same holds true for umpires. If you can't call the breaking pitches consistently, you won't make it. Don't be fooled. No matter what the baseball does, if it rises, sinks, or curves, you do *not* move. Follow the ball with your *eyes*, not your body. And no flinching or blinking." He signaled the intern to proceed.

The young man loaded the entire bucket of baseballs into the back of the machine. I got into position and prepared for the onslaught.

Thumph. A baseball shot at me and passed Jose about hip high.

"Strike!"

No comment from Morris. A few seconds later, another *thumph*, and a ball came at me, its red laces revolving vertically. Sam caught it.

"Strike," I said, and did so for the next six pitches.

The intern pressed a button in back of the machine and the next pitch spun horizontal like a slider and dipped away from Jose.

"Ball!"

The next five pitches came in like a slider and I made the same ruling.

The intern pressed another button. The pitch came in high and then broke in an arc like a curve ball. I rose up on the balls of my feet, and then down on my heels as the ball crossed the plate.

"What did I tell you about not moving?" Morris yelled in my ear. "Keep still! How can you tell if the ball crossed the strike zone if you're hopping up and down like a bunny rabbit?"

My classmates laughed. I never looked at Morris or said a word. I deserved the criticism. I then called six more curve balls, and then a few fast balls before the machine emptied.

"Not bad," Morris said. "But I expect much better next time."

"Yes, sir," I said, my thighs screaming.

By one o'clock, each member of Group D had taken a turn at calling pitches.

"Go grab some lunch," Morris said, "but I want constant improvement. Get better everyday."

I got into line at one of the mobile catering trucks.

"I must really stink," Ken said, standing behind me. "You just had to do one bucket of balls."

"Terence did two," I said.

"That doesn't make me feel better. I *have* experience."

I got a hamburger and soda, and then searched for a place to sit. There were ten picnic tables fully occupied in the shadow of the locker room. Other students sat on the grass. I spotted Beth off by herself, munching on a sandwich.

"May I join you?" I said.

"Of course," she said, patting the ground next to her.

"What're you eating?"

"Chicken salad. It's not bad."

"*Not bad*. Those are Morris Tandy's two favorite words."

"I have a feeling that when they're quiet," she said, sitting back, "or just say two words, that's a good thing.

255

So, how'd it go?"

"It was *so* cool," I said, biting into my burger. "I can't wait for the practice game. How about you?"

"It was a little rough," Beth said, finishing her sandwich. "Ben Carter told me over and over to be more firm in my voice. *You have to sound like a commander.* I can't change the voice I was born with."

"Maybe he means more forceful with the voice you have."

"Hey," she said, "I'll be hoarse tomorrow."

CHAPTER 39

After lunch, I strapped on my gear in a busy and noisy locker room. I completed my look with freshly shined shoes, pressed navy blue pants and my New Castle County Umpire Association jacket.

I carried my mask and stood outside Field 3. Like the other diamonds, it had a tall chain link backstop, and behind it, an elevated stage with a table and four chairs. Matt Fogel and the spy Wes Clinton, a retired umpire, were present and armed with clipboards and pencils.

"Good and early," Matt said from his seat. "Are you nervous?"

How should I respond? If I said yes, would Matt consider me weak and unprepared for pro ball? If I said no, Matt would sense I lied and that would be a character flaw.

"I'm a little nervous," I said.

"Don't worry," he said, "you'll do fine."

I stretched limper up as students with baseball gloves assembled on the field and two instructors divided them into Team A and Team B. Volunteers were accepted to pitch and receive and catcher's equipment was provided.

257

Jose Ramirez joined me as my base umpire. I stood taller than him, and he appeared to shake in his blue jeans and blue jacket. "I hate going first."

"Not me," I said. "Bring it on."

"Well," Morris Tandy said upon arrival. He looked me up and down, "at least you look like an umpire."

"Hey," I said. "You watch. I'm the best one here."

Morris grinned, and then escorted Jose and me onto the field. We met Ben Carter of the Triple-A Southwest League. He had been the one who criticized Beth's voice. "I'm managing Team A, and I'll be your worst enemy."

We met Jerry Aliva of the Double-A Ohio Valley League. "I got Team B, and my eyes will be on you."

"Best of luck, gentlemen," Morris said. "I'll be watching too."

"Bring it on."

Team A took the field and their pitcher warmed up. Ben Carter stood by first base and talked to Jose.

"How many warm up pitches?" Jerry Aliva asked me. "Eight."

"After the seventh pitch," Jerry said, "I want you to point at the pitcher and belt out, *one more pitch*. No, coming down or some other school yard jargon. It's *one more pitch*."

"Got it."

"Good luck."

Jerry stood by third base. The seventh warm up toss hit the catcher's mitt.

"One more pitch!"

Team A's pitcher flinched, and then looked at me as if I had lost my mind.

After the eighth pitch, I stepped to the plate and pushed down a high tide of emotion that swelled my chest. After all, I had anticipated this moment since I went on the internet and learned about becoming a professional umpire. I wanted this. I had worked hard for it. I had saved my own money for it. Now I was finally here and ready to show my worth.

"Batter!" I said, putting my mask on.

Team B's lead-off hitter stepped into the right hand-ed batter's box. Morris Tandy, from his seat behind the backstop, told the young man not to swing.

Team A's pitcher worked from the stretch. He went into his delivery. I crouched and created my imaginary rectangle above home plate. The baseball wasn't thrown much harder than the pitching machines. It crossed the plate at the batter's thighs and landed in the catcher's mitt.

"Strike!"

I anticipated a comment or two from the instructors, but none came.

Morris had me call six pitches before he told the hitter, "Swing away."

On the next pitch, Team B's hitter smacked a single to left field. Jose Ramirez hustled from behind first base to the grassy infield, with Ben Carter at his side. The batter rounded first, and kept going. The left fielder threw to second. The base runner stopped short of the bag, and then got into a rundown between first and second. Jose stayed with the play and made the call when the runner was finally tagged.

Even though the runner had been put out, Ben Carter told him to stay at first.

"This isn't a regular baseball game, guys," Ben said. "We're going to throw anything and everything at you. So be ready."

The next batter stood for five pitches before he was told to swing. On the next pitch, Ben yelled at the runner on first to take off for second. The batter did nothing. The ball crossed the plate hip high.

"Strike!"

The catcher rose up in front of me. I removed my mask and took a few steps toward third base, but kept my eyes on the baseball as it left the catcher's hand and flew to second. Jose watched the steal attempt. Team A's shortstop went to catch the throw, but the ball bounced short of the base and skipped into centerfield. The runner stayed on his feet and sprinted to third, where I waited.

Team A's centerfielder scooped up the ball and threw a missile that made a loud pop when it struck the third baseman's glove. He applied a perfect tag to the foot of the sliding runner. I waited until the third baseman picked the baseball out of his glove.

"Out!"

I returned to home plate. Not a sound came from the instructors until the next hitter approached the plate. Morris whispered something to him through the fence. I prepared for anything.

The hitter ignored six pitches. On the seventh one, he bunted. The ball went a couple feet in front of home plate. The catcher grabbed the ball and threw it over the first baseman's head because the batter had run inside the foul line. It was the same situation I had had during my first game at Christiana. The batter continued to second while Team B's right fielder retrieved the ball and ran it back to the infield.

"Time!" I said by the pitcher's mound. I pointed at the man on second. "You're out for interference. You ran inside the baseline to first."

"What?" Ben Carter said, playing his role as team manager. "What's your ruling?"

"He's out for interference. He didn't use the running lane."

"No damn way," Ben said in my face. "You can't call that!"

"He failed to run in the lane, Coach. That's the call."

"Ask your partner for help?"

"No. I got the call."

"Okay, Michael," Ben said, lowering his voice. "Just one thing, at the pro level I'd be addressed as manager or skipper, not coach."

"Yes, sorry," I said. "Old habit."

"Not bad," Ben said with a pat on my shoulder.

I wanted to jump around like somebody who had won the lottery, but played it cool. Act casual. It was just another day on the ball field.

I put my mask on and called the next batter to the plate.

I overheard Morris whisper, "Keep an eye on this kid."

I grinned. This time I didn't mind being called kid.

CHAPTER 40

The next morning, I hurried to the Conference Center bleary eyed, and with only a couple minutes to spare. I plopped next to Beth.

"I was getting worried."

"Oh, I'm sorry," I said, sarcastic, "but my roomy woke me at three in the morning to brag about his evening with some girl stupid enough to get into his van. He had, in his words, a *rockin* good time."

"Jealous?" she said with a laugh.

"What? No. I can't believe it. And the *snoring*. I need earplugs."

"He must not need much sleep. He was here when I arrived."

"I know. He comes in late and gets up early. I don't know how he does it."

"Well, if it doesn't get any better, talk to Matt."

"I don't know. I don't want to be a snitch. Besides, part of the job involves traveling and living with a partner."

"You won't be snitching. You need your sleep."

"I'll think about it," I said as the screen came down and the lights went off.

***

An overcast sky greeted us at the Daytona Speedway Baseball Facility. Class assembled on Field 1. We did our warm up exercises and umpire calisthenics, and then ran four laps. After a brief rest, we divided into our groups.

Joseph McKinney of the Triple-A International League arrived on Field 3 with two male interns.

"What happened to Morris?" Ken Dillard asked.

"He's with another group," Joe said. "You weren't expecting the same instructor every day, were you?"

"Well, no," Ken sighed. "I guess not."

"How can each instructor evaluate you if you have the same one everyday?"

"Forget I mentioned it."

Joseph taught us the proper way to leave our position behind home plate and make a call at third base. It was the same instruction I had received from Randy. "The mask comes off, then you jog about half way down and outside the third base line. Michael did an excellent job of this yesterday." My classmates looked at me. I couldn't help but smile. "Watch the play unfold in front of you. If the runner from first heads to third, you cover the base."

On a rotating basis, one student at a time crouched behind home plate while another stood in as the batter and another played the runner on first base. From the mound, Joseph pretended to pitch a ball. The batter swung with no bat in his hand and ran to first. The runner on first kept going to third. The home plate umpire practiced covering third base. By lunch, we were exhausted from all the running. I scolded myself again for not using the autumn months to get into better shape.

At lunch, Beth and I sat on the grass and split a large ham and cheese sub.

"Isn't it interesting," I said between bites, "that it's only our second day and routine has already set in?"

"Are you a student of human behavior?"

"No," I said, opening a bottle of water. "Just something I noticed."

"I'm umpiring the fourth inning on Field 3. Can you watch me and tell me what you think?"

"I can. I don't umpire until the sixth, and I got the bases."

"Good. Be honest."

"I will."

***

Start of the fourth inning, I stood in left field. Beth emerged from her separate bathroom in the locker room and arrived in full gear. She stood along the third base line. Like she had said, with the equipment on, she looked male.

Oh, crap. Robert Strauss stood next to her and tucked his hands behind his back. He stuck his chest out like a proud rooster.

"One more pitch!" Beth said, pointing.

Her soprano caused some snickering among the student-players and those seated in the bleachers. Some may have laughed from disrespect, but I believe most reacted from the sheer oddity of hearing a female voice come from a baseball umpire.

Robert jogged to his position behind first base and shook hands with Jerry Aliva.

Beth put her mask on and got behind the catcher. "Let's have a batter."

A hitter stepped into the left-handed batter's box. Matt Fogel, Wes Clinton and Joseph McKinny sat at the instructors' table. The pitcher started his delivery. Beth crouched. The ball pierced the middle of the strike zone.

264

"Strike!"

"Louder!" Wes said.

Louder? I heard her fine.

Beth called seven pitches. After each one, Wes repeated his criticism. I had to wonder if he had a prejudice against women umpires.

When the batter was free to swing, he lined out to the first baseman.

"Out," Robert said in a deep baritone that echoed.

"I heard that," Wes said.

Stupid old man, what did he want? Beth couldn't help the voice she had anymore than Robert could take credit for his.

Ken Dillard stepped into the right handed batter's box. Our pitcher threw a slow pitch inside that hit Ken on the leg. Beth awarded him first base. Robert shifted to the infield with Jerry Aliva at his side.

"Hey, ump," Morris Tandy said from the first base dugout, "the batter never moved. He has to make *some* effort to get out of the way."

"He moved," Beth said through her mask.

"He did? Really? It must've only been a hair on his arm because I didn't see anything."

"That's the call, Skipper."

Next batter, when permitted to swing, hit a sinking line drive to right-center field.

"Going!" Robert said, running to the outfield to judge a possible diving catch.

Robert had made the right decision, for a competitive baseball game. Our centerfielder, however, wasn't about to dive and risk injury. He stopped and let the baseball land in front of him. He then swiped at the ball in a half-hearted effort to catch it on the bounce, obviously missing it on purpose. The ball bounced past him. I laughed at his poor acting job as he gave chase.

Ken passed second base and reached third. He should score, but Jerry Aliva yelled at him to stop. The hitter sprinted for a triple. When the third baseman caught the ball from the outfielder he had two runners standing on his base. He tagged them both. There was a long pause, with everyone looking at Beth.

"What's the call?" Jerry said. Robert arrived and Jerry yelled at both of them. "What's the call?"

"The lead runner's entitled to the base," Beth said.

"Are you sure?" Jerry said.

"Yes," Beth said.

"Is that the call?" Jerry asked Robert.

"The lead runner is entitled to the base," Beth said. She pointed at the trailing runner. "You're out."

"Yes," Robert said. "That's the correct call."

"Fine," Jerry said. Then he addressed Beth. "It's your call, but you never gave a signal or said anything. I shouldn't have to ask. You know the rule. Enforce it."

"Yes, sir," Beth said with a frown.

Jerry took the baseball from the third baseman and walked it to the pitcher. He spoke to all. "There's a fine line between calling a play too fast and calling it too slow. Never call it too fast. There's always a pause. But that pause cannot drag on too long. Otherwise, the fans, the players, coaches and managers will think you're unsure of yourself, and that can *never* happen. Know the rules. Make the call decisively."

Robert whispered something to Beth.

"What?" she said, eyes and mouth wide open.

"What did you say to her?" Jerry said, storming off the mound.

Robert looked to the ground. He shifted uneasy on his feet.

"I asked you a question," Jerry said in Robert's face. "What did you say to her?"

Matt Fogel, Wes Clinton and Joseph McKinny joined the scene.

Robert confessed. "I said thank you for making me look bad."

"What?" Jerry said. "Oh, my God, you didn't say that, did you?"

"I did, sir."

"You're unbelievable," Jerry said. He pointed a finger within an inch of Robert's face "The only one making you look bad is *you*! Don't you *ever* disrespect your partner! Is that clear?"

"Yes, sir."

"What? I can't hear you."

"Yes, sir!"

"Five laps right now," Matt said, "and then go sit in the locker room until I come talk to you."

Robert ran the laps. Beth completed the inning alone. I then sat with her in the bleachers after I finished my inning of work.

"Well," I said, trying to make light of the situation, "you're now acquainted with my roommate."

"That arrogant S.O.B. I should've punched him. No wonder you dislike him."

"How are you holding up?"

"I need a drink. Can you believe what he did?"

"He paid a price."

"I know, but if he can't work with me, he shouldn't be out there."

"Agreed."

"I should've punched him."

"No," I said with a laugh. "The instructors handled it. Did they talk to you about it later?"

"Matt did. He was nice about it. He told me to let him know if Robert does anything in retaliation."

"Maybe they'll expel him. Then I'll get a good night's

sleep."

"Jerry's right, though. I waited too long. I know the rule, but with all these eyes watching me, I second-guessed myself. That's my problem, Michael. I'm hesitating with everything. I'm hesitating to answer the exam questions. I'm waiting too long to make calls. I can't believe how nervous I am in front of all these people. I've never been like this before. I'm a teacher, for God's sake. I speak in front of people all the time. I'm a softball umpire. Why am I so freaked out by this place?"

"I don't know. I wish I could help you with that."

"You can't. It's my problem."

We sat quiet and watched the practice game in front of us. Then for some reason, I decided to show off. "Not to confuse you, but there is a situation when the lead runner is out with two runners on the same base."

"Oh, great," she said, throwing her arms up, "thanks for telling me."

"Section 7.04 mandates that the lead runner is out if the trailing runner is forced."

Beth stared. "Are you telling me you know the rule book by heart?"

"I've been reading it for years."

"Unbelievable," she said, sighing. "But it wasn't a force play."

"Exactly. So you made the right call."

"Yeah," she said with a moan, "a little too slow. Wes hates me, probably from what I said in the van from the airport."

"Just because you asked about bars?"

"Well, it did start us off on the wrong foot."

"Stop torturing yourself. It's over. There's another game tomorrow. Lesson learned. Move on."

"Easy for you to say. You haven't been a big screw up like me. You're so confident. You're a damn natural at this. You really are."

"No," I said humble.

"Yes, you are. They ask a question, you know the answer immediately. Then on the field, you seem to know what to do and where to be without thinking."

"I anticipate."

"No, it's more than that. It's an instinct. You're a step ahead of everybody else."

"Well, thank you for saying so."

"Thank you for listening," she said, retrieving her cell phone from a pant pocket. "Excuse me. I need to call Danny."

Beth moved to a higher seat to have a private conversation with her husband. Her voice broke and I knew she was crying. I wanted to hug her and console her, but that wasn't my place. Then I wondered if I'd ever experience what Beth and Danny felt. Did I hurt my chances at love by becoming a professional umpire? After all, even in the minors, I'd travel about the country and be away from home for weeks at a time. What woman wanted to deal with that? Then again, nine of the instructors had a wife, and eight had children, so it was possible.

CHAPTER 41

Sunday was our only day off. Beth and I met at the hotel's restaurant and grabbed our breakfast from the buffet. Then we went to a Laundromat about three blocks away, each with a bag of clothes. I ironed my pants and shirts daily, but they, along with my blue jeans, underwear and socks, needed refreshing.

We stuffed our clothes into separate front-loading washers, paid the machine and then waited on a sofa. I watched the news on television while Beth picked up a celebrity magazine from a stack left on a coffee table and flipped through the pages.

"Any plans for the rest of the day?" she asked.

"No, not really."

"Well, some of us have put a study group together. You know, to help us pass all these tests. You certainly don't need it, but if you'd like to sit in, we're meeting this afternoon in the Conference Room, and probably will in the evenings too."

"Good idea," I said. "I'd love to sit in."

After the Laundromat, I returned to my room with my bag of folded clothes and a few hanging items slung over my shoulder. Robert laid on his bed and watched a

National Football League playoff game. There were two open beer cans on his nightstand and one in his hand.

Robert belched. "I can't believe you're hanging out with that dyke."

"She happens to be married to a man named Danny. And her name's Elizabeth."

He made a face. "She has no right to be here. She'll take a job away from someone more deserving."

"Like you?" I said, stuffing my underwear and socks in a drawer.

"Well, let's face it. She'll never make it to the majors, so what is she trying to prove? They should send her home and stop wasting everybody's time."

"She paid her tuition and has every right to be here."

Robert moaned. "She can't stand up to men. Hell, she sounds like a mouse out there. This job is for men and men only." He belched again.

"Don't blame her because you got yelled at," I said, wanting to throw him off the balcony. "What happened the other day was your own fault."

"She needs to go," he said.

I grabbed my copy of the rule book and left, slamming the door. I joined Beth and met four young men who sat together in a circle in the Conference Room.

"God, I hate tests," Greg Kendricks of Seattle, Washington said, squirming in his chair. "And there's so many scenarios to figure out."

"I know," Beth aside, skimming through the rule book. "That's the difficult thing about it. Keeping it all straight in my head."

"I'm going to fail if I don't stop over-thinking," Vincent Storey of Watertown, Vermont said.

"I know what you mean," Allan Frick of Lexington, Kentucky said. "This is a lot harder than I expected."

"So," I said, "what should we review?"

"I got yelled at for missing a couple balks," Allan said.

"Okay," I said, opening the 130 page paperback book, "let's look at Section 8, which governs the pitcher."

"You know the sections by heart?" Vincent said, his eyes wide.

"I know, right?" Beth said. "I said the same thing."

"Well," Greg said, sarcastic, "aren't you special?"

"Greg," Beth said. "Michael's here to help us learn. I suggest you let him."

"Sorry," Greg said. "No offense intended."

"Okay," I said. "For laughs, let's look at Section 8.04." Everyone opened their book. I read aloud, "*When the bases are unoccupied, the pitcher shall deliver the ball to the batter within twelve seconds after he receives the ball. Each time the pitcher delays the game by violating this rule, the umpire shall call Ball.*"

"Now," Beth said, "when is that rule ever enforced?"

"That would be never," Vincent said.

"Think how much faster the game would be," Allan said, "if it were."

"Yeah," Beth said, "maybe they should have a time clock like they have in basketball. Put it behind the backstop so the pitcher and base ump can see it. If it hits zero, call a ball. Maybe even use it with runners *on* base."

"Sounds good in theory," I said, "but it would really give an unfair advantage to base stealers. As the clock ticked to zero, they wouldn't be worried about a pick off throw and could get a great jump."

"Well, something really needs to be done," Allan said. "Pitchers really slow the game down once there's base runners."

"Yes," Vincent said. "It would be nice if they just got the sign from the catcher and threw the ball. Then maybe the games wouldn't take three hours."

"Sometimes it's the batter's fault," Beth said. "Do they really need to step out of the box after every pitch and adjust their batting glove, their helmet, their shirt tail and grab their crotch?"

Everyone laughed.

"Okay," I said, "the balk rule, section 8.05."

CHAPTER 42

At the end of the second week, sixteen students had quit, Ken Dillard among them. He said he hadn't expected the tough exams and almost boot-camp environment.

For me, I couldn't wait for each day to begin. I believed I stood among the top of the class. I scored perfect on the exams and received many "not bads" from the instructors. Fellow students complimented me. Even so, I couldn't relax. My rivals were clear. The better umpires had authoritative body language, the instructors tended to watch them more, yell at them more and talk to them off the field. My margin for error was so small that one mistake could doom my chances.

I had met each student, but didn't always remember their names. Among them were a couple lawyers, a civil engineer, pizza shop owner, bookstore employee, janitor, chemist, elementary school principal, bus driver, former soldier, Coast Guard member, police officer, landscaper, and several unemployed. Not all were Americans. I met an Australian, a Canadian and an Irishman.

Larry Dunn of Peoria, Illinois had been an umpire in

274

Double-A for two years when his wife demanded he get a regular job or a divorce. Larry took an accounting position with a trucking company. The marriage ended a year later. The poor man had to start the process from scratch. There was no credit for time served.

Not all students wanted to turn pro. A couple guys from Pennsylvania considered umpire school a "unique vacation, like baseball fantasy camp." Several others were content to umpire school ball and summer leagues, but they wanted to improve their skills. There were several presidents of youth organizations who wanted to learn so that they could better train their own umpires.

Surprisingly, there were students who eliminated themselves from contention by being slackers. I couldn't express it any other way. There was down time, and rather than grab a glove or bat and help out during a practice game, some guys stayed in the bleachers. They complained there was too much running. They came to umpire, nothing else. I couldn't believe it, and trust me, the instructors noticed. Well, it was their loss, but I couldn't understand why they were here. It must be nice to throw away three-thousand dollars.

Along with the study group, Beth and I started gathering with other professional wannabes on Field 1 after class was dismissed. One night we just tossed baseballs to each other. Another evening we practiced calling plays at first base. We helped each other call pitches behind home plate. Other times, we just talked.

"I don't want to waste a minute," I said to a group of seven. "I love everything they're throwing at us, but I hate these imaginary drills, when we're told to simulate a situation on the field. I'm so used to following a *real* ball, I have trouble when the instructor says, 'imagine that the catcher is standing in the infield while the ball is in left field. Where do you position yourself if the throw goes up the line between third and home and the catcher might collide with the base runner?' I hate that. I'm so used to thinking on my toes and reacting."

"I forgot to take my mask off," Clay Skelton of Bangor, Maine said. "I *never* make that mistake. But these instructors are so far up our ass, I get nervous and forget the most simple things."

"I guess they're so used to getting yelled at," Bill Vargas of Cheyenne, Wyoming said, "that this is their chance to yell back. It seems they scream more at the simple mistakes than a blown call."

"When you think about it," I said, "this entire process is a job interview, a five week job interview."

***

Of course, Mother Nature interrupted the routine. There were a couple rainy days. Field work was cancelled and we spent the day in the Conference Room, going over sections of the rule book, watching video of real situations that had happened in a game and discussing what the umpire had done right or wrong. And we took more than one test. The groans were plentiful, especially when one test focused on equipment and the size of the playing field. Such as, what were the legal parameters of a first baseman's mitt? What was the circumference of a baseball? What were the dimensions of home plate? What was the distance between home plate and second base?

"You've gotta be kidding," someone said in the back of the room.

"Do I look like I'm joking?" Matt said, pounding on the lectern. "Who said that?"

The young man raised his hand tentatively.

"Turn your test paper in," Matt said. "You get a zero."

276

CHAPTER 43

"All right," Morris Tandy said from behind the pitcher's mound, "I want groups C, E, F, J and K to form a line behind home plate." They did. "Group D, stand by first base. You'll alternate amongst yourselves and be the first base umpire." He picked up a baseball and addressed the students at home plate. "When I say go, the lead person will run full speed to first. You'll be the batter-runner. I'll be the fielder attempting to throw you out. Jose, you're up. There's nobody on, so get into position."

Jose Ramirez stood behind first base. A male intern with a first baseman's mitt stood next to the bag.

Morris looked toward home plate and yelled, "Go."

A classmate sprinted to first.

Jose moved to the infield and established the ninety-degree angle from the base and the expected throw. Morris held the ball until the runner was just a couple strides from first. Then he threw it quick. The intern put a foot on the base and stretched as far as he could, opening the mitt to receive the baseball. The runner's foot almost landed on the bag simultaneous to the baseball smacking into the glove.

"Safe!"

Matt Fogel and Wes Clinton had watched the play from the first base coach's box and they gave the out signal. Jose frowned and shook his head.

"Get ready," Morris said. "You're not done."

Jose had a dozen more chances and Morris timed each throw to make the play at first base as tight as possible. According to Matt and Wes, Jose made nine correct calls.

"Michael," Morris said, "you're next."

"Bring it on."

"Go."

The runner, who happened to be Beth, bore down at full speed, but I wasn't concerned about her. I moved into position without taking my eyes off Morris. Nothing happened without the baseball. As the runner drew near, Morris got into his throwing stance. He whipped his arm forward. The baseball never left his hand. I never looked at first.

"Not bad," Morris said with a devilish grin. He then addressed the class. "Never assume anything. Just because the play is at first base doesn't mean it'll happen there. You never know what might happen. They'll be errors committed, they'll be players who forget how many outs there are, even players who throw to the wrong base. Never *assume*, and *always, always*, keep your eyes on the ball."

I stood behind first base and suppressed a smile. Morris had tried to trick me and failed. I had to have scored points on that one.

"Go," Morris said.

The runner sprinted. I watched Morris as I moved to the infield. This time he released the baseball. I focused on the bag. The runner's foot slammed onto the base just prior to hearing the *pop* of the baseball in leather.

"Safe!"

I looked at Matt and Wes and they gave the safe signal.

I returned to my position behind first base and again suppressed a smile. Yes, I had done well, but it wasn't time to celebrate. It was my *job* to get the calls right. I had to act as if I did this everyday, and hopefully, someday I would.

I had fifteen plays at first base. I got credited with fourteen correct. The final play involved a split decision. I called the runner out. Wes had the runner safe and Matt had him out. Morris broke the tie against me.

"Oh come on," I said. "You just don't want me to have a perfect score."

"Maybe," Morris said with a grin.

"Not bad," Matt and Wes said.

When we broke for lunch, Beth came toward me, but backed off as Matt Fogel pulled me aside.

"Let's walk and talk," he said. "You're nineteen, right?"

"Turned nineteen in November."

"I'm hearing good things about you."

"Thank you, sir."

"No, thank you. You're very mature for your age. You have the right attitude. Good judgment. You handle yourself well on the field. You have the positioning down, you have a good eye, and you know the rules. I'm not often impressed by someone your age. I assume you're pursuing a pro career."

"Yes, sir. I want this very badly. Like a lot of kids, I wanted to be a player, but that was a pipe dream. Yet there's something even better about being an umpire. I love how I'm in command on the field, and have all eyes on me when they're waiting for the call."

"Yes, there is a leadership role to the job. I also see that you have the passion. But an umpire must balance that zeal with humility. The fans don't buy tickets to root for the umpires. The best games are the ones when we're not noticed."

"Yes, sir, I understand."

"Also, I'm happy to see that Beth has you as a friend. It's not easy for women to go through the program. We try and make it a great experience, but they can often feel out of place and alone. So thank you for that."

"You're welcome," I said as we shook hands.

After Matt left, Beth joined me. "What did he say?"

"He likes me," I said, sticking my chest out and grinning. "He really likes me. You know, Beth, this is going to happen."

"Was there ever any doubt?"

"And he thanked me for being your friend."

"Yeah, I told him what a great listener you are. Right after I told him I'm not pursuing a pro career."

"What?"

"I talked it over with my husband last night. I mean, I was all excited to try this, but lately I've been wondering why I came. I think that's why I'm so nervous. My body is telling me this isn't for me. I think I came here because I'm unemployed and felt sorry for myself. I needed to do something positive. But I really miss teaching."

"Are you quitting?"

"Oh, no. I'll stick it out. I can use it as education credits. We're required to have a certain number of credits each year to keep our certification. And it'll look good on my resume for the softball association. I'll teach and umpire softball. That's what I really want to do. I just need to get on the ball and find a job."

"Then that's why you're here," I said. "Coming here helped you find out what you truly love to do."

CHAPTER 44

In the third week, we still had practice games after lunch, but following them the facility hosted one or two high school or college games. The routine was the same. Student umpires worked one inning, their every action scrutinized by the instructors. Students not umpiring watched from the bleachers. These were the only baseball games in recorded history where the spectators cheered for the umpires.

I arrived at Field 1 in full gear ready to call the seventh inning of a game between Mainland High and Seabreeze High. Mainland led 8-2.

David Chance of Davenport, Iowa stood next to me and asked, "Nervous?"

"A little. I haven't umpired a competitive game since last July."

"We shouldn't expect anything bizarre, right? The instructors can't interfere."

"They can't interfere, but you should always be ready for anything."

David and I announced ourselves to Morris Tandy, Wes Clinton, Joseph McKinney and retired umpire Conrad Post, all seated at the instructor's table. We then took the field along with Seabreeze High. Seabreeze had a tall and muscular right handed hurler. I watched him during his warm up tosses to gauge the speed of his pitches. The past two weeks I had called pitches from students, interns and machines that even I could hit. This dude fired bullets.

"One more pitch!"

After the final warm up throw, I put my mask on and stood behind Seabreeze's catcher. Mainland's hitter stepped into the right handed batter's box. I raised my hand.

"Play!"

I was home. This was definitely where I belonged. Then to my surprise, I heard a rhythmic chant and simultaneous feet banging coming from the third base bleachers. "*Bring it on….Bring it on.*"

Wow, people were rooting for *me*. I had support. I had friends. My eyes watered, but I kept my composure.

"What do you know," Morris Tandy said, "he has his own cheering section."

Seabreeze's pitcher delivered from the wind-up. I crouched behind and over the catcher's left shoulder and created my imaginary rectangle above home plate. The baseball spun fast and furious at me. The catcher's mitt flashed into my sightline and the ball pounded into leather.

"Ball," I said, and turned the appropriate wheel on my indicator.

The half inning was easy. Mainland went down one, two, three. As they took the field, I removed my mask and looked at the third base bleachers. Beth grinned and waved. Seated with her were guys from our study group and other young men that hung out with us after class.

"I see you have some fans," Matt said on approach.

"Yes, sir. That was quite a surprise."

"Well," Matt said with a pat on the back, "bring it on, son."

"Yes, sir," I said with a grin, ready to burst.

***

Bottom of the seventh, Seabreeze's first hitter got on base from a walk. David Chance moved to the infield.

"Oh, come on," Mainland's coach said to his pitcher. "You have a six run lead. Let them hit it."

Seabreeze's next batter, a righty, swung late on a one ball and two strike fast ball and hit a hard and low liner toward the second baseman. David reacted late and the ball struck him in the ankle.

"Dead ball!" I said, removing my mask and stepping from behind the plate. "Batter first base. Runner, second base."

"Oh, you gotta be kidding," Mainland's coach said. He removed his cap and scratched his scalp. "Come on, ump. That was a potential double play ball. You're not supposed to be a statue."

David said nothing. Prior to the next hitter, I gave David a thumb's up to remind him we had an infield fly rule situation. He responded in kind.

Seabreeze's next batter, a lefty, then hit a lazy pop up above shortstop.

"Infield fly! Infield fly!" I said, mask off and right fist in the air. "Batter's out!"

The ball was caught. Mainland's coach breathed a sigh of relief.

Seabreeze's next hitter stood almost motionless in the right-handed batter's box as I called strike on the first two pitches.

Baseball axiom dictated: *Never let a batter get a base hit on a 0-2 pitch*. The ball should be thrown high, or low and outside, close enough to tempt the nervous batter, but never a strike.

283

Mainland's pitcher delivered from the stretch. I crouched. The baseball spun at me, and dead center in the strike zone. *Ting.* Seabreeze's hitter crushed the ball into right-center field, between the outfielders and it bounced to the fence. I moved half way between third and home. The runner from second base scored. The runner from first made it to third. The batter stood on second with a double.

"What're you doing?" Mainland's coach said. He paced and scratched his scalp harder. "An 0-2 pitch? Come on!"

Seabreeze's next hitter received a walk to load the bases. Their players were on their feet. They put their caps on inside-out and backwards as "rally caps."

"Time, ump," Mainland's coach said.

"We have time," I said.

The coach held a meeting on the mound with his pitcher and infielders. I let him talk for a moment, and then approached the mound.

"Let's break it up, Coach," I said.

"I don't have anybody warming up," the coach told his pitcher. "It's your game to finish."

Seabreeze's next hitter, a righty, received ball one, then ball two.

"Unbelievable," Mainland's coach said, shaking his head.

I couldn't help but smile.

The pitcher walked off the mound and took a moment to compose himself. I felt the next pitch would determine the game. If the count went to ball three, Seabreeze would rally. If the pitcher threw a strike, his team would prevail.

Mainland's pitcher delivered from the stretch. The baseball crossed the plate at the top of the batter's knees.

"Strike!"

"Come on, ump," Seabreeze's coach said. "That was low. If you're going to call that a strike, we'll need to use golf clubs."

Next pitch, *ting*, a line drive was caught by Mainland's third baseman. The runner on second strayed too far from the bag. The third baseman threw to second.

"Out!" David said.

Mainland's players celebrated their victory and jogged from the field.

"This is why I'm losing my hair," their coach said.

"I think you need to give that kid more lessons on the strike zone," Seabreeze's coach said to Matt.

"He knows the strike zone," Matt said.

"Then he should apply it correctly."

"He does," Matt replied, irritated.

I appreciated Matt defending me, but hoped he knew he didn't have to. I could've handled the coach's criticism.

"Good job," David said as we left the field.

"How's your ankle?"

"A little sore. I can't believe the ball hit me. I hope they don't deduct points for that."

"Well, at least you didn't cost them the game. I had visions of Seabreeze rallying to win and Mainland's coach blaming you."

"Trust me, I had the same feeling."

CHAPTER 45

During the fourth week, I had the first inning of a pick-up game on Field 3. I arrived in full gear wondering if my chicken salad sandwich had been tainted. My stomach rumbled and my face broke out in sweat.

"You all right?" my base ump, Terence Sauer, asked.

"Yeah," I said with a burp. "I'm fine."

"You look pale."

The first batter for Team A ignored five pitches before he was told to swing. He hit a ground ball to the second baseman who threw to first to complete the out. Conrad Post, who stood with Terence, told the batter to stay at first.

The next hitter swung after five pitches. He hit a weak grounder back to the pitcher, who threw to second. The shortstop caught the ball and threw to first to complete the double play. Even so, Conrad had the base runners stay on the field.

"First and second, no outs," he said.

I suppressed another burp and signaled Terence that we had an infield fly rule situation. I then called five pitches on the next batter before he hit a pop up above third. I stepped from behind the plate, removed my mask and raised my right arm. "Infield fly! If fair! Infield Fly! If fair!"

Team B's third baseman did a horrible acting job of letting the baseball hit his glove and then bounce to the dirt behind him. The baseball landed a few inches inside the foul line and in front of the bag. He bent to pick it up and kicked the ball toward the third base dugout. The two runners advanced to the next base by the time the third baseman retrieved the ball. The young man who had batted stood on first.

"Time," I said, and then pointed at the student-player on first base. "You're out by rule. You and you," meaning the runners on second and third, "stay where you are."

"Proper call, ump," Conrad said, "but I want the bases loaded."

My stomach made a horrible noise, like a growling animal. I should ask to be excused, but this was my time to show the instructors my abilities and I wouldn't have too many more opportunities.

"No outs," Conrad said. "No outs."

Just as the pitcher started his delivery to the next hitter, all three base runners took off. The pitcher stopped.

"Time! Time!" I said, jumping out from behind the plate and waving my arms. "I have a balk! All runners advance one base!"

"Good call," Jerry Aliva said, managing Team A from the first base dugout.

Wes Clinton paced in front of his dugout, and held his tongue.

Joseph McKinney, from the instructor's table, yelled at Terence. "Come on man, an obvious balk."

"Yes, sir," Terence said.

Second and third, no outs, and I felt a sharp pain in

my gut and almost doubled-over.

"You all right?" Beth asked, ready to bat next.

"Yeah, I'm fine."

"You're really sweating, and it's not that warm out."

"I'm all right."

Beth stood in the right-handed batter's box. I called six pitches before she got the command to swing away. On the pitch, the runner on second took off. The runner on third stayed. The catcher rose and threw to third. Team B's third baseman caught the ball. The base stealer stopped a few feet short of the bag, turned and ran back toward second and got himself into a run down.

Mask off, I stood half way between third and home. Terence stayed with the base stealer, running back and forth. The runner on third took off. The second baseman had the ball. He ignored the runner coming back his way and threw home to intercept the possible scoring chance. The catcher got the ball. I got into position. For safety reasons, collisions at home plate were not permitted. The base stealer slid feet first.

"Out!"

The catcher then threw the ball to third. The runner from second neither slid nor stopped. He rounded third and kept coming. Team B's third baseman caught the ball and went to throw. The runner that had tried to score remained on the ground.

"Get out of the way!" I said, almost grabbing him by his tee-shirt.

He scrambled to his feet and ran. The third baseman threw the ball high to the catcher. He jumped and missed it. The runner went around the catcher and scored. The pitcher retrieved the baseball against the backstop.

"All right," Conrad said from the infield with Terence next to him. "I want the bases loaded, no outs."

Holy crap. Would I ever get off the field?

On the next pitch, *ting*, Beth hit a fly ball to left field. I watched the runner on third. The left fielder purposely dropped the ball and all runners advanced.

Conrad loaded the bases again. "No outs! Hey, Michael, you tired?"

"Bring it on," I said, gritting my teeth and squeezing my ass cheeks together.

Team A's next hitter stood in the right handed batter's box. The pitcher worked from the stretch. Base runners took their leads. The pitcher made a motion to first base to pick off the runner, but the first baseman stood away from the bag, in his regular fielding position, so the pitcher held the ball.

"Balk!" I said, removing my mask and stepping from behind the catcher. "Runners advance one base!"

One run came home. I had runners on second and third.

"Come on, Terence," Morris Tandy said, "that's two balks you missed. Don't leave Michael to make all the calls."

Conrad loaded the bases again and I wanted to kill him. It wouldn't be long before I'd ruin my underwear and embarrass myself in front of the whole class.

Ting, the batter sent a pop up over shortstop.

"Infield fly," I said, wincing in pain.

The shortstop dropped the ball. The runners stayed.

"Infield fly, infield fly," I said with my right fist raised. "I think that's out number twenty."

Everyone within earshot laughed.

"Twenty outs, eh?" Morris said.

"I'm just guessing," I said with some anger in my voice. "My indicator stops after two."

"You're probably right," Morris said.

Bases remained loaded.   Team A's next batter hit a

ground ball to the pitcher. He scooped it up and threw home for one out. The catcher threw to first to complete the double play. I looked at Conrad, hoping to get off the field. He paused for a moment, smiled, and looked ready to extend the half inning even longer.

"All right," he said, "change sides."

"Excuse me," I said to the instructors.

I bolted from the field to the locker room and made it to a bathroom stall seconds before the worst *ass-explosion* of my life.

CHAPTER 46

Two days before evaluations, I reported to Field 2 in full gear to umpire the fourth inning of a college match up between Homestead Valley State and Daytona Beach Community College. I waved to Beth in the stands. I greeted my partner, Pete Harding, from Philadelphia, Mississippi.

"I live about thirty miles from the other Philadelphia," I said while we waited behind the backstop.

"Shhhh," he said with a finger to his lips. "I need to get into a zone."

I had worked with an umpire who always wore the same undershirt. Another that never stepped on a foul line. One gentleman, when he worked the bases, took five steps behind first base and drew a line in the dirt with his foot. With no runners on, he stood on that line. There were other umpires who carried a lucky trinket in their pocket, a family heirloom, or they wore something for good luck around their neck. One religious fellow crossed himself before he stepped onto the field. Baseball players had superstitions, but I never realized how many umpires had their own quirks. Then again, so did I, believing in the Baseball Gods.

At the end of the third inning, Pete and I took the field.

"Are you in the zone?" I asked.

"Not funny."

Matt Fogel, Morris Tandy and Jerry Aliva sat at the table behind the backstop, clipboards at the ready. I wished I had the eyesight to read whatever they wrote. I had a near perfect score on the written exams, but I'd have to wait like everyone else on how I scored on the diamond.

Homestead Valley batted with a 5-2 lead. It took only seven pitches for DBCC to record three outs. In the bottom half of the inning, DBCC's first two hitters popped out to shortstop on two consecutive pitches. Pete and I hadn't been on the field ten minutes and we were one out away from completing our session. With only today and tomorrow left to prove my worth, I hoped for something to extend my stay.

DBCC's next batter hit a single to right field. Next hitter, on a one ball, two strike count, sent the ball over the head of Homestead's first baseman and it bounced along the fair side of the right field line. Mask off, I moved toward third base. The runner from first turned the corner at second and continued. The right fielder picked up the ball and threw to third. I positioned myself for the call.

Homestead's third baseman, glove on his left hand, stepped to the infield side of the base and caught the ball at his ankles. The runner slid past his left side feet first. The third baseman did a swipe tag to the runner's calf.

"Out!"

Inning over, I spun around and jogged toward the

exit gate by the third base dugout.

DBCC's coach cut me off. His eyes bulged, his body shook, his arms waved about and he spat. "Bullshit! What the hell are you looking at? You can't be serious! What kind of call is that?" He boiled over and became incoherent. "Wh..no…bull. tis…non… ye…what? Get…fu..real!"

"Coach," I said, seriously worried that he'd have a heart attack, "he got him on the leg."

DBCC's coach took a deep breath to collect his senses. He put a hand along each side of his face and formed his words loud and clear. "But he *dropped* the ball! My guy was lying on it!"

What? Oh, no.

I turned. Homestead had cleared the field. DBCC's player sat on third base with his arms folded around his knees.

"Pete," I said as he joined me, "did you see the ball come out of the third baseman's glove?"

"No, I was watching the runner at second."

"Where's the baseball?" I asked with sweat seeping from every pore, my heart pounding.

"It's on the mound."

"Yeah," DBCC's coach screamed, "it's on the mound, God damn it! They ain't stupid! They tossed it there as they ran off the field! You didn't see that either!"

"Inning over," I said, trying to sound convincing.

"You son of a bitch!" the coach said. "He dropped the ball and you weren't even looking! That's just incompetent! It's inexcusable!"

I ejected him. He got in my face, pointing a stiff finger within inches of my eyes, and released a cussing tirade that I just stood there and took.

Matt Fogel arrived and got between us. "Roy, that's

enough, calm down."

It took all my strength not to run crying from the field. Not because of what the coach screamed, but because I had committed a cardinal sin of umpiring and it would ruin my chances at getting hired.

"Matt," DBCC's coach said, "we play these games as a courtesy to your school. We know they're just students. But this is incompetence! *In-com-pe-tence!*"

"Put your team on the field," Matt said.

"I'll put my foot up his ass!"

"One more outburst," Matt said, "and you're forfeiting the game."

DBCC's coach thought about it for a moment. Then he yelled at his team. "Go on, get out there! Joe, take over. Seems I've been ejected for telling the truth."

Matt gave me a sympathetic pat on the shoulder. I couldn't look at him. I had to get off the field before the flood gates opened.

Beth joined me on the long walk to my car. I couldn't look at her either. I thought about driving home. Why stay? I had been humiliated in front of the entire school and committed an unforgivable error.

"Michael," Beth said, "you all right?"

I struggled to breathe, my chest hurt and my lower lip shook.

"Michael?"

"Please," I said, putting a hand up, "leave me alone."

I reached my car, unlocked the driver's side door and got in with my equipment still on. I grabbed the steering wheel and put my face between my arms and cried like I had never cried in my life. Just two days from graduating and I had destroyed my dream.

CHAPTER 47

On the final day of school, I stood behind first base with Wes Clinton on Field 1 and prepared to umpire the third inning of a pick-up game. There was no high school or college match up scheduled because a graduation banquet was set to take place at six o'clock in the Conference Center. Attendance at the catered affair was mandatory. Otherwise, I'd skip it. My glaring error had been the talk of the student body and it made me the brunt of jokes. "See the ball yet," some teased. Robert Strauss called me, "Quick call McGraw." Beth was compassionate. The instructors were kind enough not to mention it.

Fortunately, one of baseball's redeeming qualities was that it allowed for a quick recovery. Its game a day season left little time to celebrate a victory, but more important, little time to dwell on a loss or a costly error. A new day had dawned, and a new game, time to forget my mistake and the derogatory comments made by DBCC's coach. I had blown my chance at a pro career, but I still had a job to do.

The first two batters hit routine grounders to shortstop. I called them out at first base.

I then hustled around the infield with the next batter who hit a triple. That was followed by a single, the runner on third scored. On the next pitch, the man on first attempted to steal second. The batter took the strike. The catcher threw to second. The shortstop caught the ball over the bag and applied a quick tag that hit the runner's foot before he reached the base. And yes, I waited for the shortstop to show me he still had possession of the ball.

"Out!"

I heard a mock cheer from a couple classmates in the bleachers, but I left the field able to smile about my performance.

"You all right?" Beth asked when I sat with her in the bleachers.

"Yeah, I'm fine. It's not the end of the world. I'll go home, back to college, umpire games, and then return next year. Who knows, I might even be a better umpire because of it."

"That's the spirit. I was so worried yesterday. You looked like you might kill yourself."

"Well, that was yesterday."

***

That evening, I wore a suit and tie and knocked on Beth's door. She opened it a moment later.

"Wow," I said. "I'm sorry. I thought this was Elizabeth Bridger's room."

Beth wore a full-length, sleeveless red dress and carried a small red purse. She had applied a tiny amount of cosmetics to her face and I smelled an intoxicating perfume.

"Oh, it's me," she said, adjusting my tie. "You look very handsome."

"Wow again. I can't believe the difference."

"Is it too out of character?"

296

"Are you kidding? It's nice."

"I figured we might as well go out in style."

"Good idea. Let's celebrate our friendship, not our failures."

"Agreed."

We took the elevator to the first floor, and then entered a dimly-lit and crowded Conference Center. The rows of tables had been replaced by large circular tables, each with eight place settings and chairs.

Beth and I mingled with other well dressed students and instructors near a cash bar. Everyone looked twice at Beth. "Is that you?" was their standard reaction. She smiled and accepted compliments.

"I can't wait to get out of these clothes and into a pair of jeans," she whispered.

"Oh, don't spoil it. You look fantastic."

She pretended to gag, and then laughed.

At the appointed time, the instructors, some with female companionship, took a seat at one of the long tables on stage. Matt, wearing a tuxedo, stood at the lectern. I half expected the screen to appear with a test question.

"Please be seated," Matt said into the microphone.

There was no assigned seating, but students tended to sit with friends they had made. Beth and I were joined by Jose Ramirez, Sam Pleasant and Terence Sauer. A couple young men from our study group joined us. To my surprise, Robert Strauss occupied the last remaining chair next to me.

"Can you believe he's sitting with us?" Beth said, seated on my other side. "I thought he was Mister Popular."

I just shrugged.

"Welcome to our graduation banquet," Matt said. Light applause. "Let me express my congratulations. Although only eighteen of you will find out tomorrow that you're moving onto professional baseball, it doesn't take away from the fact that you *are* graduates of the Matt Fogel Umpire School."

I joined the applause, but with a heavy heart because I wouldn't be among the lucky eighteen.

"I know my instructors and I got up close and personal with some of you," Matt said. "Maybe too close. We yelled and screamed, but it was for a good reason. We had your best interests at heart. Congratulations and enjoy tonight. You earned it."

Everyone applauded.

Men and women from the catering service delivered garden salads in a small bowl. Water was poured, along with champagne. A couple hundred voices in conversation filled the air.

After salads, the next course consisted of chicken marsala with green beans or a vegetarian alternative. The food was well prepared and tasty, but I was anxious for the event to end.

Following the meal, Matt returned to the microphone. "Let's have a big hand for our servers, the cooks, the bartenders, everyone that helped make this a memorable evening."

The audience obliged.

"As you know," Matt said, "tomorrow is evaluation day. You'll have a final interview, and then you'll be free to leave. For those of you who told us you're interested in a pro career, you'll find out where we ranked you and whether or not you earned a job. But tonight, we like to hand out a few awards." Matt reached inside the lectern and removed a trophy. It was a foot tall, bronze figure of an umpire in full gear. "Receiving the award for first in class is Taylor Jordan."

Taylor had served six years in the marines. He had

the physical presence that would make any player or manager think twice about arguing with him. He marched to the stage under everyone's applause. I couldn't help but think that should be me.

"He was such a kiss ass," Robert said. "He should be First in Class."

Taylor received his trophy and shook hands with Matt. A professional photographer snapped a picture.

"Receiving the award for Second in Class," Matt said, "is James Trefold."

James leapt from his seat and jogged to the stage. There was another handshake with Matt and another photograph.

"And our third award is for Best Return Student," Matt said. "This winner was here two years ago. So come on up here…."

Robert pushed his chair away from the table and started to rise.

"Clay Upshaw," Matt said.

Robert sat. I suppressed a laugh.

"Maybe next year I'll win Best Return Student," I said to Beth.

"And our final award is for the highest grade average on the exams," Matt said.

Oh, really? Perhaps the evening wouldn't be a total loss.

"It's what we like to call The Rule Book Genius Award," Matt continued. "The winner had an average score of 98.5."

"Your grade average should be around that," Beth said, and I agreed.

"And the award goes to," Matt said.

I leaned forward, ready to push my chair back and dash to the stage.

"Michael…."

I lifted my butt off the seat.

"Hopkins."

I slumped in my chair. Robert laughed.

"Don't worry," Beth said, "you'll be in the majors someday and he won't."

CHAPTER 48

Evaluation Day, my appointment was scheduled for 10:45, but I woke at eight because Robert moved about the room packing his clothes. He and I hadn't become friends, so his departure was quick.

"Come see me in the big leagues," he said with a handshake.

I rolled out of bed and showered. I thought about the long drive home and the start of spring semester, and snow on the ground. Last night's email from my parents had included another weather report. Five inches of the white stuff had fallen. I had written about my blunder at third base and their reply appeared to express joy at my failure. *We look forward to you coming home and continuing your education.*

I dressed casual, said goodbye to my temporary home and packed my belongings into my car. I checked out of the hotel, and then Beth and I met for breakfast at the hotel restaurant.

"Are you leaving after your evaluation?" I asked over a plate of pancakes.

"No, I'll wait for you."

"You don't have to."

"I know I don't have to," she said. "I want to. Okay?"

"Okay. Thank you."

"And thank you for helping make this experience better than I could've hoped for. If it weren't for you, I might've quit, but I'm glad I stuck it out. So thank you."

"You're very welcome," I said.

After breakfast, Beth stood in a short line outside the Conference Center. I sat on a chair in the lobby and flipped through a sport's magazine that had been left on a coffee table. My stomach churned and my hands shook and I couldn't understand why. I knew my fate.

Beth waved just before she disappeared behind closed doors. She returned five minutes later.

"How'd it go?"

"They ranked me 43rd in the class."

"Not bad."

"Oh, please," Beth said with a laugh, "I don't ever want to hear those two words together again."

We then sat, browsed magazines and watched fellow students come and go from the Conference Center. Most came out wearing long faces. Some appeared relieved, while a few carried manila envelopes and boasted that they had been hired.

Robert entered the Conference Center at ten-thirty. When he came out, he had a clenched jaw and a red face. His hands were balled into fists.

"He doesn't look happy," I said.

Robert threw open the hotel door and stormed out.

"It's a real shame," Beth said, sarcastic, "it truly is."

"He was so certain he had a job."

"Yeah," Beth chuckled, "a real shame."

As my time approached, I stood and brushed off my

pants.

"Good luck," Beth said. "I want to get a little sun before I leave. So I'll wait for you out on the boardwalk."

"Okay," I said, and got in line behind Jose Ramirez.

"Nervous?" Jose said.

"A little."

"Do you think you made it?"

"No. My grades are good, but that disaster the other day."

"Yeah, that's tough, man. You coming back next year?"

"Absolutely."

Jose's turn came and he entered the Conference Center. I prepared for disappointment so that I wouldn't get emotional in front of the instructors. Be dignified. Listen to their critique. Speak if they ask a direct question. Be formal, all business. Anything else and I might lose it.

Jose emerged a few minutes later with a sullen expression. "They want me to get more experience, and then come back next year."

"Then I'll see you," I said. "Maybe we'll be roommates."

We shook hands and said goodbye. I took a deep breath and then stepped inside. A divider wall had been put in place that cut the Conference Center in half. Using the temporary wall as a backdrop, three long tables were connected, with each instructor seated. Matt occupied the center chair. He had a stack of loose papers in front of him. The interns were present at a couple side tables, joined by four men I had never seen before.

A lone chair waited.

"Mister Briggs," Matt said, pointing at the vacant chair, "have a seat."

303

I did, grabbing the sides of the chair to keep anyone from noticing my shaking hands.

"How are you?" Matt asked with a broad smile.

"Okay."

"Nervous?"

"Yes."

"As you know this is your evaluation. Each instructor and I reviewed your classroom and field work during these five weeks." Matt looked at his notes. "Your exam score is exceptional, 98, second-highest in the class." Light applause from all. "Your knowledge of the game, your awareness on the field, your ability to anticipate were also impressive."

I waited for the "But."

"But, you had an incident the other day that can never happen. Why do you think you made the type of mistake in week five that's made in week one?"

I took a deep breath. "I did a lot of thinking about that. I mean, I had always waited for a play to complete itself. Why didn't I on this occasion? I can only say that I got too cocky and took the play for granted."

"That sounds like a valid conclusion. I hope you learned your lesson."

"Oh, yes, sir."

"Good," Matt said. He became somber. "It's unfortunate. We had ranked you among the top ten. Putting you through to pro ball was a no-brainer."

"I'm sorry," I said, my heart breaking. "I let you all down."

"You let yourself down," Matt said. "You're better than that. We know you're better than that. You're a good young man. You stood out as a leader. You're honest and you have integrity and a sense of fairness. All excellent qualities and what we're looking for."

I wished he'd get to the point. I couldn't hold back

304

the waterworks much longer.

"Yes," Morris Tandy said, interrupting, "he's a fine young man. And I'm betting he learned his lesson. He won't ever make that mistake again. Right, son?"

"Never again, sir."

Matt looked to his right, and then his left. Each instructor smiled.

"That's what we thought," Matt said. "That's why we're willing to overlook the mistake and have you report to the Pirates facility in Brandenton, Florida in two weeks. You'll receive further training and orientation into the New York-Penn League."

"What?" I said. I stared for a moment while my brain confirmed what my ears had heard. "I'm hired?"

"We ranked you twelfth in class," Matt said, standing and extending a hand. "And since you live in the mid-Atlantic region, we decided to start you in the New York-Penn League. Congratulations."

I stood in a daze, shook Matt's hand, but still doubted my senses. "This isn't a joke?"

Matt and the instructors applauded.

"It's real?" I said. I put my hands over my mouth to keep from screaming. My eyes watered and my heart pounded.

"Go see Mister Greenbank," Matt said, pointing at a portly gentleman in a gray suit who sat at a corner table with the interns.

I raised my arms like a football referee signaling touchdown. I jumped around like some crazy game-show contestant who had won the grand prize. "I made it, I made it, I made it, I made it! No kidding?"

"No kidding," Matt said.

"Oh, my God, I made it! I'm hired!"

"You're not on the payroll yet," Mister Greenbank said, holding a pen.

Everyone laughed.

"Sorry, sorry," I said, grabbing a chair next to him.

Mister Greenbank opened his briefcase. He handed me a packet of information about the training facility at Brandenton. Another manila envelope contained details about the New York-Penn League, a Rookie A affiliation that played its games in June, July and August. I also signed a contract and received a benefits package.

"Isn't that less than minimum wage?" I said about the salary.

"Just about," Mister Greenbank said.

I couldn't have cared less about the money, but I could hear Dad question my sanity.

"We'll be in touch," Mister Greenbank said. "Be prepared to work spring training and work harder than you've ever worked in your life."

"Oh, I will, sir. Thank you. This is *so* great."

I shook hands with Matt and each instructor, and heard in return, "Congratulations, Mister Briggs."

I danced out the door with envelopes in hand. Students in line noticed the packets and my ear to ear grin.

"Congratulations," they said. "Good job."

I thanked them, and continued my happy dance to the hotel's exit. I flung open the door. The sun hit my face and the bright blue ocean spread out before me.

Beth sat on a bench, facing the hotel. Our eyes met. She smiled and stood. I started to walk to her, but I had so much energy surging through my body that I took off running, giving Beth the envelopes in passing.

"Michael! What're you doing? Where're you going?"

I ran onto the beach. My sneakers kicked up chunks of sand as I cut in front of a car and ran between two guys who tossed a football. I didn't stop running until I splashed into the Atlantic and a wave slapped me in the chest and almost knocked me over.

"Michael," Beth said at the water's edge, laughing. "Are you crazy? You got in with all your clothes on!"

"Who cares," I said, shivering in the cold water. I jumped up and down with my arms raised. "I did it, Beth! I did it!"

PART 4

GOING FOR HOME

CHAPTER 49

Five minutes to game time, a security guard escorted George Evanshire and me in full gear down a narrow tunnel beneath the stands at Cal Ripken Stadium in Aberdeen, Maryland. We stepped through an open gate by the third base dugout and emerged onto a manicured grass and dirt field. Old Glory flapped in the breeze next to a tall videoboard behind a green fence in right-center field. A black scoreboard resided behind the same fence in left-center. With the blue sky as background, the flash of colors in the bright sunshine stunned and thrilled my eyes. It was as if I had been seeing the world in black and white, and then stepped outside to a glorious explosion of color.

I looked behind the home team's dugout and spotted Austin and his girlfriend Cindy. Next to them were Mom, Dad, Granddaddy William and Grandma Julia. They were part of a packed house of 6,000 spectators.

My family waved. Dad did so with less enthusiasm. He wouldn't be happy until I reached the majors and earned a six-figure salary. Until then, he worried that I'd never make enough money to move out.

At home plate, George and I met the manager for the Aberdeen Ironbirds and the skipper for the Hudson Valley Renegades. The New York-Penn League consisted of fourteen teams from New England to Maryland. Their rosters were populated with young men drafted from college, free agents trying to make it, or talented high school graduates. Like myself, each player had aspirations to climb the ladder to full season A ball, to Double-A, to Triple-A, and the Major Leagues. A player, if good enough, could skip levels on his way to the majors. Not so for an umpire.

I accepted the line-up cards from the two managers and saw a familiar name batting sixth for Aberdeen.

"I don't believe it," I said under my breath. "It can't be."

Led by Aberdeen's manager, we went over the stadium ground rules. Once completed, the starting nine for Aberdeen took their position on the field as the public address announcer introduced them to the audience. The body that belonged to that familiar name jogged to left field.

George wished me good luck and strolled to his position behind first base. I stood along the third base line. The public address announcer introduced the umpires to the spectators. I grinned as my name echoed throughout the stands. It was followed by a loud outburst from Granddaddy William. "You did it!" He, Mom and Grandma Julia stood and clapped. Dad remained seated.

Everyone then stood for an instrumental rendition of the "Star Spangled Banner." I listened to the notes and experienced a mixture of patriotic zeal and the ecstasy of accomplishment. I hadn't made it to the majors yet, but I was on my way.

Following the National Anthem, the audience retook their seats, except for Dad. He stared at me. Then with sincere purpose, he clapped. It was a steady, rhythmic applause that seemed to echo throughout the stadium.

My chest swelled and my eyes watered. I mouthed the words, "Thank you."

He nodded and sat.

I took a deep breath and focused on the business at hand. In just a moment, I'd be responsible for the start and finish of a professional baseball game. The players, managers, coaches and fans counted on me to be fair and impartial. I felt the weight of responsibility on my shoulders, yet welcomed it.

"One more pitch," I said to Aberdeen's hurler.

Hudson Valley's lead-off hitter approached home plate. He carried a *wooden* bat. It was odd how the bat's material signified the difference between amateur and pro ball.

I put my mask on and stood behind Aberdeen's catcher. Hudson Valley's right-handed batter dug in. The pitcher looked in for the sign.

Although I had umpired spring training games, they had been practice. This was it. My debut in professional baseball!

"Play!"

CHAPTER 50

Bottom of the second inning with one out, that player with the familiar name approached the right-handed batter's box.

"How's it going?" Joe Forrester said, grinning. "I heard your name announced and thought, no way, it couldn't be him. But it is. How the hell are you?"

"Just fine," I said through my mask. "I thought you had a scholarship at Virginia."

"I do. I just finished my freshman year. But why wait? I mean, if I'm going to play pro, why wait four years? Let's talk after the game."

"Can't. No fraternizing with the players."

"*Fraternizing*," Joe said, laughing.

Musclehead stepped into the batter's box. I stared at his helmeted profile and remembered the hurtful words and physical abuse he had dealt and how much he had enjoyed it. He had better swing.

Hudson Valley's pitcher delivered from the wind-up. I crouched. The baseball came in fast and thigh high, but veered outside of Joe's strike zone.

"Ball."

No matter what my personal feelings were, I couldn't violate the integrity of the game. The pitch had been close, but it wasn't a strike on any other batter. It wasn't a strike on Joe.

Next pitch, Joe swung overtop a fastball to equal the count at one ball and one strike. He then swung and missed the next two fast balls. He cussed loud enough that people seated around home plate heard him.

I should take great satisfaction in Joe's failure, but didn't. After all, this was baseball. A batter could fail two out of three times at the plate and yet qualify for the Hall of Fame. Whatever Joe and I had been to each other, it had been high school and those days were over.

***

The game progressed at a nice pace. Hudson Valley had a 5-2 lead by the sixth inning. Aberdeen scored one run in their half of the sixth and another in the eighth to cut their deficit to 5-4.

Bottom of the ninth, Aberdeen's first batter hit the first pitch for a single to left. The fans cheered and looked on with hope.

Aberdeen's next batter, on a two-one pitch, smacked a single to center field. Now the fans stood.

The next batter, on a one-one count, put down a perfect sacrifice bunt that moved the runners to second and third. The fans were on their feet, cheering.

Hudson Valley's manager ordered his pitcher to intentionally walk the next hitter to load the bases and set up a possible double play. The game then paused while Hudson Valley brought in a new pitcher.

When play resumed, Aberdeen's batter worked a two ball, two strike count before he hit an "infield fly" caught by Hudson Valley's shortstop. Two outs. A huge groan rose from the standing crowd.

Joe Forrester approached the plate. The announcement of his name over the speakers was followed by another groan from the spectators. Joe had struck out swinging on all three visits to the plate. But the Baseball Gods had set the stage for Joe to redeem himself and tie or win the game with a base hit.

Joe stepped up to the plate. He and I made eye contact. I saw something I never thought I'd see, fear. How ironic. *He* was afraid. Aberdeen's manager should pinch-hit for him.

Joe took a deep breath. Hudson Valley's pitcher threw from the stretch. I crouched. Joe swung over the ball.

The crowd turned merciless. They had already seen this and had no desire to see it again. Their angry shouts and boos drowned out any words of encouragement that came from Aberdeen's dugout.

Hudson Valley's pitcher threw a curve ball that started high and broke late and wide.

"Ball."

Joe hadn't come close to hitting a fast ball and this pitcher threw a curve? I wasn't the only one confused. Hudson Valley's manager yelled at his battery mates in some pretty colorful language.

Hudson Valley's pitcher and catcher got the message. A fastball pierced the air. Joe missed it. The crowd became enraged.

Joe stepped out of the batter's box and took a long breath.

Baseball was considered a team sport, yet much of it had individual components. A fielder worked alone when the ball came to him and he had to make the play. A base stealer ran alone when he attempted to advance. Yet the loneliest feeling had to belong to the batter and pitcher. The pressure could be enormous on the person who held the baseball and the one who wielded the stick. Just one could prevail. And it was this battle that made me love the game and love being the home plate umpire.

Joe stepped into the batter's box and stared down the pitcher. The crowd noise dissipated.

I actually found myself cheering for Joe. Come on, man. Just like you did in high school. Send it over the fence.

Hudson Valley's pitcher delivered from the stretch. I crouched over the catcher's left shoulder and anticipated another fast ball. The baseball whistled at me, a beautiful pitch dead center in the strike zone. A pitch any major leaguer would send five-hundred feet in the opposite direction.

Joe flinched, but didn't swing. The ball smacked in the catcher's mitt.

I had no choice. "Strike three!"

The catcher jumped up and ran to congratulate his pitcher. The fans booed.

Joe turned on me. His eyes looked ready to pop from their sockets. Veins bulged in his neck. He released a torrent of verbal abuse and set a record for the amount of times the F word was used in a single tirade. He questioned my eyesight, my ability to umpire and my ancestry. Yet I almost laughed because I sensed it wasn't real hostility. Joe acted as if he wanted to send me to the hospital, but I suspected his real purpose was to redirect the blame for his failure onto me and hopefully divert the fans anger as well.

Oh, well, let the spectators believe I made a bad call, but I doubt they did. The pitch had been right down Broadway and Joe knew it. I ejected him, which seemed irrelevant, given the game was over, but league rules meant he'd be suspended for the next game.

315

Aberdeen's manager got between us and shoved Joe toward the dugout.

"This isn't over!" Joe said, pointing.

***

An hour later, George and I had changed into casual clothes. We left the locker room and headed for the stadium exit.

"Hey, Michael."

It was Joe. He stood alone in the concourse.

"I'll catch up," I said to George, tossing him my car keys. George hesitated.

"Don't worry," Joe said with a chuckle, "I won't kill him."

"It's okay," I said.

George rattled my keys and left.

"Sorry about that," Joe said with the first ever handshake between us. It was almost unnatural to see him humble. "The pitch was perfect."

I could've danced on Joe's grave, laugh and tell him what a lousy player he was, just as he had done to me, but why stoop to that level? "Yes, it was."

"Ironic, isn't it? Looks like you'll make it to the majors instead of me."

"It's just one game, Joe."

"One game was enough. But you're good. Everybody in the dugout said so. You had a consistent strike zone. We all knew what to expect when we went to bat. Good job."

"Thank you, Joe. That's the nicest thing you've ever said to me."

"Yeah, I'm beginning to realize what an asshole I've been."

"But why?"

"Not sure. Maybe I'm jealous. And mad as hell."

"What?"

"My brother's a surgeon. My sister has a full scholarship to Penn's Wharton School of Business. I'll never be on their level. I hate family events because I always get compared to them. I hated you because you reminded me of them. I thought you were plain crazy to throw all that brain power away and be a jock. I still think it's nuts, but it's your life. So again, I'm sorry."

"Apology accepted," I said, shaking his hand again.

"Thank you," Joe said, turning to leave.

"Hey."

Joe stopped and looked at me.

"When I make it to the majors, I'll save you a ticket."

Joe playfully poked me with a finger into my breastbone. "You better."

ABOUT THE AUTHOR

William Francis is a writer of fiction and history, and had pursued a career as a professional baseball umpire. His novels can be found on Amazon.com. His books of vintage photographs related to Delaware history are published through Arcadia Publishing and available at book stores throughout Delaware or online at www.arcadiapublishing.com. For the latest news about book releases, appearances, interviews or book signing events, log onto the author's website at www.authorwilliamfrancis.com

CPSIA information can be obtained
at www.ICGtesting.com
Printed in the USA
BVHW040924091118
532661BV00017B/385/P

9 781495 493577